C000130141

Congratulations

Ash Hartwell
x

www.stitchedsmilepublications.com

ACKNOWLEDGEMENTS

I'd like to say a massive 'THANK YOU' to Nicki for her constant encouragement during the writing of this book and Kirstii, Sophie, Xenia, and Nathan for putting up with my grumpy writer moments. Thanks should also go to a multitude of other people who have encouraged and, when it was due, critiqued my writing over the years. I can't possibly list all of them here, but they know who they are.

In addition, special thanks to Stitched Smile Publications and its wonderful staff for believing in my dream and for putting so much work into the final, finished story without whom I doubt it would have ever come back from the dead.

Dedication

For my beautiful wife, Nicki
and our wonderful kids,
Kirstii, Sophie, Xenia, and Nathan.

And for all those who found eternal peace at sea.

One

The rich aromatic smoke formed a heavy veil obscuring the features of the two rough-looking men sitting opposite Patrick McGowan. He shifted slightly in his seat, taking one last glance at the cards in his hand before placing them face down on the curiously stained and deeply scratched table. Lady Luck had favoured him this night, and he sensed he was about to overstay his welcome in the Belvedere Arms.

A small lamp hanging above the table cast shadows across Patrick's only remaining opponent, a wizened old sailor, whose facial features gave him the gnarled appearance of an ancient wizard. He leant forward saying, "Okay, Belfast Boy, let's see what thee has." His voice was deep and harsh, the words creaking like an old schooner's rigging.

"I'm from Dublin," Patrick replied coldly, flipping his cards over and fanning them out in one smooth motion to reveal four jaded kings. "And I'm not a boy!"

An awkward hush descended across the room. It started with the small group huddling around their table, and like ripples on a pool after a stone is cast into its depths, spread outwards through the squalid dockside pub. The wizened old sailor remained hunched forward, looking down at the cards laid out before him as if unable to trust his tired, old eyes. Then, twitching his tobacco-stained moustache, he threw back his head to emit a deep roar of laughter, his deep-set eyes sparkling as they caught the light of the gas lamp overhead. His laughter

immediately defused the tension in the room as people returned to their own private conversations. Throwing his cards down to reveal a pair of aces, he watched as Patrick gathered his winnings.

"You're a bloody good liar, Belfast." Waving away Patrick's attempt to correct him, the sailor continued, "and I'll wager, thee's in town to gain passage to the land of opportunity in search of your fortune?" Fixing Patrick with an inquiring stare, which made the younger man feel uncomfortable, the weather-beaten sailor searched Patrick's face for answers. After a short while, the sailor leant back in his chair, obviously content with his findings, and uttered, "and I fancy you'll find it, too."

Patrick nodded respectfully to the man, aware this might be his opening gambit in an attempt to win back his money. Taking care not to give too much away, he replied, "Indeed, it is true that I plan to travel to America and the point of that endeavour is always to be seeking a fortune. But you knowing these facts hardly qualifies you as a mind reader. We are in Southampton the night before a ship sails for New York, and I'll warrant she'll be full of immigrants." Patrick flashed the old sailor a warm smile. "If you hanker after a chance to refill your pockets, old man, then you'll have to engage me better than with a cheap trick and lame flattery."

Patrick got to his feet and was busy stuffing the meager collection of coins that constituted his winnings into his pockets. As he bade his host a good day and was turning to leave, the old man's voice boomed across the crowded bar.

"I have no wish to play any more games with you. I can ill-afford to lose any more money. If you doubt this then you have never met my missus." The sailor joined in with the laughter around the table.

Smiling, Patrick replied, "Then we have ended our business, and I shall be on my way." Walking through the smoke-filled pub he was aware of his vulnerability as an outsider in the roughest part of a strange town. An outsider who had some of their hard-earned wages weighing down his pockets. He was of the opinion people do not take well to losing money, especially to a stranger.

"Hold your horses there, Belfast," the old sailor's voice carried over the general chatter and commotion present in the run-down pub. "I like ya. Think ya 'ave balls. I got a little present for thee to take with ya." Patrick stopped. He was aware it might just be a simple ploy to stop him from leaving the pub so the sailor's cronies could steal his winnings, or worse, give them time to arrange an ambush in one of the many narrow lanes or dark alleyways riddling the dockside slums. But Patrick was curious, and curiosity didn't always kill the cat.

Turning to face his would-be benefactor, Patrick quickly scanned the crowded bar looking for potential threats. "Why would you want to give me a present? We only met but a few hours ago, and if truth be known, you've already given me so much." He tapped his bulging pockets, smiling broadly as he did so. The assembled locals joined in with his mirth, a few shouted

comments lambasting the card players still gathered around the table.

Raising his hands as if to protect himself from the barbed comments, the old sailor was again laughing, "You see, Belfast, you've a sharp wit and I daresay a sharper tongue when there is a need. There's nay many walks in 'ere take our chink and 'ave the guts to play the wag." Motioning for Patrick to re-take his seat, he continued, "Yesterday fortune sailed my ship, much to the misfortune of a naive young mariner just docked from journeying Africa's eastern coast. He'd with him a rare treat that I fancy will serve you well in your pursuit of happiness and wealth." He shrugged theatrically, adding, "And one my good lady wife would not tolerate in our 'ouse." Again, there was general merriment around the table as he shared what had obviously become a private joke.

Patrick was finding himself becoming more intrigued the longer the conversation continued but was mindful of the man's need to tell his story. Besides, he wasn't in a position to force the issue despite the apparent general good humour of both the old sailor and the pub's other regular patrons. A word out of line on his behalf would alter the situation, and not in a good way. Satisfying himself he was in no direct danger for the present, Patrick remained seated as he glanced around the room, alert to possible threats. It was getting late. Patrick noted many of the men had drunk to excess, and as a result, the pub had a raucous atmosphere making normal conversation almost impossible.

The sailor continued with his story, his voice booming across the table. "Fact is, the rarity of his stake matched the rarity of his skill, and so, I now have his exceptional treat; something he surprisingly didn't seem too disheartened by." He fixed Patrick with a quizzical stare and continued, "At the time it seemed a fair conclusion to our evenin' but with the harsh light of day, and a sober mind, I ain't so favourably disposed to the notion. However, I'm sure a man of your talents will see the potential of what this opportunity offers."

Patrick felt the time had come for him to press the sailor for a few details, but as he began to speak, the old sailor's thunderous voice drowned him out, shouting instructions to the innkeeper. Before Patrick could even draw breath, let alone make himself heard above the general clamour that followed the sailor's gruff order, a large wicker basket, its top secured by a thick leather thong, was placed on the table in front of him.

Two

Esme Jackson couldn't sleep. She'd retired to bed early to be fresh-faced and alert when reporting for duty the following morning. But with the pandemonium from the street revelry below her bedroom window, mixed with her own excitement, she'd found sleep elusive. Tomorrow marked the beginning of her new life, a life full of hopes and dreams. Hope for the future—she'd had precious little the past two years—and dreams of marriage to a wealthy, handsome, but mainly wealthy, young man. Today she was Esme, the wench and occasional good-time girl from the Belvedere Arms; tomorrow she would become Miss Esme Jackson, chambermaid, *RMS Titanic*.

Rising from her bed, she crossed to the window and looked down on the narrow, cobbled street below. A group of young men, all so drunk they couldn't stand without help, were toasting one another and their new lives in America. Smiling, Esme looked skyward. Despite the lateness of the hour, the spring sky retained the dying embers of daylight: a distant glow on the western horizon, and here and there, a star sparkled in the darker sky to the east. Her father started her dreams of travel. He used to sit by her bed at night when she was no more than an infant, recounting tales he'd heard while working the docks. He unloaded ships from the farthest reaches of the Empire but always preferred to talk about the cruise liners sailing back and forth across the Atlantic. He always spoke to

her of his dream of a better life in America, a dream he was never destined to fulfill.

Esme's father died after a swinging crane struck him while unloading one of his beloved liners. He'd plunged into the sea, trapped in the vicious swirls between the ship and the wharf. When they eventually pulled Esme's father from the water, he had already drowned. Now, whenever she missed him, Esme would look to the stars shining down on the world's oceans and imagine him sailing the globe, living out his adventurous stories. Tonight, as she looked out towards the stars and thought about it being the eve of the maiden voyage of the world's biggest liner, a liner she would be on as it set sail for America, she imagined she could feel her father's presence.

"What is it, Esme? What's going on out there?" Charlotte, Esme's younger sister sat up in bed, rubbing her eyes.

"Just some drunken lads, all off to America. It got me thinking about Father and his crazy dreams, but just now they don't seem so crazy anymore,"
Esme said, moving to the bed she shared with her sister, perching on the edge.

Charlotte hugged Esme and whispered, "He'd be right proud of you." She felt the damp tears on Esme's cheeks mingling with her own. Breaking away, Esme used the sleeve of her nightgown to gently dab the tears away. She took a deep breath, trying to keep her own emotions from revealing themselves in her voice, then added, "Anyway, it's about time I

had a room to myself, what with you coming and going all hours."

Charlotte was going to miss her elder sister who, lately, had become her sole parental figure and closest friend. Following the tragic death of their father, their mother had sought solace in the bottom of a gin bottle and scarcely found time to acknowledge her daughters, let alone care for them or grieve with them. It was Esme who got a little job cleaning cabins after the cruise liner's passengers disembarked, which was offered by an old drinking partner of their father, either out of kindness or because he had designs on his late friend's widow. After much hard work, Esme secured a position with the White Star Line to work the Trans-Atlantic crossing. Meanwhile, she also found work as a barmaid at the Belvedere Arms, serving thirsty sailors eager to sup a beer, or a good deal more, with a beautiful young woman.

"Don't you be getting too comfy. I'll be back in a few weeks and might never get a second trip," Esme told Charlotte. Although the tone of Esme's voice was light and humorous, Charlotte detected an underlying tension. Esme made no secret of being unhappy at leaving her young sister at home with their gin-soaked mother, or of her own fear of failure. Esme paused for a short while, before adding, "Still don't seem real."

"It's real alright, the *Titanic*, your job, everything," Charlotte replied. Esme could see Charlotte's eyes twinkling mischievously in the half-light.

"Why don't we go down to the docks and sneak ourselves a peek? No one will mind, and she'll be all lit up pretty." Charlotte's enthusiasm caused her words to come out faster and faster the more she spoke, "Please, I can't sleep anyway, and you're so excited I 'spect you'll never sleep again."

Esme laughed aloud and nodded her acceptance of the younger girl's plan. She sensed somehow, after tonight things would never be the same again, and this moonlit adventure would mark a watershed in their lives.

"Alright, but we can't be out too late. We'll just go down to the docks, have a quick look, and come back. No loitering, it's no place for a young girl this time of night. Now get dressed quickly!"

Fifteen minutes later, the two young women walked briskly down the alleyway that ran along the back of their small terraced house, heading towards the main thoroughfare down to the docks. The sky had darkened, and although not cloudless, was clear enough to allow the pale moonlight to illuminate their way, not that they wouldn't be able to find the route on the darkest of nights; they'd travelled it so often.

Esme pulled her woollen shawl up over her head before pulling it tight around her shoulders. "It's a cold night, Lottie. Make sure you stay well wrapped up, I wouldn't want you catching a chill."

"I think you may have much colder nights to look forward to," said Charlotte as they left the enclosed alley and turned

onto the wide cobbled street. Even at this late hour of the evening, the road was busy. Men staggered home after drinking in one of the many dockside pubs, and young couples were out walking, no doubt taking the opportunity to view the unsinkable goliath moored alongside the pier.

As the sisters walked arm-in-arm past the open ground separating the narrow terraced houses from the large warehouses and shipping offices of the busy commercial dockyard, they noticed a small group of local children gathered around what appeared, in the monochrome moonlight, to be a large bundle of rags. The evening was quiet, and a gentle sea breeze carried the children's excited voices to them, bringing with it a refreshingly clean salty tang which prickled their faces. The children, their voices raised and angry, were involved in a disagreement so intense and animated they didn't notice the sisters who, attracted by the commotion, were now walking towards them; not, that is, until Charlotte hailed them.

Recognizing a few of the older boys, Charlotte picked on one in particular and shouted, "Billy Cooper! Does your mother know you're running around making a nuisance of yourself?"

The boys, unsure who was approaching them, stopped their arguing and faced the women. As if on some unspoken command, they formed a semi-circle between the intruders and the pile of rags, like wild dogs protecting a prized carcass. Billy Cooper looked ready to protest his innocence until he saw Esme, who was by now close enough to fix him with the

withering stare she usually reserved for rowdy dock workers or crapulent sailors.

"We ain't doing nothing, miss." Billy Cooper spoke to his well-worn boots, unable to meet the young woman's stern stare.

"If that's so, Master Cooper, then you must be doing something! What causes so much excitement you try hiding it, despite us being no more than ten feet away?" Esme's voice was calm and authoritative, demanding an answer.

Billy, a snotty urchin about twelve years old, looked confused. He opened his mouth to answer her but his expression took on a perplexed stare, and after an awkward pause, he shut it again without uttering a sound.

"Does anyone care to enlighten us?" As Esme's stare passed to the assembled children, mainly boys close in age to Billy, not one tried to either make eye contact or offer any explanation. After a short while, Esme lifted her long skirt to reveal her booted ankle. "Very well. I shall take a look myself, but if the devil has found work for idle hands, I shall ensure your fathers beat his evil from your souls."

She walked around the line of boys carefully avoiding the muddier areas and approached the dark bundle. Her sister followed closely, stepping around the boys' cordon with exaggerated importance.

Charlotte had always been in awe of her sister and was happy living in her shadow. Esme was charming, witty, and intelligent with all these qualities neatly packaged in a lithe, yet

gracefully curved frame that disguised her strength. She disarmed men and women alike with her beauty, the shining emeralds in her eyes, highlighted by the soft, jet curls framing her face, captivating stokers and sea captains alike. So striking were her eyes most people, meeting her for the first time, couldn't remember anything else about her countenance, which did her high cheekbones and delicate, slightly upturned mouth a huge disservice. Once a man had fallen under her spell, he would feel compelled to either spend a small fortune just to remain in her company, a situation favoured by the Belvedere's landlord, or propose to her in an extravagant fashion. Some would do both before staggering back to their ship to sleep off the night's excesses.

Esme got her first clear sight of the rags heaped haphazardly on the damp ground and put out a restraining arm to prevent her sister from advancing any closer. "Don't look Charlotte. It's not a sight to be filling a young girl's head as it will summon the darkest of terrors and haunt her dreams. Please take the boys back to the road." Esme pushed Charlotte away, propelling her in the direction of both the assembled boys and the main road.

"What is it?" Charlotte asked; Esme's reaction had piqued her curiosity. She pushed back against her sister's arm, craning her neck to catch a glimpse of the hidden horrors her sister had witnessed, but Esme held firm, pushing Charlotte back. Charlotte finally accepted the inevitable and reluctantly walked away, signalling for the boys to follow.

Esme watched Charlotte walk away, the gang of boys trailing in her wake as she headed towards the warm yellow glow of the gaslights lighting up the thoroughfare. Then she turned her attention to the large pile of rags and the body concealed within.

Three

Patrick eyed the basket with suspicion, disinclined to touch it. The men, gathered around their table, had fallen silent and the old sailor, sitting opposite Patrick, had the look of an expectant grandfather handing out presents to his grandchildren on Christmas Day. Inspecting the basket, he was impressed by its sturdy construction and the workmanship involved, and although Patrick was no expert, he guessed the basket originated from the African continent. Despite his reservations, Patrick stretched out his hand and ran it over the basket's lid. He felt the wood's undulating smoothness, each twist expertly finished with none of the sharp, jagged snags that blighted old or cheaply made baskets.

Something inside the basket moved. A faint scurrying sound was accompanied by a gentle creak as the wooden staves rubbed together. Patrick quickly withdrew his hand and stood up, knocking his chair over. The sailor and his cohorts standing around them roared with laughter. Patrick joined in nervously, unsure whether he was the butt of the joke or if there was some secret he was not yet privy to.

The amusement was such, it took a minute or more for everyone to settle, and even the weather-beaten old sailor had to wipe a tear from his eye, using the threadbare cuff of his overcoat. When he'd regained his composure, the sailor said, "I like you Belfast. You're off to conquer the world all full of pretentious swagger, but deep down you're just a nipper not

long off his mother's tit." He motioned for Patrick to retake his seat before continuing, "Take my advice lad, travel through life like it's a game of cards. Hold 'em or fold 'em, but do it with belief, not fear." Gently tapping the top of the basket, he fixed Patrick with a challenging stare, then added, "So Belfast, are you gonna hold on and believe or are you folding with fear?"

Patrick met the old man's stare and began undoing the leather thongs that held the lid down. All the while, he heard something scurrying about within the basket and briefly thought he heard a baby's whimper. He pulled the last thong free and placed it next to the basket on the table, keeping one hand on the lid to ensure it remained closed; at least until he was ready. He felt the hairs on the back of his neck bristle in response to the oppressive weight of expectation in the now silent hostelry. Patrick sensed this was a defining moment in his life; if he bottled it now he would always be an emotional coward unable to seize the moment, to take the risks that would bring life's greatest rewards. Pretentious swagger or not, the time to step into manhood was now.

With a deft flick of Patrick's wrist, the basket's lid swung up and over to land on the table with a soft thud and the familiar creak of shifting willow. The sound, although barely audible, sounded like a door slamming shut on his childhood. All the while Patrick had returned the sailor's stare, and rather than feeling intimidated, he sensed the old man's pride and admiration; an unspoken bond had formed between kindred

spirits. But now, Patrick looked away, stealing a glance into the basket.

Huddled in one corner was a tiny monkey. Its long tail curled around its body, either for protection or possibly warmth, and its saucer-like, mahogany brown eyes looked wide and terrified as the poor scraggly creature tried to make itself look small and invisible. Patrick looked up at the sailor, momentarily speechless. Of all the things he'd imagined being in the basket, some more macabre or bizarre than real, he'd not expected a monkey. He had thought perhaps something hideous and grotesque, maybe reptilian, a dragon or a shrunken head, but certainly not a cute little monkey. He smiled and reached into the basket to pick up the tiny bundle of fur.

The sailor's hand stayed his. "I suggested you shouldn't act out of fear, I didn't suggest you should become a fool. That animal, however small and dainty it may seem, has the devil within it. When it has the will, it can become the most disagreeable of creatures. Only this morning it took a liking to the finger of a crew member of mine. It bit down to the white of his bone, and it wasn't long before the evil spread through his body, sending the poor man into a delirium."

Patrick withdrew his hand and looked around the assembled crowd seeking confirmation of the sailor's warning. He felt relieved not to see a delirious madman glaring at him, although several of the tough looking sailors and rougher looking dockers were nodding in silent agreement. A few of these world-weary men, who thought nothing of gambling their

skills against Nature's violent seas to earn a shilling then brawling in the bars and brothels of the world's ports to spend it, looked scared or at least apprehensive. Their eyes clearly focused on the basket and its enigmatic contents. He returned his attention to the monkey and wasn't afraid to admit his confusion. His eyes told him of a cute monkey held captive far from his home, lost in a confusing world, but his ears told of a savage beast capable of a fury powerful enough to take down a grown man. The curiosity cat within was scratching to be let out, and Patrick was about to open the door.

"Where is this man so afflicted by this evil curse?" Patrick asked. "Without proof, all you have is a story, a clever and intriguing story I grant, but a story nonetheless. I will take this animal off your hands thereby saving you from the wrath of your wife, which I suspect is more terrifying and because I, like you, see the potential return on this investment once in the new world." As if to emphasize his point, Patrick flipped the lid shut and began rethreading the leather thong.

Again the old sailor laughed, his eyes twinkling in the gloomy gaslight. "Aye, I fear you may be right about my wife, however, the story I tell is true. The man in question felt light-headed with a fever so high his blood may have boiled. He left earlier to return to his lodgings and sleep it off." The old sailor paused long enough to signal to the barman then continued. "It's rare I meet a man who reminds me so much of my own youth. It has been an honour to make your acquaintance,

Belfast, and I wish you God-speed on your journey. Will you join me in a last drink before we go our separate ways?"

Doffing his cap respectfully to the ancient mariner, Patrick replied with a smile, "I would be honoured, although I'll be payin' as you lost all ya money to me four kings." Again, the tobacco-stained moustache tilted upwards at the ends as the gnarled old sailor's deep laugh boomed across the crowded pub.

Four

Sixth officer James Moody stood silently on the Poop Deck of the *Royal Mail Ship Titanic*. The day had dawned fine and clear; the early morning sun, although bright, had yet to warm the air, and Moody was glad he'd chosen to wear his heavy overcoat. He looked at his pocket watch and patiently waited for the second hand to tick round towards the hour. In the distance a church's bells began to peal, announcing the approaching hour as the hand on Moody's pocket watch ticked on past the Roman numeral IX.

"Stand by, Mr. Callahan!" Officer Moody issued the command in a loud, clear voice despite Mr. Callahan standing only a few feet away.

"Aye, aye, sir." Mr. Callahan's accent identified him as American, indeed the one fact Officer Moody knew about Callahan was he was the only American enlisted on the ship's crew. The distant bells stopped ringing for a moment, then the first dull chime rang out across the harbour, signalling the hour.

"If you would be so good, Mr. Callahan?" Moody watched as the American expertly hoisted the Blue Ensign up the flagpole. As he tied off the lanyard, Moody briefly saluted before wheeling away just as the church clock struck for the eighth and last time. He was due to meet with Captain Smith in fourteen minutes to collect the Captain's report verifying the ship's readiness for sea, and Mr. Moody was not in the habit of being even one minute late for a meeting.

As he walked briskly across the Poop Deck heading for the Captain's quarters located just aft of the Bridge, Officer Moody stole a glance over the handrail at the quayside far below. Even at this early hour, the White Star Dock around Berth 44 was crowded with smartly dressed well-wishers and rougher looking navvies, all eager to watch the world's largest vessel set sail on her maiden voyage. A band was setting up on a raised dais close to the main gangway and occasional notes of disjointed music floated up to Moody as the musicians tuned their instruments. He sensed he was about to embark on something momentous, something people would tell their grandchildren about in years to come, and a soft tingle of pride ran down his spine.

"Gee, will you take a look at that? We don't sail for another four hours and the passengers don't board for two." Able seaman Callahan walked quickly, half a stride behind Moody, matching the young officer's pace.

"I'll remind you, Mr. Callahan, you are here to do a job, and to do it professionally." Moody's pace didn't falter, as he firmly fixed his gaze straight ahead. "We will all be under great scrutiny: from passengers, the company, even our peers. You will do well to remember that and act accordingly, not gawk at the crowds."

"Yes sir, I apologise. I've never before born witness to anything as spectacular as today's events and, for a moment, it got the better of me." Mr. Callahan's tone matched his apologetic words, and Moody sensed his chastisement may have sounded a little too harsh.

Lowering the volume of his voice, Moody looked directly at the American, his eyes sparkling with excitement "Neither have I, Mr. Callahan. Neither have I."

Mrs. Bridget Grafton modestly pulled the crisp Egyptian linen sheet up to her neck as her husband of barely two months collapsed beside her on the bed, a slight wheeze evident in his laboured breaths. She had awoken less than five minutes before to find him knelt between her legs fumbling with the cord of his pyjama bottoms, and out of some sleepy wifely duty, or just plain pity, she'd finally relented. After all, it was his honeymoon too and only the second time she had allowed his obvious excitement to get the better of her. Now, lying next to him in the hotel's king-sized bed, she realized he'd not once kissed her or shown her any real affection, just basic, and frankly, disappointing sex.

She listened to his wheezing breath for a minute or so before venturing to speak. "Could you ask Violet to draw me a bath."

Rising from the bed without answering her, Captain William Grafton refastened his pyjama trousers before donning the Oriental styled housecoat Bridget had bought him at an exclusive London tailor. Once suitably dressed, he gave the call bell's sash a sharp tug, summoning their maid. There was a brief pause, followed by a gentle knock on the bedroom door. "Come in," William responded with the confidence of an upper-class English gentleman schooled at Harrow and educated at

Cambridge. At fifty years old, he was the sole heir to the Grafton steel empire reportedly worth £100 million, and almost thirty years the senior of Bridget, who had only celebrated her debutant ball the previous spring. Captain Grafton was a man with a reputation for getting what he wanted and when introduced to the belle of the ball, he had known exactly what he wanted. A whirlwind romance followed, attracting much gossip on both sides of the Atlantic. Many people in London's society had openly expressed their shock at his choice of a woman young enough to be his daughter, fearing the marriage was doomed to fail. But they quickly became one of society's golden couples, the wealthy dashing Captain and the beautiful and outspoken American with Boston new money connections.

"Good morning, Violet." William barely looked at the servant as she entered the room. "Could you please draw a bath for Mrs. Grafton and have Cecil meet me in my dressing room in five minutes?" Then he walked into the connecting bathroom, firmly shutting the door behind him.

"Good morning, Mrs. Grafton. I trust you slept well." Violet smiled at her mistress. Bridget wasn't sure if she detected a hidden meaning in the words, and she wondered if the maid had overheard her and William's hurried love making.

She chose to assume not and stretched, letting out a fake yawn before replying, "I'm sailing home on the *Titanic* today, Violet, of course I didn't sleep well; I'm far too excited."

Violet smiled politely, a faraway look in her eyes that Bridget thought both odd and a little rude. Despite the two

women being so close in age, they had failed to strike up any form of relationship since Captain Grafton had taken it on himself to employ Violet as his wife's personal attendant.

Bridget remained lying in the warm, comfortable bed while Violet, excusing herself with a perfunctory curtsey, began running the bath. Taking a glance at the wall clock, Bridget noted she had almost an hour before the South Western Hotel stopped serving breakfast and at least two before they needed to make the short cab ride to the White Star Pier. After a few minutes, Violet returned to the bedroom and began laying out Bridget's clothes for the day. Bridget turned lazily onto her side and, propping up her head with a delicate arm, asked, "Have you finished packing?"

"Yes, ma'am. Your suitcases for the voyage are already in the lobby. I will escort them to your cabin in advance and unpack for you whilst you and Captain Grafton are at breakfast." Violet continued bustling around the bedroom gathering the last of Bridget's possessions together.

After a few minutes, Bridget finally threw back the sheets and climbed out of bed. She walked into the spacious bathroom pulling her nightgown up over her head, casually discarding it on the linoleum covered floor before stepping into the bath. Sinking into the warm, lavender scented water, she stretched out her still sleepy muscles, letting the water's warmth soothe out the night's knots. She stared down at her slightly rounded belly and gently rubbed the developing bump, allowing the water to lap back and forth across her body.

Violet stood in the doorway, the discarded nightgown in her hand. She had seen her mistress naked many times in the last few months and had herself noted the growing bulge and slight swelling of Bridget's breasts. "Forgive me for speaking out of turn, ma'am, but you'll find it hard to disguise your pregnancy much longer. I fear you'll be 'aving to tell Captain Grafton sooner rather than later."

"What makes you presume I've not already told my husband of our impending good fortune?" Bridget asked, casually making small ripples in the bathwater with her hands.

"Because …" Violet paused pursing her lips, obviously unsure whether to proceed with her observation.

"Because?" Bridget repeated, turning slightly to face Violet. She looked troubled, her expression reflecting her inner turmoil. Then her verbal dam broke, the words flooding out unabridged.

"Because he would not treat you in the manner he does if he knew you were carrying his child." Violet's speech was rapid, and she hardly drew breath before continuing, "I mean the way he treats you when he believes you to be alone."

"I'm at a loss to understand what you are gibbering about. Your master is a well-respected gentleman who always behaves impeccably," Bridget replied angrily. Mortified, she turned away to hide the telltale flush colouring her cheeks, waving a dismissive hand at Violet, signalling their conversation was at an end. How dare she be so presumptuous to make

suppositions about her employer's marriage? But what really irked her was the accuracy of Violet's words.

Bridget sank deeper into the soothing, warm water and pondered her predicament. She knew she would have to tell William soon, but the timing needed to be just right.

Five

Like all seaports, Southampton was a chaotic collection of quays and piers, warehouses and cranes, and in the harbour, tugboats and tenders crisscrossed the grey-blue water leaving frothy, white wakes. At the centre of this chaos floated the majestic hull of the *Titanic*, her white superstructure glistening in the sunlight. Three of her four mighty funnels smoked lazily as the plumes drifted away on the gentle breeze. She had sailed into port the previous week, quickly becoming the harbour's focal point as she took on a seemingly never-ending list of supplies. Even now, just a few hours before her scheduled departure, the firemen and stokers were busy loading and trimming the last of the coal.

Into this maelstrom strode Patrick. He carried a battered suitcase, which contained almost everything he owned, and a hastily purchased secondhand valise. Inside the valise was Pandora. He'd always liked the name Pandora and it seemed a suitable name for a grumpy, ill-tempered, bag dwelling monkey. He had covered the valise in old hessian sacking he found behind one of the large warehouses so as not to draw attention to it, and he hoped, subdue Pandora.

Patrick weaved his way through the crowds of well-wishers, street sellers, and passengers saying emotional farewells, and walked purposefully towards the White Star Line's purpose-built passenger terminal. As he walked, his eyes scanned the faces around him, searching for any sign the police

were on to him. He presented his second class ticket at the gate and began climbing the stairway up to one of the *Titanic*'s gangplanks and his new life in America.

Patrick sensed the mounting excitement; the warm sunshine that bathed the quay below added to the crowd's general good humour and made the cheerfully coloured bunting appear more vivid. He took a deep breath and smelt the usual mix of tar and sea salt mingling with the strong scent of the freshly caught fish being hawked around the quayside for a ha'penny. Pausing for a moment to look down on the crowds below, Patrick absorbed the atmosphere and was struck by the enormity of the moment. He was leaving England's green fields the way his grandfather left the Emerald Isle: on a promise of a better life, and to evade the police.

Patrick quickly checked the clasp on Pandora's valise then walked confidently across the gangplank, nodding a friendly greeting to the officer who stood welcoming the second and third class passengers aboard. All the while, Patrick waited for Pandora to screech or become restless, giving her presence away.

His legs turned to jelly, and his heart threatened to jump up through his mouth as he stepped off the gangplank and onto the ship's spotless deck. He exchanged hasty pleasantries with the burly master-at-arms, the palms of his hands feeling damp and sweaty as he awaited his illicit luggage's inevitable discovery and their resulting removal from the vessel.

But it never came. Instead, he found himself directed to a stairwell with further directions to his second class cabin. As he hurried away from the welcoming committee, his battered suitcase in one hand and the tatty valise wedged firmly under his arm, Patrick's smile got broader with every step.

Patrick McGowan and his unusual traveling companion were on their way to America.

Esme's first three hours as a White Star employee aboard the *Titanic* were a whirlwind of frenetic activity. She'd exchanged several tearful hugs with Charlotte before walking across the crew member's gangplank into the bowels of the ship a minute or so after her allotted time. Once inside, she was met by a stern-faced woman who, although probably in her late fifties, had the wrinkled skin tone of a woman far older. She wore her hair pulled into a tight bun, with not a single gray strand daring to step out of line. She introduced herself as the head housekeeper, Miss Wilson, while looking down her pointed nose at Esme, her frosty expression falling somewhere between disapproval and outright contempt.

After what seemed like an age, Miss Wilson nodded, seemingly satisfied that Esme passed muster. "Here are your cabin details. You will find your uniform there. Please change and report to the first class dining saloon by eight thirty, sharp." She snapped impatiently before striding away. A second, younger woman thrust a sheet of paper into Esme's hand

before scurrying off after Miss Wilson, leaving Esme to find her own way to her cabin.

If Esme had been expecting luxury accommodation, then her expectations were about to take a battering. At first, she walked the length of the narrow corridor mistaking her cabin for a broom cupboard and then, upon entering, discovered she shared the broom cupboard with another maid. A haphazard pile of clothes lay across the top bunk, and a pair of boots lay discarded on the floor. There was no sign of the woman herself, and Esme flung her small suitcase onto the lower bunk before hastily changing into the uniform neatly folded at its foot.

Esme finally ran into the lavish Dining Saloon on D Deck a little over ten minutes late, breathing heavily. A stone-faced Miss Wilson stood on the Grand staircase's second step; arms behind her back. She glared at Esme who started to mumble an apology, then seeing the rising anger in the older woman's wrinkled face and realising she was only making matters worse, stopped herself. She quietly joined the other housekeepers assembled at the foot of the stairs and was secretly relieved when two minutes later, another three women rushed in to join the group.

"Now that you are all finally ready, albeit sixteen minutes late, I would like to formerly welcome you to the crew of *RMS Titanic* and inform you of our expectations." Miss Wilson then droned on for the next half an hour frequently mentioning words like, 'tardy, punctuality' and 'fraternisation', but Esme found it hard to concentrate, her thoughts drifting back to the

events of the previous evening. If finding a dead body hadn't been strange enough, the events that followed were so curious and gave her such a fright; it left her with an unnatural chill that still flowed through her veins.

Once she had ordered the children away, she quickly checked the body and found it to be very definitely dead. A fact she felt sure of due to the stench of death lingering around the corpse. Then she and Charlotte took the younger children home before stopping at the Belvedere Arms to ask a few regulars to escort them back to the body's resting place. However, when they arrived back on the waste ground, the body had vanished, leaving a pile of discarded rags to mark its earlier location. The men from the pub had been sceptical of her story; after all, dead men didn't just get up and walk away. They pointed out with some hilarity that maybe she'd supped a little too much Mother's Ruin, but did, after some persuasion, agree to search the immediate area; although, Esme suspected they were only humouring her. They trampled around for a few minutes before succumbing to the lure of the distant hostelry, but it was long enough to prove there was no dead body in the vicinity. A fact Esme found worrying, leading her to conclude either a deranged killer or a firm of body snatchers were at work in Southampton.

Esme knew she had seen a dead body. There was no trick of the light, no drunken hallucination, just a dead man lying in a bundle of old rags. She would never forget his face, what with those strange markings and the smell; the vile smell of rotting meat left in the summer sun. She supposed the dead man had

died some time ago, but if that were the case, why were his remains not discovered before? The waste ground was a regular playground for the children and a busy shortcut home from the docks. Surely, if the body had been there long enough to rot, then someone would have discovered it earlier, unless the children disturbed the killer during the act of disposing of the body. Maybe the killer lurked in the shadows while she and Charlotte took the children away, before swooping in to reclaim the body. She remembered her father telling her stories of Jack the Ripper and how he just slipped away. What if he had escaped abroad but now had returned to Southampton aboard a liner, free to kill again?

For a brief moment, her thoughts turned to Charlotte, and she uttered a silent prayer for her safety.

"Miss Jackson!" The sound of someone shouting her name with such venom roused her from her thoughts. She looked up in time to see the head housekeeper steaming towards her. Miss Wilson's palm sounded like a whip cracking as it connected with Esme's cheek, snapping her head to the side. For a split-second, Esme thought Miss Wilson had missed. Then the pain surged across her face leaving a stinging sensation that brought tears to her eyes.

Through the ringing in her ear, Esme heard Miss Wilson's muffled voice, "How dare you daydream when I am talking to you, you insolent little girl! We should have left you in the gutter where you belong."

Esme lifted her head and stared defiantly back into Miss Wilson's baggy, bloodshot eyes. She could see the fury and hatred burning deep within the woman's soul. It was more than just Esme's idle daydreaming fuelling the rage. There was resentment etched in the woman's face along with a lifetime of regrets, a deep desire for retribution, and maybe even a little bit of jealousy simmering below the surface. All of it waiting for that one spark that would send her emotions into a bubbling turmoil, hurling the demure Miss Wilson into a raging frenzy bordering on insanity.

A smirk twitched at the corners of Esme's mouth. She had the very things this sanctimonious old bitch craved the most: youth, beauty, vitality, and opportunity. At that moment, as the other chambermaids looked on in hushed awe and Miss Wilson turned an interesting shade of apoplectic purple, Esme believed she had the whole world at her feet.

Miss Wilson was at a loss for words. She opened and closed her mouth several times before uttering, "Well I never …!" before turning on her heels and storming off towards the kitchen.

Goaded by the presence of the other women, and despite the pain still stinging her left cheek, Esme muttered, just loud enough for the assembled chambermaids to hear, "No, I don't suppose you ever did."

Several of the young women looked shocked, a few sniggered quietly. The woman, who'd earlier directed Esme to her cabin, now handed her another sheet of paper. She tried to

hide her smile as she spoke "You are to help with housekeeping duties in first class." Lowering her voice to a whisper, she added quickly, "If you want to be on the return trip, I suggest you stay well clear of the Old Dragon." Then she was gone, hurrying after Miss Wilson, every inch the loyal assistant.

Esme checked her assignment before handing the list to a nervous looking girl of about fifteen standing next to her. Esme gave the young girl a brief, reassuring smile, before climbing the Grand staircase in search of the first class Staterooms on A Deck where she was expected to welcome the passengers aboard with champagne, before assisting them with their unpacking.

Six

Captain William Grafton had decided he and his wife should walk the short distance from the hotel to the White Star Pier because it was "the British thing to do." He also secretly hoped the pleasant stroll would help digest the large breakfast he had devoured. After he finished his large breakfast, Captain Grafton ordered a second helping of bacon and a third of toast, which caused the already generous cut of his suit to feel uncomfortably tight. Casually, he ran his thumb around the waistband of his trousers just below his decidedly middle-aged belly, hoping to relieve the tightness of the waistband.

Captain Grafton waited in the hotel's plush reception area for Bridget, who had ordered her lighter breakfast be sent to their room once she had bathed. In all his adult life, he had never been a man expected to wait. During his lifetime, people rushed to do his bidding, but having to wait on Bridget to finish her bath, dress, and have breakfast made him feel self-conscious sitting alone in the plush reception area. He made a mental note to speak to Bridget about her timekeeping, but that would have to wait until they were alone. Some things between a husband and wife were best resolved in private where the master of the house could wield his power, unhindered by moral indignation.

Bridget finally walked into the reception area, having kept William waiting for almost an hour. He glanced at his pocket watch, noting it was well past eleven o'clock. Bridget stopped to

thank a few members of the hotel staff, another trait he found annoying. William hated the direction in which Edwardian society was heading. As he waited for Bridget to make her way towards him, he thought to himself that it was these people's place to serve the upper classes, and they did not need fawning over. He was firmly of the belief young women had become far too opinionated with a tendency to be overly friendly with servants, and American women, in particular, were especially guilty of this.

William stood and coughed politely, signalling for his wife to join him. She walked towards him with a broad smile. He suppressed his anger and forced a smile in return before offering his young wife his arm. Together they walked out of the hotel; his grip on her forearm so tight she whimpered in pain.

Politely, through a false smile, William mumbled, "We need to hurry my darling otherwise we shall be late. I am sure White Star will not delay the ship's departure, even for us."

Bridget felt her arm going numb below the pinching grip of William's strong fingers. She nodded in agreement. "I'm sure you are quite right, my dear. It was remiss of me to dally so long while dressing. I shall endeavour to be quicker in the future."

William eased his grip, content he'd successfully made his point, and began marching down the road at a brisk military pace, which Bridget found hard to match. A few scruffy sailors, intent on getting one last drink before joining their ship, stumbled across their path. William smelt the beer oozing from their pores as they staggered out of his way, raising their caps in

an exaggerated, drunken apology. One fixed Bridget with a leering smile which lasted too long for William's liking, and he quickened his pace. He knew Bridget was a beautiful woman; he could see that for himself, and the polite attention she got from his gentlemen friends flattered him, but he didn't appreciate some lower-class plebe openly lusting after her. If he had his way, the impudent imbecile would be beaten to within an inch of his miserable life, but again, the fine structures of Victorian society were gradually eroding away as the twentieth century gathered pace.

William settled for simply flashing a warning glare at the sailor who stumbled away, leaving William to almost drag Bridget across the road. He hissed menacingly at her to "Hurry up," then added sarcastically "or would you prefer spending your time entertaining sailors for a penny a go?"

Bridget blushed, shocked at her husband's suggestion and embarrassed by his behaviour, but most of all, she felt scared. William had changed almost as soon as the doors closed behind their last wedding guest. She mumbled another well-rehearsed apology; she was fast learning the privileged position of Mrs. William Grafton came with a heavy burden. As she hurried along behind her husband, she kept her eyes fixed demurely on the path in front of her, anxious not to draw unwanted attention and risk another of William's little lessons in discipline.

William believed he did it for her own good, and she needed to understand that. It was important for a wife to

support her husband, to look pretty and be entertaining without making him the object of ridicule. He was teaching her to be a better wife, a better person. She was lucky he understood she was young, and he was prepared to allow for that. She didn't deserve such a patient and understanding husband, but it still hurt when he disciplined her.

Bridget didn't lift her gaze from the port's cobbled street until William led her into the White Star Line's large reception building. As he presented their tickets and completed the formalities, she gazed out through the tall windows at the vessel towering above them. Even she couldn't help feeling a shiver of excitement and expectation running up her spine. This was going to be something to tell her unborn child about. Subconsciously, she rubbed her belly, her thought momentarily drifting to idyllic dreams of motherhood.

"Are you alright, my darling?" She hadn't noticed William approaching, a look of concern etched on his face. Bridget knew it was only for the benefit of the other passengers waiting to board. He was never this attentive when they were alone.

"I'm perfectly fine, thank you. Why do you ask?" Bridget smiled sweetly at her husband, playing along with his little act. She looked into his eyes, searching for any hint that he knew about her little secret: about her precious, unborn child.

"Well, my dear, you drifted off to another world, and you have rubbed your stomach several times since leaving the hotel." Then smiling at two elderly ladies seated on a bench

close by, he added, "And, as your husband, I am naturally worried."

"Oh! I believe I may have eaten breakfast with too much haste, and I now have some trapped gas. Just like the Mona Lisa, my expression was enigmatic as opposed to distant as you implied." A White Star employee arrived and ushered them towards the gangplank. Bridget added in the brashest American accent she could manage, and just loud enough for the two elderly ladies to overhear as she walked away, "Nothing a good fart won't cure."

The two ladies' jaws dropped open in shock, one even went as far as placing her hands over her ears in case the uncouth American woman should continue her crass observation. William turned the colour of pickled beetroot as he tried to apologise for his wife's comment before hurrying to catch up with her before she could embarrass him further. Bridget kept walking without so much as a backward glance at either of the two outraged women or William, who firmly grasped her arm as she stepped onto the gangplank. She knew he would take his revenge the moment they were alone but now, deep inside, she danced a waltz. She spun around and around in a giant ballroom celebrating her little victory, every turn getting faster and faster as her mysterious partner guided her around the floor.

As they stepped onto the ship's deck, one of the ship's officers welcomed them aboard before introducing them to the chambermaid who would show them to their cabin. Bridget

noticed the chambermaid was a similar age to her with well-defined features and piercing green eyes hinting at wisdom far beyond her age. The left side of her face appeared slightly reddened, and her eyes looked puffy as if she had cried recently, but she smiled politely as she introduced herself as Esme before requesting they follow her to their Stateroom on A Deck.

As Bridget followed Esme along the wood paneled corridor with her obviously still furious husband bringing up the rear, Bridget felt like a condemned woman being led to the gallows thinking so much for the romantic fairy tale of marriage to a dashing army officer. If this was her honeymoon, she wondered what the rest of her life would be like. Would William continue to dole out punishments and discipline or would she, in time, learn to be the perfect, submissive wife he obviously wanted?

Seven

Patrick had just finished the unfortunately short task of unpacking all his worldly possessions in the cramped second class cabin and was pushing Pandora's valise into the storage space below the wooden bench when the cabin door swung open. A large man dressed in a brown tweed suit almost fell into the cabin, his feet tripping on the doorway's raised lip. Belatedly, he grabbed the iron framed bunk, taking on the comic appearance of a music hall mime artist as he swung helplessly from the framework, his feet skidding across the floor as he struggled to pull himself upright. Once he regained his balance, he calmly returned to the doorway to collect his baggage, dragging it into the cabin before slamming the door shut with his foot.

Standing in the centre of the cabin, the intruder finally acknowledged Patrick's presence with a mock theatrical bow. "That, dear boy was not the grand entrance I planned, but no doubt more memorable." The man's speech was slow, deliberate, his tone deep, the aristocratic accent a little too polished with the words rumbling out from under the bushiest walrus moustache Patrick had ever seen. The man's pale blue eyes were so deep set they appeared to be peeking out over his ruddy cheeks, and atop his head, he sported a slightly frayed deerstalker, which, presumably due to his dramatic entrance, sat at a comically, rakish angle.

Patrick stared at the man in astonishment for a heartbeat longer than necessary before erupting with laughter. The man, old enough to be Patrick's father, stared back in disbelief for a brief moment before he too started to chuckle.

"Aye, it was memorable," said Patrick, still laughing as he held out his hand to introduce himself. "McGowan. Patrick McGowan."

The stranger politely removed the deerstalker before accepting Patrick's handshake. "My name is Astor. Sir Bernard Astor."

Patrick struggled to regain his composure, then replied with a smirk, "Oh, a Knight of the realm. I didn't realise we were being so formal. In that case please address me as Pope Gregory." A smile spread across Bernard's face and he joined Patrick in laughing at their shared joke.

Bernard raised his finger suggesting he was about to speak. Patrick tried to look serious. "I like you ... Your Holiness ..." Patrick stifled a snigger as Bernard raised his finger again in mock reproach. "You are intelligent and quick of wit, a useful combination. My real name is of no importance, it's so long since I used it, I hardly remember it myself, and so Bernard will have to suffice. I'm traveling to the new world in search of a new me. One that is a damned site richer than the old me, and a new name, with a shiny title to hang it on, might just be the key to unlocking New York society."

Patrick nodded knowingly, the ridiculously over-the-top country gentleman look and fake upper class accent were all

part of a cunning ruse, a deception that started the moment he boarded this vessel with its exclusive passenger list.

"Let me get this straight, just to avoid confusion. You're a con man with lofty ambitions of tricking your way into New World riches."

Bernard removed a shiny hip flask from his pocket, taking a brief swig, he offered it to Patrick. "I prefer the term artist … con artist, but essentially you are correct. As I alluded to earlier, you're not fooled easily, a condition of great value in my occupation. Unless, that is, you have other plans on your arrival in New York?"

Patrick took a shot of the unexpectedly smooth whiskey and returned the flask to Bernard who slipped it back in his pocket without breaking eye contact. Patrick sensed Bernard was awaiting a response. Was he about to unmask him as the amoral reprobate he undoubtedly was, or were they cut from the same cloth? Patrick couldn't deny the suggestion intrigued him, and going to America with an ally, someone to watch his back, was a much safer plan. Hell, Patrick didn't even have a plan, just an ill-tempered monkey.

Just as Patrick was about to respond to Bernard's quizzical stare, two shrill blasts from the ship's whistle interrupted their conversation. He looked at his pocket watch and noted the time. It was noon precisely. With a wry smile, he said, "I believe we have much to discuss, Sir Bernard, but right now I would like to view our departure from the upper decks. It is a sight I wish to remember for the rest of my life."

"Of course, dear boy. Would you mind if I joined you to witness this historic moment?" Bernard stepped back from the door with an exaggerated sweep of his arm.

"I would be delighted," replied Patrick as he accepted Bernard's gracious invitation to lead the way. He headed for the stairway up to the second class deck area, hardly sparing a thought for Pandora and the valise stowed under the bench.

William heard the ship's whistle sound as he stood in his first class Stateroom on A Deck. Bridget was clinging to his leg begging him to stop. He could barely make out her words as she sniveled an apology for her disgusting behaviour at the boarding gate. William couldn't abide snivelling, it wasn't the English thing to do, but he couldn't afford the time to further correct his errant wife now. He carefully placed his riding crop in the top drawer of Bridget's dressing table so she will see it whenever she opened her drawer. It would serve as a reminder of the consequences of her ill-discipline.

He pushed his wife's tear-stained face away from his thigh then walked to the door leaving Bridget, curled up in a protective ball, on the plush Axminster carpet. "We are to dine with the Captain at eight sharp. Please try to look presentable." Then without so much as a backward glance at his wife, William left the cabin, slamming the door behind him. He had plans for the afternoon, plans that began with a full bodied red and ended with a full bodied blonde.

As he strolled along the wide corridor, William was vaguely aware of the mighty ship's movement, a gentle sideways nudge as the tugs began the job of gingerly guiding the vessel down the River Test and out into The Solent. He nodded politely to an elderly woman dressed in the traditional black of mourning, who stood patiently waiting for her chambermaid to open the door to her stateroom. She responded with a discreet nod and a faint smile, although her eyes remained sad and lifeless. William remembered doing business with her late husband and had met her several times, although he couldn't remember her name. He was about to offer his assistance when, to his relief, the servant pushed the door open and ushered the widow inside, sparing William the awkwardness that comes when speaking to someone you should know but whose name you just can't recall.

Once the door had clicked shut, he continued his stroll, heading for the aft lounge which, according to reports, was as fine and lavish as any hotel in Europe.

William wasn't disappointed. Even with his expensive tastes and ostentatious style, which he'd become renowned for flaunting at any given opportunity, the room's design and craftsmanship took his breath away. The room, lit by four huge bay windows and a large central chandelier, boasted an ornate white marble fireplace that provided the main focal point. Carved oak paneling, with large inlaid mirrors that would not have looked out of place at the Palace of Versailles, surrounded the fireplace. The room also contained an extensive library and

a bar where William ordered a glass of Beaujolais before choosing a comfortable seat facing one of the bay windows. Here he planned to while away an hour or so inspecting the passenger list for business associations, both past and future, and peruse the library for a little light reading before his secret rendezvous.

Eight

The time-consuming task of collecting the luncheon trays from half of the upper deck's thirty-six luxurious staterooms had been allocated to Esme, and by mid-afternoon, she still had the last few rooms to clear. She felt sure the horrible ogre, Miss Wilson, had singled her out for this task as punishment for her earlier insolence. Her mother always said she had a tendency to be overconfident, a trait she apparently inherited from her father, and this would one day lead her headlong into trouble. Esme was sure that day had come. She'd had plenty of time to reflect upon her earlier outburst and realized how stupid she had been. Esme pondered the thought she would never get hired for the return voyage, let alone future crossings, because of her earlier outburst. This job had been her dream since she and her father watched the cruise liners sail out of port bound for exotic locations when she was still a little girl. It was going to be her and Charlotte's way of escaping the life of poverty and prostitution, which so often ensnared young women living in the Victorian slums that surrounded the port.

Feeling a little despondent, Esme surmised she had screwed that up on the first day, simply because she couldn't keep her big mouth shut. She knew the frustration and anger she felt came from her own stupidity, but she still focused her hatred towards Miss Wilson and her haughty, holier-than-thou attitude. She fought back tears every time she replayed the incident in her head, wishing she could go back and do things

differently, like groveling apologetically as was expected of her and toeing the line like any other young girl desperate to keep her job.

As she stood outside the door of the next stateroom, Esme took a deep breath and forced her anger into a tight ball before burying it deep inside herself. She quickly ran her hands down her new uniform and smoothed out her starched pinafore before darting a finger around the inside of her collar trying to relieve the irritation where the material's newness rubbed at her soft skin. Then she knocked firmly on the door.

There was no reply.

Esme waited a respectful ten seconds then knocked again, only harder this time. A woman's voice, muffled by the thickness of the door, answered inviting her in. Turning the cold brass doorknob, Esme gently pushed the door open and stepped inside to find the suite's lavishly decorated reception room unoccupied, the luncheon tray sat on the table, its food untouched. As she hurried to gather the tray, she heard movement from the bedroom.

"Hello?" she called out. "Maid service. I've come to collect the luncheon tray."

There was no answer. As she listened for a response, Esme craned her neck trying to peer through the half-open bedroom door. Her hearing picked up a feint rustling sound, like something dragging across the room's deep carpet followed by a brief moment of silence, broken only by a low moan and a gentle sigh.

"Hello?" Esme called out again, her annoyance returning. Surely, whoever was in the other room must have heard her call the first time? This time there was a definite response to her call. It started as a low groan then grew into barely coherent speech punctuated by loud gulping sobs. Esme took a few tentative steps towards the door before asking in a loud voice, "Are you alright in there? Do you need any help?" As her palm touched the smooth surface of the door, her confidence drained away, and she fought the urge to turn and run back to the safety of the corridor. Summoning all her resolve, she gently pushed the door inwards.

She was completely unprepared for the sight that greeted her.

A young woman sprawled face down across the bed, the back of her expensive dress torn open to reveal not only her pale skin but several painful-looking wounds. A few of these thin, dark lesions had split open, soaking the dress' bodice and forming little dark rivulets of blood on the dazzling whiteness of the new sheets. The young woman's tousled hair, clumsily pulled from its style and left hanging like a lopsided bird's nest, obscured the woman's face, preventing Esme from identifying her.

Esme gasped involuntarily, momentarily backing away, unsure whether the woman was alive or dead, the ghastly image of the dead body from the previous evening still hauntingly fresh in her mind.

The young woman on the bed let out another low moan and tried unsuccessfully to lift her head. Esme remained rooted to the spot, unable to run away and unwilling to advance. She tried to speak, but like her feet, her throat was paralysed with fear. She opened her mouth, but the simple words she formed so easily in her head failed to rise past the lump in her throat. She took a deep breath, forcing the air deep into her lungs, holding it there for a second, before allowing it to escape slowly through pursed lips as she concentrated on her disobedient legs, urging them into action.

Esme knew this was not the time for feint hearts, the woman obviously needed her help. After a fleeting moment of hesitation, she pushed her fear aside and ran to the bed. Crouching next to the prostrate figure's head, she carefully moved the mass of dark hair away from the stranger's face. Esme immediately recognised the tear-stained face of Mrs. Grafton. Offering soothing words of comfort, she gently stroked Bridget's dishevelled hair.

Esme had only shown the young woman and her handsome new husband to the suite a few hours ago. How could someone get into the room and attack a woman without discovery? Locked iron gates protected the first class section of the ship, preventing the steerage passengers from being able to mingle with the upper class. Even if someone from first class entered the cabin intent on attacking Mrs. Grafton, which Esme thought unlikely, then surely her screams would have alerted someone.

Esme had spent the last couple of hours clearing trays from nearby cabins and the corridors had been a constant hive of activity with servants attending to their employer's needs and people returning, having witnessed the ship navigate around the Isle of Wight, from one of the cafés or restaurants on the upper decks.

"Who did this?" Esme asked as she glanced fearfully around the room, suddenly aware the attacker may still be in the suite.

"I cannot say." Bridget's voice was barely a whisper. "But you are quite safe; he left some time ago." She winced as she tried lifting her head from the tear-stained pillow, but the effort was too much, and she slumped forward with a frustrated cry.

"But you must!" Esme said, "You need to be seeing a doctor, and reporting the attack to the proper people, the beast that done this, he must be caught."

"If I speak up he will only punish me more, and I fear there is not a living soul who would believe me." As she listened to Bridget's voice, Esme thought her words were more for her own benefit than Esme's, convincing herself silence was the safest course of action.

"Any man capable of such a despicable act against a lady such as yourself is too dangerous to be allowed to roam freely about the boat. If you know his name you must speak up. You are not without considerable influence, and your husband wields immense power. Who'd dare dismiss you as a liar, and the wounds … well, they speak for themselves?" Esme was

trying to keep her voice calm and reassuring, aware of both Mrs. Grafton's lofty status and the obvious fragility of her mind.

Bridget attempted to sit up again, gratefully accepting Esme's help with a half smile that transformed into a grimace of pain. She swung her legs off the bed with a stoical moan then wiped her eyes with a silk handkerchief before replying. "I barely have influence over my own household, and as to my husband, well there lies the problem." As Mrs. Grafton spoke, Esme moved around the large bed to take a better look at her injuries. She gently peeled away the edges of Mrs. Grafton's garments to reveal three distinct red welts; each had torn the flesh sufficiently to cause considerable bleeding.

Bridget Grafton paused, flinching while Esme inspected her back, and then added in a soft voice, "It was his hand wielding the riding crop." She fell silent again allowing Esme to grasp the significance of her words, then after a lengthy pause added, "So you see my dilemma?"

Stunned, Esme stopped her inspection of the wealthy socialite's wounds. She had witnessed firsthand the injuries caused by a drunken sailor's fists, returning from the pub to find his supper not ready. Esme was aware of the violence a man could use on a woman he claimed to love, but for an officer and a gentleman to use a riding crop on a lady of breeding was beyond her understanding. Esme took a moment to gather her thoughts before replying, unsure whether Mrs. Grafton had asked her a direct question or had simply made a statement. "Yes, I do, ma'am." Then with more conviction, she added, "I

still think you should see the ship's doctor. These wounds need cleaning and a dressing."

"It would only raise awkward questions, and I'm sure the physician will be duty bound to report such injuries, especially with them happening to the wife of one of the ship's wealthier passengers." Bridget unbuttoned the front of her dress but struggled to pull the sleeves from her shoulders, her face contorting in pain. Seeing her distress, Esme hurried around the bed to help. She gently eased the dress off one arm at a time then carefully peeled away Bridget's torn and blood-soaked undergarments.

"Well, if you'll not speak with the doctor then I must insist you allow me to treat you. I have some experience tending injuries obtained in accidents and drunken fights. I could use spare laundry as temporary bandages." Esme, realising she may have spoken out of turn, added in a more deferential tone, "I mean, if that would be agreeable to you, ma'am."

Bridget allowed a small smile of relief to brighten her face for a moment, "That would be very agreeable … I'm sorry, you must think me rude, but I have forgotten your name?"

Giving a brief, self-conscious curtsey to the half-naked patron, an act that obviously amused Mrs. Grafton, she answered, "Esme, ma'am. And I do not think you the slightest bit rude."

"I think we are beyond social niceties, Esme," Bridget hunched forward, her arms folded across her exposed breasts.

"I suspect you know who I am, as it was you who escorted us to our cabin, but please call me Bridget." Then, seeing Esme's look of discomfort, added, "Or Mistress Bridget, if you are happier with that." She gave another half smile, half grimace as Esme nodded her acceptance. "I suggest then, we continue with some haste as I am due to dine with the Captain this evening, and I do not want you to get in trouble for not completing your tasks."

Nine

The Dining Saloon's main reception area was lavish to the point of pretentiousness with Chesterfield settees set around a Steinway grand piano. The three elevator doors were paneled with oak and the grand staircase, down which William and Bridget walked, swept majestically through the room. As they awaited their turn to be seated, Bridget admired the elegant white Jacobean styled ceiling and white oak walls which added to the room's modern, spacious feel. Although large, the design gave the room an intimate atmosphere with carefully positioned alcoves creating an illusion of privacy.

An immaculately dressed waiter escorted the couple to one of these alcoves with a large circular table laid with the finest china and sparkling silver tableware. Even William, with his privileged upbringing, couldn't help but feel impressed, whereas Bridget, with her more sheltered background, was in complete awe and just kept gawping at the expensive oak furniture and fine linen tablecloths. A couple had already taken their seats on the far side of the table and the gentleman rose politely as she and William took theirs. Bridget nodded politely, responding to his act of chivalry.

"Allow me to introduce myself?" The man spoke with an educated Boston accent which Bridget recognised from her childhood, before her parents sent her off to expensive European schools and an even more expensive English finishing school. "I am Benjamin Guggenheim and this ..." he bowed

towards the lady seated next to him, "is my companion, Madame Aubart."

"Good Evening Mr. Guggenheim. I am Captain William Grafton and this is my wife, Bridget. May I say how honoured we are to meet you; your reputation crossed the Atlantic well in advance of your good self." William smiled at Madame Aubart and added, "And what a delightful companion you have chosen to travel home with."

"I understand, from the London gossip rags, that you two only recently married. Is that correct, my dear?" Guggenheim spoke directly to Bridget to the obvious annoyance of William.

"That is correct, Mr. Guggenheim."

"Then let me order champagne to celebrate the joyous union." Then added in a conspiratorial tone, "If I am not mistaken by your accent, although you do hide it well, Mrs. Grafton, you are also from the colonies ... Boston, maybe?"

Bridget leant forward with a smile, and joining his conspiracy replied, "I won't tell if you don't."

Guggenheim threw his head back and laughed loudly, disturbing some of the other diners seated around them; not that he appeared to care. "Excellent. You have chosen well there, William. You don't mind if we drop the stuffy formalities, do you? She will serve you well as a wife, and I fear become quite a pain in the ass, as brash young American women can be. And I, for one, would not have them any different." He raised his finger to attract a nearby waiter's attention and curtly ordered two bottles of the ship's finest champagne.

Although William leant in close to his wife, his hand gently caressing her back while he whispered quietly in her ear, Madame Aubart noticed Bridget looked uncomfortable, even pained. She decided to say nothing, choosing instead to place her hand in the billionaire's lap. A gentle reminder that, although a beautiful young society girl may look appealing in the dining room, when it came to the bedroom, or the veranda of their exclusive Parisian hotel, it was experience that counted. She felt Benjamin respond and removed her hand giving him an innocent smile, confident she'd got her point across.

"Well, Madame Grafton," Madame Aubart's English was perfect, although she deliberately kept a sultry French accent, believing it gave her an air of continental mystery, which proved popular with rich American men. "I do believe the gentlemen will begin to talk business and politics if we do not establish some ground rules. So I propose we ban both subjects until after dinner when you boys may retire to some smoky backroom to bore each other to death." She paused, allowing the gentlemen a moment to digest her words, then just as William was about to respond, she continued, "And if you do not adhere ..." she looked uncertainly across the table at Bridget, "is that the right word? Adhere?" Then, buoyed on by Bridget's polite nod of confirmation, she continued, "Oui, yes. If you do not adhere to our proposal, and either by accident or deliberate intent, venture forth on such a conversation then, as punishment, you'll have to take us dancing. There will be no adjourning to the library for a cigar."

"Madame! I am deeply saddened you could even suggest we would not wish to take you dancing. How can dancing with a beautiful woman be a punishment?" Guggenheim feigned outrage and, becoming animated, threw his napkin to the floor in a theatrical gesture before folding his arms across his chest like a recalcitrant child, much to both William and Bridget's amusement.

Bridget winced as she laughed, the lesions on her back bearing testament to William's skill with a horsewhip. He'd already warned her about the consequences of becoming too familiar with the debonair billionaire. The outwardly loving caress on her back, while he whispered in her ear, had been far from caring. The pressure he applied to the wounds, while not excessive, was enough to cause her discomfort, and his words contained a thinly veiled threat. Bridget was sure Madame Aubart had noticed her discomfort and was now discreetly trying to lead the conversation, allowing Bridget time to compose herself.

During their light-hearted conversation, the champagne had arrived and Guggenheim insisted on proposing a toast to the happy couple, wishing them good health and a long, happy marriage. When she raised her glass to accept the other couple's good wishes, Bridget felt the constricting tug of the linen dressing applied by Esme earlier and hoped no one noticed her smile was one of irony, not happiness.

As they retook their seats, the Captain and his party joined them at the table. Captain Smith wore his full dress

uniform and oozed the kind of authority that put people at their ease. He politely introduced himself to William and Bridget in a soft, yet confident, voice before greeting Guggenheim like an old friend. He checked the champagne bottle to ensure he'd ordered something palatable, because as he put it, "An American wouldn't know the difference between a fine wine and dirty bathwater." The two men laughed as they shook hands before Captain Smith introduced the rest of his party.

"This fine fellow is," he pointed to a middle-aged man with an unimpressive handlebar moustache standing slightly aloof from proceedings, "Mr. Bruce Ismay. He is the managing director of The White Star Line and the man who, for the next few weeks at least, pays my wages. And the gentleman to my left will no doubt captain this ship himself in a few years, but for now, he is the ship's Sixth Officer, Mr. Moody." The men all exchanged cordial handshakes as Guggenheim introduced Madame Aubart and Captain and Mrs. Grafton before everybody took their seat. The young officer, Mr. Moody, appeared taken aback by Captain Smith's approval and couldn't help but smile the entire way through dinner, but more than held his own with the social elite assembled at the table.

Throughout dinner, both William and his newfound friend, Mr. Guggenheim asked questions about the *Titanic* and her capabilities. These were answered enthusiastically by the ship's officers, and when questions involved financial matters, less enthusiastically by Mr. Ismay. Bridget thought he appeared shy and uneasy in the presence of such confident traveling

companions. On one occasion, Madame Aubart jokingly chided Guggenheim for sailing too close to the wind about a question on the politics of shipbuilding and the struggle to command the North Atlantic route. Her intervention prompted an intrigued Captain Smith to ask about the lady's proposal regarding after-dinner dancing. When supplied with the details, he told her that if the gentlemen chose to abandon such beautiful women, then they must suffer the consequences.

He added, "I'm sure any one of the ship's officers would be honoured to escort them in a dance." At this, Officer Moody stole a furtive glance at Bridget, briefly catching her eye, before hurriedly looking away. It was a moment Bridget hoped had gone unnoticed by William who was busy trying to ingratiate himself with Mr. Guggenheim's wealth.

The evening ended with Captain Smith regaling the table with stories from his distinguished career. Being a self-effacing man, he described his forty years at sea as 'wholly uneventful,' but his natural humour and well-practiced delivery did entertain his guests well past the sumptuous cheese board served with finely blended coffee.

Despite the quality of the evening's revelry, Bridget was glad when William stood, announcing, "I regret to break up such an interesting gathering, but it has been a fulfilling, yet ultimately tiring, day. Therefore, I think it time Bridget and I retire for the night. Thank you for such a wonderful evening. I'm sure I speak for my wife when I say that we look forward to our next meeting."

He took Bridget by the arm, escorting her through the half-empty dining room, many of the guests having long since left it in search of alternative entertainment or simply to take a stroll on the promenade. From the painful way he gripped her elbow, Bridget knew she'd somehow displeased him, and for Bridget that rounded the evening off perfectly.

Ten

Patrick breakfasted alone at the smartly laid table in a suit he had borrowed from Bernard. It was not usual for him to dress so smartly for breakfast, but then the second class dining saloon on the *Titanic* was not his usual breakfast haunt. Bernard had insisted he go to breakfast looking presentable, proclaiming, "Image is everything, dear boy." The shirt's over-starched collar caused his neck to itch, despite him being able to run his fingers around its inside, while the trousers were so big, the belt he'd borrowed with them stretched almost twice around his waist.

Patrick took a quick look around the room, checking nobody was watching, before deftly flicking the thick pork sausage off his plate and into his waiting napkin. This he folded casually before placing it in one of the cavernous pockets of Bernard's trousers. Patrick tried to look nonchalant as he finished his second cup of tea in one navvy-like swig before rising from the table.

He had arranged to meet Bernard on deck for a midmorning coffee, while they were at anchor off Queenstown Harbour, so he could say a final farewell to the old country, and to the old Patrick McGowan. By early afternoon, the *Titanic* would have weighed anchor and headed for the open sea and New York.

But now, he had a far more pressing engagement. He needed to check on Pandora. He had elected not to tell Bernard

about his furry companion, at least not for now, as he wasn't sure how the older man might react. If he reported Patrick, which Patrick thought unlikely, because of their having only met twenty-four hours ago, then both he and Pandora would be put ashore at Queenstown. This would scupper his plans of welcoming a new life before he had a chance to say a fond farewell to the old one.

Patrick entered the sparsely furnished cabin and tossed his jacket onto his bunk before sitting on the hard bench occupying the opposite wall. He was pleased by Bernard's absence, he either had not yet returned from breakfast or had already left to take a constitutional stroll on deck before their planned meeting. Taking advantage of Bernard's absence, Patrick retrieved the battered valise from its hiding place under the bench, sliding it out into the middle of the narrow cabin. He fished the napkin containing the breakfast sausage from the depths of his pocket, placing it beside him on the bench, before fumbling with the valise's brass catch.

Finally working the catch open, Patrick heard a soft whimper from within the coarse fabric's interior. Cautiously, he pulled the bag open just enough to peer inside. Pandora was curled in a tight ball at the bottom of the bag, her sad looking brown eyes staring inquisitively up at him. Making what he hoped were reassuring noises, he broke off a small piece of sausage, dropping it into the bag. Pandora cowered deeper into the dark interior, her eyes wide with terror, her lips drawn back

to reveal razor-like teeth and a particularly vicious-looking set of canine fangs.

"It's alright, Pandora. I've brought food," he gently dropped another, this time smaller, piece of meat into the bag's depths.

The tiny monkey tried to appear even smaller by curling her tail tightly around her body and hunkering down into the valise's darkest corner. She ignored the meat, her eyes remaining fixed on the bag's narrow opening. After a few minutes of gentle coaxing, all of which was to no avail, Patrick admitted defeat.

"Alright Pandora, have it your way. But I'll leave the meat in the bag in case you're just being shy." Patrick refastened the valise and gently slid it back under the bench.

Patrick, aware of his own discomfort in the oversized, borrowed suit, took a few minutes to change back into his own clothes, taking time to carefully place Bernard's suit back in the compact cupboard they shared. He checked his pocket-watch, realising it was already gone eleven, before quickly brushing his hair and charging out of the cabin.

Officer Moody had just left the bridge in the capable hands of First Officer Murdoch following his two-hour watch. The *Titanic* was riding at anchor two miles offshore, her mighty bows turned into the brisk south-westerly wind. It would fall to Murdoch to notify the Captain when the last of the passengers embarked and the barge had safely returned to shore, taking

with it the well-wishers and hawkers that came aboard to sell fine lace, fresh fruit, and general knickknacks. On the Captain's command, he would then weigh anchor and set a course across the Atlantic.

Moody felt a pang of jealousy. How he would have loved to tell his grandchildren stories of how he sailed the mighty *Titanic* out into the open sea on her maiden voyage. But Moody, a patient, level-headed man, was smart enough to know he was still young, his time would come.

Officer Moody made his way towards the first class promenade. It was White Star's policy that officers, while not on watch, should be visible about the ship, especially in the first class areas. It helped to reassure the passengers, giving them a sense of security. It also allowed passengers to ask many and varied questions about the voyage and the ship's progress, and therefore he had developed a brisk, but unhurried, walk that deterred all but the most ardent of passengers. He smiled politely and returned the passengers' greetings with a slight touch to the peak of his cap, a movement he had practiced in the mirror for several hours to ensure it portrayed the correct gravitas.

Moody walked almost the entire promenade during which he helped two elderly ladies position their deck chairs and explained to an obnoxious young boy and his stern-faced nanny which side of the ship was port and which was starboard. Moody then left the promenade, descending two decks to the first class dining saloon, where he spent some time conversing

with the passengers who had decided to take an early lunch. Spotting William seated at a table on his own, he approached the educated, military man, "Good morning, Captain Grafton. So good to see you again so soon."

"Officer Moody?" William Grafton greeted the young officer with a forced smile. "I trust you slept well? I was sorry we could not stay for a dance, but Mrs. Grafton felt tired. A combination of fine food and sea air, I expect. Not to mention the fine champagne," William gave a polite but, Moody thought, hollow laugh.

"I retired early myself, Captain Grafton. I was due to take the morning watch." Moody replied, aware that William wasn't really listening, his attention focused on the door as if waiting for somebody. With a little more excitement in his voice than was necessary, he continued, "Will Mrs. Grafton be joining you for lunch?"

"No, she will not!" William replied curtly. Then, realising his rudeness, he added in a softer, calmer tone, "I'm afraid she felt a little out of sorts this morning. I think, regretfully, she enjoyed herself a little too much last night and is suffering the consequences today."

Moody was taken aback by his own feelings of disappointment at this news and wondered whether his impromptu stroll had, in fact, subconsciously brought him to the dining saloon with the intent of seeing Mrs. Grafton. He also sensed that William's words contained a carefully disguised,

almost sinister, message, certainly his demeanour appeared hostile.

The rising tension between the two men eased abruptly as Benjamin Guggenheim walked into the saloon. William rose from his seat, and without bothering to even look at Moody, asked with a dismissive tone, "Would you be so good to invite Mr. Guggenheim to have lunch with me?"

"It would be my pleasure, Captain Grafton." As he gladly hurried away to intercept the billionaire before a steward could seat him at another table, Moody added under his breath, "But not, I sense, for Mr. Guggenheim."

The gregarious American greeted him with a warm smile, "Mr. Moody, how are you this fine day?" His handshake was firm and genuine, his left hand lightly touched Moody's elbow adding vigour to the perceived friendship.

"I'm well, thank you, Mr. Guggenheim. I have a message from Captain Grafton for you." He began to signal towards the now vacant chair at William's table.

Guggenheim interrupted him, a comical look of panic on his face, "Please do not tell me he has invited me to join him for lunch."

Moody tried hard to mask his smile, and choosing his words carefully, replied, "I'm delighted to inform you he has, Sir, yes."

Guggenheim gave a resigned sigh and smiled in William's direction before whispering just loud enough for Moody to hear, "He's an odious little man. I only spoke with him because I

had the misfortune to sit at the same table, and his delightful wife is a fellow American." He took half a step towards William's table then, almost as an afterthought, turned and added with a wink. "Such a pity you didn't get to dance with her, maybe an agreeable young man like yourself could make her see the error of her ways." Then he was gone.

Momentarily flustered, Moody couldn't reply; a tingling feeling of warmth spread through his cheeks, and into his earlobes. For a brief moment, he thought he should follow the American, reprimanding him for his inappropriate comment. After all, Bridget was a married woman with a reputation to protect … Bridget, he had thought of her as Bridget. Not as Mrs. Grafton. Now it was he who was being inappropriate, but he did have to agree with Guggenheim on one thing. Captain Grafton was indeed an odious little man and Bridget deserved so much better.

Moody checked his pocket watch and saw he had just enough time to get something to eat before he was expected to welcome the new passengers on board. As he negotiated a path through the saloon, he tried in vain to get the image of Bridget's soft cornflower blue eyes and slightly crooked smile from his mind. He resolved that politely avoiding the fair Mrs. Grafton for the rest of the voyage would be the best course of action for all concerned.

Eleven

Patrick stepped out onto the second class promenade located on the aft section of the boat deck directly to the rear of the similarly fashioned first class promenade. The only real difference between the two sections was the wealth of the passengers who strolled along the expertly crafted pine flooring. The sun shone brightly, momentarily deceiving Patrick into believing it to be a pleasantly warm afternoon until the invigorating sea breeze, cooled by its journey across a thousand miles of Atlantic seawater, buffeted him backwards. He thrust his hands deeper into his pockets, pulling his overcoat tighter about his body, then, aided by a strong gust of wind, headed aft in search of Bernard.

Patrick stole a glance at the rear mast towering above him. The ensign of The White Star Line fluttered frantically at its top while the rigging below creaked as its ropes swung back and forth, occasionally smacking loudly against the mast. Slightly forward of his position was the rearmost of the four black-capped, tawny brown funnels, a thin wisp of lazy smoke drifting skyward until, caught by the wind, it disappeared into the fluffy, silvery-gray clouds.

As he stepped around the corner into the relative shelter afforded by the raised building housing the stairwell and carefully folded deck chairs, he smelt the unmistakable seafaring blend of canvas tarpaulins and tar. The harsh burnt-coal smell of the tar irritated the back of his throat, causing him

to cough, while the sea-salty tang in the air stung his lips, making them feel dry and cracked. Patrick swept his gaze across the few passengers, hardy enough to brave the wind, until he spotted Bernard propping up the railing, staring out across the white-capped waves at the distant shore. He scurried over to join his new friend.

"Hello, my dear boy. Come and witness the end of our old-world lives, for soon, we'll be reincarnated as new Americans. Free from the shackles of class and the manacles of poverty. Free to shape our own destiny and realise the American dream." Bernard threw his arms wide as his voice rose in a crescendo before plummeting into a limp, sarcastic laugh, his words blown away on the wind. "What a load of, if I may be so bold as to borrow a word from our adoptive nation, bunkum!"

"You do not strike me as a man full of optimism for his new life. Did you not embark on this great adventure to advance your station in life, to climb above those holding you back?" Patrick eyed Bernard with confusion which gave way to suspicion as he added cautiously, "Or did you have too much wine with your lunch?"

Bernard looked hurt and took a moment before replying. "To answer your last question first; no, I did not. If the truth be known, I didn't have enough wine with my lunch and to answer your more pretentious first question, the answer is again, no. I embarked on this great adventure because I am running away. Not from poverty or oppression, but from the police who would

like to ask me some awkward questions regarding certain funds which, as happy circumstance would have it, came into my possession."

Patrick laughed aloud and applauded the older man. "You're wanted for common theft." It was a statement, not a question, but Bernard was quick to tender an answer.

"I have never stolen anything in my life, except maybe a few hearts. The money was given to me in good faith, albeit misplaced, as I may have misled the dear, sweet lady who gave it to me, on one or two small details." His eyes met Patrick's, and he winked. "Namely, who I was and what I wanted the money for. It was not a common crime; it was sophisticated in detail and rich in deception."

"I knew you to be a fraud at our first meeting, but I have my suspicions you were never the English country gent your appearance makes you seem," Patrick replied, smiling broadly.

"Oh! Far from. My father was a poor man, a farm hand from Lincolnshire. Sadly, all I inherited from him was poverty." Bernard laughed, his mood becoming more pensive. "It's the English social order. We rely on class to ensure society runs smoothly. The working class works to make the upper class rich while the middle class actually works for the upper class, and the upper class themselves drink champagne, ignorant of the rising power of the masses. They remain ensconced in their ivory towers enjoying a halcyon lifestyle while we remain downtrodden and oppressed, all because of birth."

Patrick listened intently to Bernard's words while he stared at the distant Irish coastline. Somehow, it looked even more beautiful than he remembered; the green pastures were a deeper emerald shade while the ploughed fields were a richer brown. "That's why there are so many people on this ship, and not just from England. All of Europe is the same. People believe it is somehow better to be a poor American than a poor Englishman or Irishman or Italian."

Bernard nodded his agreement. "That is true, but I do not intend to be a poor American. It is the poor Americans who gave their lives building the American dream, the railroads, and the skyscrapers while rich Americans live the American dream. The rich ones become politicians, and the rich politicians become president; a rich king presiding over rich men with economic power, a feudal system of wealth. It's serfdom by another name." Bernard became more animated as he spoke, his eyes afire with passion. "Even here, as we sail to our freedom there is segregation of class. Not just by ticket price but by real, physical barriers. Servant's quarters are located away from their masters, sparing their employers the ignominy of having to make small talk over dinner. Locked gates separate first and second class areas of the ship from steerage areas, preventing the common man rubbing shoulders with the gentry. We, my young friend, are interlopers, traitors to our class; me by fraud and I know not how you paid your way, but I wager it wasn't earned by hard work alone."

"And to avoid becoming another poor immigrant you are going to do ... what exactly?" Patrick pointedly ignored Bernard's veiled invitation to tell his story. Then, before the Englishman could reply he added, "My apologies ... Sir Bernard Astor intends to do ... what exactly?"

"My plan ..." the bushy moustache tilted upwards as he smiled, "is to marry a rich, gullible, and preferably attractive widow."

"Am I to assume that description also applied to the lady who told the police about your inattention to detail?" Again, Patrick found himself laughing, enjoying his conversation with the older man. He felt that a strong bond of friendship had already formed between them, one that could be of great mutual benefit.

Bernard looked aghast, "Why no! She was rich and a widow, that much is true, but she was also as ugly as sin and sadly for me, not as gullible as I thought."

The shrill sound of the ship's whistle drowned out their laughter. The two men gradually fell silent, taking a last lingering gaze at dry land as the propellers far below churned the water into a foamy white spray and began inching *RMS Titanic* out towards the vast ocean.

William felt the almost imperceptible increase in power as the two massive steam engines began to turn the ship's three solid bronze propellers, pushing the vessel through the water. She crept forward, slowly at first, her vast bulk taking time to

respond to the helmsman's orders, but she soon picked up speed, leaving Cork Bay in her wake. As he almost danced up the grand staircase with a joyous smile, William reflected on his luncheon meeting. He had dined on the most exquisite food and with none other than the hugely respected philanthropist and businessman, Benjamin Guggenheim, as his guest. He was confident he had secured Guggenheim's friendship and the support of one of America's most influential men. That, coupled with his clever marriage to a Boston socialite, would undoubtedly smooth his passage into the higher echelons of society on both sides of the Atlantic, helping him make a notable sum of money into the bargain.

On reaching the top of the grand staircase, he looked down the corridor towards his cabin before pointedly turning on his heel and walking confidently in the opposite direction. He headed to the identical staterooms on the other side of A Deck. He was in the mood to celebrate, but not with his new wife, she was a convenient business arrangement, and an immature and irritating one at that. No, he wanted to enjoy himself with someone who understood his needs, shared his passion.

He stopped outside the cabin next to the Writing Room, pausing to allow an elderly couple to pass. He gave them a courteous nod and waited for them to enter their cabin a few doors along the corridor before knocking gently on the door. He listened carefully but heard no response. Without bothering to knock a second time, he quietly opened the door and slipped inside. The reception room was in semi-darkness, the thick

drapes closed tight preventing the bright afternoon sunshine from entering the room, and the sickly-sweet smell of freshly burned opium hung heavily in the air. William moved to the well-stocked drinks cabinet and poured himself a generous shot of Scotland's finest export before removing his jacket and draping it over the chaise longue.

He took a sip of his drink, savouring the gold liquid's rich taste as it caressed his pallet before burning a path down his throat to ignite a fire in his stomach, then strolled through to the adjoining bedroom. Again, William discovered the drapes shut with a single lamp, secreted behind a red silk modesty screen, bathing everything in the room in a deep, blood red hue. From the doorway, the room appeared unoccupied, the smell of opium growing stronger with each tentative step.

William was only a few steps over the threshold, his eyes not yet accustomed to the darkness, when he felt the subtle sensation of warm breath tickling his neck. He froze; a shiver passed down his spine as the tiny hairs on the back of his neck stood erect. His nose detected the light flowery aroma of an expensive perfume above the opium's heavier odour, and he thought he heard the faintest of sighs close to his ear. William remained rooted to the spot, unwilling to move. He had no desire to turn around. He sensed the faintest of movements then something brushed lightly against his shoulder.

"Where have you been? I've not seen you for so long I thought you'd got a new plaything and forgotten about me." The voice was soft and feminine, the words whispered in a

sulky, licentious tone. "You know I behave so badly without anyone to correct my ill-discipline." The woman's intoxicating scent mixed with her thinly veiled threat of misbehaviour—behaviour apparently so bad it required chastisement—had altered William's emotional state. He had become frustrated, eager to turn around and take control, but the anticipation was his exquisite punishment for not attending to this matter sooner.

He didn't have to wait long before Violet glided silently past him, her hand running seductively across his shoulder and down his chest. She turned to face him, her fine silk dressing gown hanging open to reveal her naked curvaceous body to his lingering gaze.

William could contain himself no longer. Scooping his new wife's maid up in his arms, he carried her across the room before throwing her face down on the large bed. Holding her down with a firm hand, he used the back of her wooden hairbrush to punish her for her perceived indiscretions until he could endure it no longer. Then, in a violent, opium-induced haze, they shared the delights of one another's bodies.

Twelve

Esme had risen shortly before five and was finally nearing the end of her morning duties. She had spent almost six hours making up the beds with fresh linens, picking up wet towels, and clearing breakfast trays. She also helped a sweet old lady put on her jewellery while listening to stories about the woman's recently deceased husband. In another stateroom, she felt compelled to exit the room in a hurry after discovering a gentleman and his butler in a delicate position. She deliberately chose to leave the Grafton's stateroom until last.

Bridget was waiting for her by the door and quickly ushered her inside. "I've waited so patiently for you, but now feel I may burst if I do not tell you my news." Bridget paced back and forth as she spoke, her hands gesticulating wildly.

"Please try not to, Mrs. Graf ... Bridget. I would 'ave to clean up the mess." Esme was laughing as she steered Bridget towards one of the couches. "I'm here now; so please sit yourself down, and take a deep breath before you begin."

Bridget accepted Esme's advice, taking a seat on the couch; although, she remained sitting upright with her hands outspread in her lap. She took a few slow deep breaths, composing herself so when she spoke, her words were measured and thoughtful, her voice calm, almost accepting.

"My courtship with William was brief to the point of whirlwind, and the romance briefer still. The man is a pig ... and saying that is to do pigs a great disservice. He sees fit to

interfere in every facet of my life, by bullying and manipulating everything to his advantage. You yourself have witnessed the results of his handiwork if I displease him in even the minutest of ways." Bridget paused, her distress obvious in her expression.

"And yet you carry his child," stated Esme, then before she could stop herself asked, "It is his?"

Bridget looked at her hands for a moment then shook her head. "I had the briefest dalliance at Christmas with a fine young gentleman from Boston, whom I grew up with. It was brief, but we did … you know?" Bridget's face flushed a dark pink, causing Esme to giggle.

"You should come visit me when you're next in England," said Esme. "I know a few men who would gladly relieve you of your embarrassment over such matters. You might even earn yourself a pretty penny." The shock on Bridget's face brought tears to Esme's eyes as she struggled to keep her laughter bottled up.

Bridget launched a cushion at Esme. "You are a cow for having such fun at my expense, and I will not continue my story until you have regained your senses." She tried to preserve a suitably disapproving visage, but the maid's laughter was infectious.

"My apologies, Mistress Bridget, please do go on." One hand still covered Esme's mouth, stifling a final small giggle, as she replied.

"We dined at the Captain's table with Mr. Guggenheim, who William couldn't stop fawning over, and his little French

plaything. Obviously, the Captain himself, with the unbearable Mr. Ismay and the delightful Officer Moody who, I must say, is a dashingly handsome and perfectly charming gentleman." Bridget's voice had risen in pitch as she rushed through the final few words even surprising herself with such a brazen statement of attraction.

"He is that," said Esme, "and a whole lot more, I daresay, if given half the chance." She winked at the American socialite who feigned a disapproving look.

"Captain Smith suggested Mr. Moody dance with me so William and Mr. Guggenheim could adjourn for a cigar, but William cleverly put a stop to that." Her mood quickly changed as she looked down, inspecting her fingernails as her eyes filled with tears. Esme rushed to her side and placed a comforting arm around the distraught woman's shoulders. She gently drew Bridget's face into her chest allowing her to sob uncontrollably for a few minutes, until finally, she composed herself enough to snivel, "And I thought that ironic, as I'm sure he has a mistress."

"But if you do not love him, why do you care? Maybe he will realize the error of your marriage and you could divorce ..." Seeing Bridget shaking her head furiously, Esme added, "Or at least live separate lives. Perhaps you could stay in Boston on the pretence of a family illness when he returns to England."

Bridget smiled wistfully at the one person in the world she felt she could trust. "I do not care for him, but I do care about myself. To fail in a marriage before the honeymoon is even over is not something I'm proud to admit. How could I

have been so blind, so blinkered to his infidelity even as he courted me? Although I see now it was not me he courted but my father's connections. William Grafton is nothing but a worthless sycophant."

"I would agree wholeheartedly, I'm sure; however, there is not much call for such posh words in the Belvedere Arms."

Bridget let out a little chuckle and took a handkerchief out from her sleeve which she used to dab her eyes. "That's what I like about you, Esme, what you see is what you get. No airs or graces, just honesty and kindness, and despite being wise beyond your years, you have retained an almost childlike sincerity."

"Thank you for your kind words; however, I must admit I can be rash and, at times, too forthright for my own good, and I fear it will be those qualities that get me dismissed on our arrival in New York." Esme felt a lump rising in her throat, then it was her turn to cry, the tears rolling unchecked across her cheeks.

Bridget rose quickly from her seat reaching out to embrace the distraught maid. "What on earth is the matter?" She rubbed Esme's back sympathetically and made soothing noises as the other woman cried uncontrollably into her shoulder. It took Esme several minutes between sobs to tell Bridget about her fears for Charlotte, their plans for a new life and how, in a matter of hours, she'd jeopardized it all by upsetting the head housekeeper, Miss Wilson.

Bridget listened carefully to Esme's tale of sorrow without interrupting. Even though she was intrigued by the notion a dead body could simply disappear, she remained silent for a short while after Esme finished speaking, pondering her new friend's predicament. When she gingerly sat back trying not to aggravate the bruising left by William's riding crop, she had an almost triumphant smile on her face.

"It seems we both have problems that individually appear insurmountable; however, I believe I could, using a few of my rich and powerful connections, wipe clean your earlier misdemeanours with regard to Miss Wilson." Bridget let the statement hang in the air between them for a moment, before adding, "But in return, I would like your help in resolving the awkward quandary I have engineered for myself." She looked deeply into Esme's sparkling emerald green eyes, searching for a deeper understanding before finally asking, "Would that be acceptable to you?"

Bridget had to wait for her answer.

Thirteen

Violet looked at William lying next to her, a wicked smile tugging at the corners of her mouth. His eyes were closed, but he didn't yet have the deep regular breathing he usually did when sleeping. On the contrary, he was still breathing hard, struggling to regain his breath following his recent exertions, his perspiration adding a healthy sheen to his lightly tanned skin. She felt pleased with her afternoon's endeavours; William had the stamina of a man half his age and wasn't easily satisfied. She bit his exposed nipple playfully, giggling when he flinched in surprise.

"What did you do that for?" William asked, rubbing his injured nipple ruefully.

"You have always told me pain is an aphrodisiac. I wondered if it would be the same if you were the one experiencing the pain." She lifted the silk sheets and peered at his naked body. With another little giggle, she answered her own question. "It would appear not."

"I would love to teach you the error of your ways, Violet my dear, but I must return to my cabin and prepare for dinner. It is important I keep up the pretence of a happy marriage, as even in these enlightened times, many people find it distasteful doing business with a known philanderer."

William swung his legs out of bed and walked naked to the bathroom, something he had never done in front of his

wife. There he relieved himself before splashing refreshingly cold water on his face.

When he returned to the bedroom, Violet had moved to the dressing table where she sat admiring her naked breasts and delicately pulling a brush through her tousled hair. She had a nonchalant, almost distant look in her eyes as she asked softly, "Will the baby change anything between us?"

Shocked, William stopped picking up his clothes and slowly turned to stare at his young mistress. He tried to gather his thoughts, to formulate an appropriate response, but it was like his mind had shattered; the ideas, opinions, and values that together formed his ability to produce reasoned, coherent thoughts were nothing but broken fragments, scattered across his psyche.

After several seconds of catatonic stupor, he finally uttered, "Baby? What baby?" His thoughts rushing back, fighting to reform inside his head; a dozen voices, all clambering for attention.

"Your baby," replied Violet innocently. Secretly, William's obvious discomfort pleased her. It meant, just as she'd suspected, he hadn't known about Bridget's pregnancy. She knew William detested children as they had talked about it on several occasions. He viewed them as nothing more than parasites, eating into their parents' wealth and giving nothing in return. 'Let the poor have children; they have nothing to lose,' had become his mantra on the subject.

"You ... are ... with child?" William asked slowly, his finger pointing vaguely at the slight paunch of Violet's alabaster-white stomach.

"Me? No, perish the thought." She added an almost imperceptible shudder for dramatic effect, carefully ensuring it was not too subtle for William to notice. He had never been good at understanding the subtleties of feminine body language. "Mistress Grafton. She is the one carrying your child!" Violet brought her hand to her mouth with a soft gasp, adding in an incredulous tone, "Surely you knew? I'm so sorry if I've spoken out of turn."

William sat on the bed with the look of a prisoner listening to the judge sentencing him to hang. His normally ramrod straight back and military bearing had, for the moment, deserted him, leaving him hunched and withdrawn. He wore a stunned, almost blank, expression on his pale, blood-drained face as he wrestled with the news of his impending fatherhood.

"Bridget! Mrs. Grafton ... is pregnant? Are you sure?"

William stared at Violet quizzically, the intensity of his gaze scaring her. She could see his confusion of earlier turning to anger; his eyes had darkened, his jaw hardening to the point it could have been hewn from granite. Suddenly, conscious of her own nakedness, she reached for the silk gown she had discarded so seductively only an hour or so before and slipped it on, covering her own vulnerability.

She was beginning to wish she had kept quiet and not tried forcing his hand. What did she expect would happen? Was

he going to abandon his wife and unborn child for her, a mere chambermaid in his employ? Even if they did share certain interests in the boudoir, it would be social suicide for a man of his position. Violet suddenly realized his question hadn't been rhetorical, he still stared at her, expecting an answer from her.

"I ... I saw the bump myself, and sh ... she has suffered from sickness in the morning." Violet stammered as she sought the correct response, thinking it prudent not to mention the conversations she and Mrs. Grafton had shared on the subject. She did not want William thinking she had been in some small way disloyal to him, she had witnessed firsthand the bruises he had inflicted on his wife's fair skin and did not want the same happening to her, at least not out of anger.

Without warning, William sprang into action. Almost jumping from the bed, he gathered his clothes from all four corners of the exquisitely furnished bedroom before quickly dressing in silence. Violet watched him without further comment until he'd laced up his shoes and downed the last of the Scotch he had poured himself on entering the suite.

"Are you all right, my love?" She ventured, tentatively, regretting the words even as they left her mouth.

William stared at her for a moment with a look of contemptuous disdain then, slamming down the empty glass, he stormed from the room. Violet jumped as the thick oak door slammed shut behind him. She couldn't help but wonder if she would ever see him again. Flinging herself angrily onto her

unmade bed, she sobbed into the pillows that still bore the musky scent of his cologne.

Fourteen

In the musky darkness of the valise's interior, Pandora lay shivering, her bushy tail curled tightly around her fragile little body. Each minor convulsion rippling through her caused the tip of her tail to flick uncontrollably, but she wasn't cold. She felt frightened, but that wasn't the cause of her uncontrolled shivering.

No, Pandora understood the shivering was a physiological response to the raging heat threatening to consume her from within.

It flowed through her tiny body like molten rock, scorching her internal organs and boiling her brain in its own fluid, causing a savage combination of searing pain and mind-bending confusion. She could only think of the emptiness, and the emptiness she felt wasn't through lack of food. She had devoured the sausage Patrick had given to her earlier. This emptiness ran deeper than that, much deeper. It was a craving, an insatiable desire for fresh meat.

Pandora craved fresh, raw meat.

Every fibre in her frail body screamed at her to sate her hunger. She needed to feed, to hunt, to kill. And Pandora needed to do it soon.

A soft knock on the door disturbed Captain Smith in the middle of the chief engineer's report. They were never exciting at the best of times, but this one was particularly boring with

the only highlight, if he could call it that, being the small fire still smouldering in the starboard coal store. As a result, Smith welcomed the disturbance.

"Enter!" Captain Smith raised his voice and lowered his tone to give the word a suitable amount of authority. After a moment of hesitation during which Smith considered repeating his command, the door swung open and Bruce Ismay, the chairman of White Star, entered the room followed by Thomas Andrews, the ship's architect. Captain Smith felt ill-at-ease with the intrusion when he realized who his visitors were and immediately felt his authority to command the vessel was going to be tested.

"Good evening, E. J., Mr. Andrews and I were on our way to enjoy an aperitif before joining Sir and Lady Duff-Gordon and the Countess of Rothes for dinner and thought it might be an excellent idea to garner your assessment of our progress, as I'm sure the topic will arise."

Mr. Ismay spoke with the same assured arrogance of privilege and wealth that had led the English to build an Empire that spanned the globe. He was used to getting what he wanted when he wanted it, even from the Captain of the world's largest ocean liner.

"I'm certain you will make sure it does," replied Captain Smith dryly.

He was well aware of the importance of this voyage to his employers. They had invested heavily in *Titanic* to make it the largest and most luxurious vessel ever to put to sea, and they

needed this first voyage to be an unequivocal success. "I am reviewing the reports now and so far, except for the smouldering coal store, everything is progressing exactly as expected."

Captain Smith handed the chief engineer's report to Ismay, who glanced at it with seemingly little understanding of the nautical parlance and engineering configurations it contained.

After taking a brief moment to feign interest in the document, Mr. Ismay handed it back to the Captain muttering a perfunctorily, "Excellent."

An awkward moment of hesitation followed, during which the ship's owner looked at Andrews for support. Then, no doubt buoyed by the architect's presence, Mr. Ismay continued in his usual, more confident air. "I understand the engines are not yet running at their full capacity. Is there a reason for this?"

Captain Smith fought the urge to let out an exasperated sigh. He knew his visitors were keen to make New York on Tuesday evening as opposed to the scheduled Wednesday morning. The early arrival of the *Titanic* would mean the most luxurious method of crossing the Atlantic was also the fastest, and more conveniently, would also make the morning editions of the New York papers. Both Ismay and Andrews were aware of Captain Smith's opposition to pushing the engines too soon. Even the rich and powerful Bruce Ismay didn't have the authority to order his captain to increase speed, and as this was

Smith's last trip before retirement, he didn't feel the need to acquiesce to the chairman's wishes.

In the tone a schoolmaster might use to explain a simple problem to the class dunce, Captain Smith offered his reply. "You are absolutely correct, Mr. Ismay. The engines are not yet running at full capacity; however, we have been running at 70rpm which allows the *Titanic* to sail at exceptionally good speeds, often in excess of 21 knots. Meaning we could cover as much as 480 nautical miles in the day, and that's in less than ideal weather. Tomorrow the weather forecast is for calmer conditions, and if that holds true we will increase the speed to 72rpm following the officers' noon briefing. But please note, I'm responsible for this vessel and the lives of everyone aboard; if I have to slow or alter course for safety reasons, then I will. We don't want to throw a propeller shaft or risk a collision because we were going too fast to alter course, do we?" Captain Smith cocked his eyebrow as he turned the final sentence into a question, almost daring his visitors to disagree with him.

Boxed into a corner, Ismay reluctantly found himself agreeing with the captain's assertion that the vessel's safety was of paramount concern. He congratulated Captain Smith on his diligence and for making such excellent time between Southampton and Cherbourg then looked, awkwardly, to Andrews to continue the conversation.

"I agree the safety of the passengers and crew is of the utmost importance, as proved by the ship's revolutionary design which makes her almost unsinkable. It would take an

unfortunate series of events to breach enough compartments to actually sink this immensely strong, well-engineered piece of British industrial ingenuity." Andrews spoke in the quiet easy manner of a man who had total confidence in his design and the men who'd laboured night and day to make it a reality.

Andrews paused for a moment to allow Captain Smith to understand fully the implication of his words. Then, like a defence barrister about to blow a hole in the prosecution's supposedly watertight case, he continued. "It's this design and superior engineering that makes the *Titanic*, not only the safest vessel to cross the Atlantic, but also the fastest. She can withstand everything the North Atlantic route can throw at her and still make good time. I admire your sense of caution, Captain. It is a commendable trait in someone who holds other people's lives in their hands; however, this ship is capable of so much more. Speaking as one of those people whose life you commendably hold so dear, I think you should throw caution to the wind. After all, the kudos of reaching New York early would be a glorious end to your illustrious career." Andrews, who'd become more animated the longer he spoke, opened the door and left the room, as if signalling to the others that the decision was made.

Captain Smith was first to break the awkward silence Andrews' departure had left in its wake. "I will not allow myself to be bullied into making a rash decision, Bruce. You've known me long enough to understand that."

"Yes, I do, E. J. I also know you are not one to shirk a challenge, and reaching New York on Tuesday night is definitely a challenge, but you do whatever you think is right. This vessel is certainly magnificent; she will have other chances to be fast." With that, Ismay stepped through the door in pursuit of Andrews and a long overdue aperitif.

Captain Smith studied the reports on his desk thoughtfully for a while. Then, making a mental note to check the iceberg reports with the duty officer before turning in for the night and to have someone inspect the damage caused by the smouldering coal store fire, he dressed for dinner. There was no way he was going to even consider throwing caution to the wind on an empty stomach.

Fifteen

William's mood hadn't improved by the time he reached his own stateroom. His confused thoughts had tumbled and twirled around inside his fractured mind. He detested children and the idea of having one of his own simply abhorred him. How could Bridget have let this happen? He'd enjoyed the company of many women while studying at Cambridge and again later serving first Queen, and then King, and country in the colonies. Not to mention most of the scullery maids his parents, and later he, himself had employed and, to his knowledge, not one got pregnant. In fact, he had even begun to doubt the fact he could father a child.

What if he couldn't? What if Bridget was carrying the bastard offspring of another man, after all, how well did he know her? She was young and beautiful—much the only reason he'd married her, that and her influential Boston connections— and she undoubtedly attracted the attention of other men. He had witnessed that himself, both on their way to the port and only last night at dinner. It was obvious both Guggenheim and that jumped up serving boy, Moody, were both besotted with her. William noticed this was something she did little to discourage. If she was pregnant from another lover and it should somehow become public knowledge in London society, then the scandal would do him great harm, if not completely ruin him.

He crashed recklessly through the door, pushing it open so violently it swung inward and bounced back off the small Queen Anne styled reception table, catching him on the elbow. He swore loudly as the pain exploded in the sensitive joint before shooting down into his fingers with a tingling jolt that left his forearm in a strange juxtaposition of searing pain and total paralysis. Storming through the suit's antechamber into the bedroom, his right hand clutching his left elbow as he tried in vain to get any sensation in his lower arm that wasn't agonizing pain, he found Bridget. She sat at the dressing table with the pretty chambermaid, Esme, who had shown them to their cabin when they'd boarded, in close attendance. His dramatic entrance had obviously surprised them, and William was convinced in his own mind of his wife's attempt to undermine the servant's respect for authority by engaging her in common, idle gossip.

"My dear, whatever is the matter? You came in here as if the devil himself were chasing you." William did not respond to his wife's greeting, choosing instead to direct a thundersome glare at Esme.

"Leave us!" William almost spat the words in her face.

Esme held her ground defiantly. She had handled far rougher, far drunker characters while pulling pints in the Belvedere Arms, and she wasn't about to leave Bridget at the mercy of this cowardly bully.

"I said, leave us!" William repeated, this time shouting into the young woman's face. His voice rose to a crescendo, his face turning an interesting shade of puce as the veins in his neck throbbed with anger. This was exactly the disrespect you deserved when you fraternized with the help; they get above their station and became insolent and unruly. He would have to do something about that.

William lurched menacingly towards Esme, his hand raised as if ready to strike; his sheer physical size forcing Esme to take a few steps backwards. His warm breath bore the distinctive sickly-sweet smell of alcohol and the smoky, almost flowery aroma of burning opium, scented his clothes. Both of these were common and familiar smells to the former barkeep.

Esme realized with horror Captain Grafton was far too drunk to exercise restraint, even to a woman, and briefly wished she had taken the opportunity to slip away at his first command. All she managed to do by spurning the chance to leave was antagonize the beast. She might as well have jabbed a large stick into the heart of a bee's nest. She was dreadfully aware she had only succeeded in making Bridget's predicament far worse than it already was.

"Go!" Bridget's shrill voice cut through Esme's thoughts, spurring her into action. Esme ducked nimbly past William and darted to the door. Once there, Esme paused to look back at her new friend with anguished concern, but Bridget waved an arm signalling her to leave. "Just go! I'll be fine."

Even as Esme ran from the room, pulling the suite's main door shut behind her, both women knew Bridget wouldn't be fine.

Sixteen

Much of the ship's vast bulk was still shrouded in darkness as Esme fastened her pinafore before carefully pinning her cap in place. She stole a quick glance in the tiny mirror provided and decided it would have to do. She was already two minutes late reporting for duty, and the grisly Miss Wilson had, on several occasions, already made plain the consequences of tardiness. The head housekeeper already had a beady eye focused on her following their less than cordial meeting on the day of sailing. On several occasions since that first, and so far, only direct meeting, Esme had experienced the strange feeling of being watched, only to look up and discover Miss Wilson's shrivelled features observing her from afar.

Esme pulled open her cabin door, surprising Mable, one of the other maids, who was about to knock, her fist poised just inches from Esme's nose. A startled look flashed across her baby-faced complexion then, sheepishly, she lowered her fist and stood with her hands clasped firmly together in front of her starched pinafore, her weight rocking nervously from one foot to the other.

"What is it, Mable?" Esme couldn't disguise her irritation as she pushed past the younger woman, firmly shutting the door behind her.

"I ... I'm truly sorry, Miss Esme," stammered Mable. Since she had stood up to the matriarchal Miss Wilson, Esme had gained a level of respect from the other, particularly younger,

housekeeping staff that was more usually reserved for the ship's upper class passengers.

"Why are you sorry?" Esme asked as she hastened along the corridor with an out of breath Mable struggling to keep up. Sensing the younger woman's distress at the pace she had set, Esme slowed a little adding in a more compassionate tone, "I can't stop. I'm fuckin' late, and the Old Dragon is lookin' for an excuse to burn me." At this, Mable stopped suddenly in the middle of the passageway. Esme, glancing over her shoulder, discovered her young escort on the verge of tears.

Mable gave an apologetic shrug as she blurted, "It was the Old Dragon what sent me. She told me to fetch you 'cos you'd crossed the line." If she said anymore, a wailing sob drowned out her words as the tears flowed unchecked down her rosé-mottled and rather chubby cheeks.

Mable's words opened a bleak, despondent chasm deep in Esme's soul. She felt all her hopes and dreams, the new life for her and Charlotte, her dead father's unspoken pride, her fantasy of marrying a rich, handsome officer, all of it, just sliding away, replaced by gut-wrenching despair. She felt sick. Her legs, no longer able to support her, buckled at the knees and she stumbled forward, clutching Mable's arm to prevent her from crashing to the floor.

"Sweet Jesus! Are you alright, Miss Esme?" She detected the concern in Mable's voice, and possibly a touch of panic. "Would you like me to get anyone for you, a doctor, maybe?"

Esme forced a smile, but even she knew it was hollow and meaningless. "Yeah, I'm fine. Just came over a little queer for a moment, that's all. I'll be right as rain in no time at all, you'll see." She filled her lungs and forced the air out slowly, allowing her cheeks to puff out. Once she regained her composure, at least enough to put on a brave face for the shell-shocked Mable, she turned and strode off with a confident air. But inside, she felt empty, devoid of emotion. Like she stood on the edge of a precipice with nowhere to turn, condemned to take that final step certain in the knowledge she would soon plummet into the abyss.

Mable had taken a few faltering strides in pursuit of her, but Esme waved her away, not in the mood for company. The quicker she could get this over and done the better, as far as she was concerned. Why drag it out? She had ordained her own demise, written it herself, in a heated moment of petulance on that first day, and none of Mrs. Grafton's influential friends would be able to save her. A stupid little girl from Southampton who, dazzled by the opulence and wealth surrounding her, elevated herself above her station, and she felt, was about to be unceremoniously booted out of the Promised Land.

Five minutes later, and with much trepidation, Esme knocked on the door of Miss Wilson's small office just off the main pantry. She waited patiently for a moment and was just about to knock again when the head housekeeper's dry croaky voice bade her, "Come in."

For once, Esme did as instructed and pushed open the door to find Miss Wilson seated in a worn leather chair. She wore thin, wire-rimmed spectacles, which perched on the end of her nose as if defying gravity, and a navy blue dress, fastened at the neck and held in place by a small, understated lace scarf. She was reading as Esme entered the room and continued to do so, pointedly Esme felt, ignoring her presence.

Finally, Miss Wilson placed the papers down on the desktop with meticulous attention to detail and then looked up. Esme felt the woman's cold steely-grey eyes examine her. As if dissatisfied with her discovery, Miss Wilson sighed deeply. "Well, Miss Jackson, as I feared, it did not take very long for you to sully your reputation and worth with us. Not only were you insolent beyond belief at the embarkation meeting, but now it seems, you have become too familiar with the ship's guests."

Esme opened her mouth to offer some form of rebuttal, but Miss Wilson's glare told her there was more to come, so she shut it again. "I refer, of course, to your friendship, although I use the term in its loosest possible sense, with Mrs. Grafton. It has come to my attention that you have spent quite some time with her discussing her marriage while, it seems, trying to seduce Captain Grafton."

Esme remained quiet, too stunned to even deny the allegation. She stared back incredulously at Miss Wilson, who met her stare with a satisfied smirk and at that point, she realized the truth didn't matter to the craggy old housekeeper. She'd set her mind to dismissing Esme the moment they first crossed swords and this accusation was just the ammunition she needed.

Miss Wilson removed her glasses and settled back in her chair. She was obviously enjoying the moment intent on savouring every last second of Esme's dismissal. "I suppose one ought to congratulate you on making it all the way to Friday. Your parents must be so proud." The sarcasm in her voice was beginning to anger Esme, and she knew it. "I will have to find a suitable replacement; although, with White Star's insistence on employing common harlots from the dockside, that shouldn't be too taxing. Girls like you are ten-a-penny."

The blood pounded in Esme's ears, and her fists were balled up so tight her knuckles had turned white, but Esme was determined not to rise to the old woman's taunts. It was all she could do not to dive across the pompous bitch's desk and pummel her sanctimonious face. She forced herself to relax, focusing her thoughts on New York, as she mentally pried her fingers open. Esme became so engrossed in her thoughts, conjuring up images of skyscrapers, cranes, and the welcoming figure of the Statue of Liberty, that she barely heard Miss Wilson terminate her employment, effective on their arrival pier-side in New York where she must disembark. Miss Wilson's voice droned on about the company's expectation that she will continue with her duties in a more fitting manner until formally dismissed, eventually asking Esme to show herself out. Before she knew it, Esme stood outside the pantry, her dreams crushed.

It was then the emotion welled up inside her, and she felt the telltale sting of salty tears in the corners of her eyes. She hurried through the pantry, which buzzed with activity as maids, waiters, and cooks prepared for the busy morning ahead, her hands covering her face, masking her distress. She vaguely remembered hearing Miss Wilson warn her about returning to the first class staterooms, saying they would assign her alternative duties, but she didn't care. She couldn't possibly get in any more trouble. Besides, what could they do? Throw her overboard?

The heels of her boots rapped out a steady beat as she strode purposefully along the narrow passageway linking the pantry to the first class quarters. The tears she had held back in the presence of the Old Dragon, now streamed unchecked, blurring her vision and stinging her cheeks. She rounded a corner and, paying little attention to where she was going, collided full tilt with the ship's doctor heading in the opposite direction on his way to breakfast.

Doctor Sampson was a stout middle-aged man with a balding pate and a voracious appetite, both for exquisite dining and attractive women. It was rumoured, while on his previous commission, he got the ship's nurse in trouble and then, in the back room of an Irish tavern, performed illegal surgery to absolve his own indiscretion. It was a rumour he fiercely denied, but the young woman in question never reported for duty again.

"Whoa! Steady on there, missy. You need to pay more attention to where you're going." The soft Irish lilt gave his voice a lightness that was incongruous with a man of his girth.

Esme mumbled an apology and tried to sidestep the doctor's large frame, but seeing her red-rimmed eyes and the distressed look on her face, he moved to block her path. He smiled broadly, a boyish twinkle dancing in his eyes as he spoke, "Why missy, whatever is troubling that pretty, young head of yours?" His hand lightly brushed her chin and gently lifted her head so his eyes stared down into hers.

"It's nothing, Sir. I was just given some upsetting news, that's all. Now, if you'll excuse me, I have duties to perform." Esme kept the remark vague, believing the ship's doctor would care little for her plight, even siding with Miss Wilson, and she didn't care for another lecture.

Doctor Sampson held his ground, his eyes searching her face for clues to her distress. "Is it bad news from home?"

She responded with the briefest shake of her head, hoping it would satisfy his curiosity and he would step aside.

Doctor Sampson paused for a moment but didn't move from her path, then asked, "Has the Old Dragon given you one of her 'England expects' speeches she's so renowned for?"

This time she looked away, her jaw quivering as she fought back a renewed torrent of tears. She felt embarrassed at crying in front of an officer, it only served to distress her further. She tried edging past him, but his hand found hers, holding her back.

"Did the sour-faced bitch call you a whore then sack you?" The doctor, having discovered the cause of her unhappiness, pushed home his advantage. The only response Esme could muster was a timid half-nod before the dam burst and, letting loose a despondent wail, she allowed the tears to wet her cheeks again.

"I'm s ... sorry," she sniffed as she fumbled in her pinafore for a handkerchief.

"That's quite alright, my dear. She can be a very scary woman, but her bark is worse than her bite. I'm sure, with the right amount of charm and cajolery I could persuade my dear colleague to rethink her decision."

Esme dabbed her face with the screwed up handkerchief and tried to smile. "Thank you for being so kind, but I don't think any amount of charm, and whatever else you said, will change her mind. She appeared certain of her bite."

Doctor Sampson laughed aloud. "I'm so sorry, I do not mean to laugh at your expense, but you are such a delightful creature." He paused briefly, then closed in for the kill. "Perhaps I could have a word with her on your behalf, that is, if you would like me to?"

Esme looked up at the doctor with a coy smile. He still had hold of her hand, their bodies, due in part to the narrowness of the corridor, were a little closer than would be acceptable in normal society. "I don't believe, not for one moment, you would do that for me, not without getting something in return."

The doctor's confident expression flickered for the briefest of moments and then returned with another of his broad smiles. "I fear I may have met my Waterloo. Here I am, believing I'm luring you into my net, while all along it was you who controlled the line."

"But the facts remain, I will be put ashore in New York, and you would like to study … what is it you doctors study?"

"Anatomy?" The doctor offered helpfully.

"Yes, that's it. And you would like to study my anatomy," she finished, forcing a faint smile that brightened her tear-stained features.

"So, miss, do we have an understanding?" The doctor could hardly contain his excitement at the prospect of exploring the young chambermaid's voluptuous curves.

"We do," she whispered. "But with one condition. You speak to Miss Wilson and get my job back before Sunday evening. I believe I have some free time then." With that, she withdrew her hand from his with another coy smile.

The doctor stepped aside to allow her to pass, whispering as she did so, "I fear it is I that now has cause to fear the Old Dragon's bite."

Esme walked away, a smile briefly dancing on her lips as she thought of Doctor Sampson trying to charm Miss Wilson, but quickly vanished with the self-abhorrent anguish she felt as she considered her deal with the devil.

Seventeen

The early morning sunlight crept slowly into the spacious suite, gently waking Bridget with its persistence. The warm rays prising their way under her swollen eyelids until she finally relented and rolled onto her back before pulling herself into a sitting position. She gently plumped her soft pillows, taking special care not to wake William, before settling back against the headboard.

The morning's first wave of nausea swept over her and she rubbed her silk covered bump tenderly. Fleetingly, she considered rushing to the bathroom, but before she could even reach for the edge of the top sheet, the feeling rolled away as quickly as it had arrived. Experience had taught her it would be back. Like the waves on a beach, it would keep washing in, each wave stronger than the last until, inevitably it would overwhelm her.

She yawned, taking a deep lung full of air and winced as the pain tore through the thin scars and thicker bruising on her back, the result of William's drunken handiwork. He had been too inebriated to effectively wield his riding crop, resorting to slapping her with his bare fists, beating her repeatedly as she cowered against the bed. Somehow, she had managed to half-stagger, half-crawl to the relative safety of the bathroom, where she had locked the door until, cursing her like a common navvy, William stumbled from the room. She took the opportunity to change quickly into her nightgown and climb into bed, believing

William would inevitably return too drunk even to walk. She pretended to be asleep when he did finally return, pointedly ignoring his incoherent mumblings, as he quickly passed out on top of the eiderdown still fully clothed, having been able to remove only one of his shoes.

Looking across at her husband's sleeping form, she noticed he had not managed to finish undressing during the night. She briefly considered removing his other shoe at least, but another wave of biliousness put a stop to her deliberations, and forced her up from the bed, with one hand covering her mouth as she dashed to the bathroom. Bridget tried frantically to gather her flowing nightdress in her other fist so as not to vomit down the intricate embroidery forming the exquisite garment's loose bodice.

As she returned from an uncomfortable few minutes of stomach twisting retching, gently dabbing her face with one of the ship's fluffy white towels, she found William lying on his side, head propped up on one arm. He glared at her as she approached the bed, and she forced a smile, "Good morning, darling. I hope I didn't wake you?"

"As a matter of fact, you did!" His voice was gruff and a little croaky. William cleared his throat with a polite cough then added in a more conciliatory tone. "But that's not your fault. It must be damned beastly waking up feeling so sick every morning." He paused, letting the words hang in the silence, then asked in a quiet, yet menacing voice, "And it is every morning, isn't it my dear?"

Bridget felt her blood run cold. Had he guessed, or was she reading more into his words?

Not waiting for an answer, he rose from the bed and casually wandered into the bathroom, stretching out his sleepy shoulder muscles as he walked. He didn't bother to shut the door, a trait he knew annoyed Bridget who thought it uncouth and common, while he emptied his bulging bladder.

Deciding to ride it out, hoping he was simply making an observation about the state of her health, she ignored his question, deliberately steering the conversation back towards his behaviour. "I wish you would be so good as to close the door when you do that."

In the bathroom, William mimicked her admonishment silently into the mirror as he rinsed his hands, then said aloud, "I wish you'd close your fucking legs, you cheap whore!" He strode out of the bathroom, revelling in the stunned look on his wife's face. "You see, I know your dirty little secret. Did you think you could keep it from me, convince me that little bastard is the fruit of my loins?" When Bridget offered no response to his accusation, he shouted in her face, so close she felt droplets of his spittle strike her cheek.

"Well?"

"You have me at a disadvantage as I have no idea what you are talking about, but I do know this is no way to speak to your wife." Bridget felt the blood flushing her cheeks. Her anger and surprise at the coarseness of his insulting revelation paled into insignificance at the fear that gripped her chest and knotted her bowel. She had felt his wrath several times over the last few days and was aware of his abilities. If he could beat her for perceived, minor indiscretions, what would he do for this? He detested the idea of having a child, he'd made that abundantly clear, let alone another man's child.

"A lady would not carry another man's bastard offspring up the aisle," said William beginning to remove the creased trousers he'd worn to bed. "I am glad that you at least have the decency not to insult me by denying the pregnancy, but I am none the wiser about the father's identity. Perhaps we could discuss that over breakfast?"

Bridget stared at her husband as he selected an expensive cashmere suit. She'd expected him to take the riding crop to her bare flesh, not talk about discussing the situation over breakfast like it was an irritation, and nothing more. After an apprehensive pause, she asked in a soft voice, "You want me to go with you to breakfast?" His behaviour confused her and she felt the need to remind him of his daily routine. "You're always so insistent on dining alone at the breakfast table."

"I do." William chuckled softly. "Ironic choice of words, they sound so hollow now. I want you to accompany me to breakfast for two reasons. First, in case we should have a chance meeting with Mr. Guggenheim. He likes you and your presence might help cement a favourable relationship. Second, I wish to preserve, at least the pretence, of a happy marriage. I absolutely refuse to be the subject of society scandal and a figure of derision within my own home. So if you would be so good as to get dressed?" He phrased his last statement as a question but left Bridget in no doubt it was an order she best not disobey.

William gathered the clothes he had chosen to wear and strode resolutely from the suite's boudoir into the larger reception room, where he proceeded to dress. As he pulled the door closed behind him, he remembered how long she had kept him waiting at the hotel before they walked down to the docks, so he added firmly, "Do not dawdle. Otherwise, we shall miss breakfast altogether."

No sooner had the door clicked shut, Bridget became aware of the tension within her own body. Her fists gripped her nightdress, twisting the cream-coloured silk into tight twirls and pulling the soft fabric tight against her thighs. Her delicate shoulders and smooth neck were so rigid and knotted she was aware of the blood pulsing through her arteries, and her entire body radiated heat, so much so she detected a soft sheen of perspiration. It coated her skin and formed a small rivulet, which trickled gently south through the soft valley of her breasts and on towards her swollen baby belly.

Bridget was so convinced William would resort to violence that she still shook with a mixture of pent up anger and fear. The adrenaline she felt coursing through her body set her very soul on edge and shredded her nerves. She made a conscious effort to breathe, forcing the air deep into her lungs before pushing it out with an exaggerated sigh, willing her sore muscles to relax. Finally, she slumped into the upholstered chair provided with the elaborate dressing table.

Studying her reflection in its gilt-edged mirror, Bridget was shocked to see tired, red-rimmed eyes staring back at her. She knew she had not slept well. Pain and fear were never good bedfellows and the pregnancy was beginning to take its toll on her, but she hadn't realized how tired she looked until now.

Bridget took a few moments to regain her composure before rising from the chair. She hurried to the bathroom, pulling the nightgown over her head, dropping it to the floor on her way, before quickly splashing cold water over her face and rubbing her body down with a damp towel. Once she was satisfied she had at least removed the unladylike sweat, she patted herself down with a clean towel pulled from the pile and inspected the still bright red welts on her back from William's last, overzealous beating. Relieved to see they were at least not bleeding, she gingerly pulled on her undergarments, taking great care not to remove any of the scabs forming over her wounds. Over this, she buttoned a plain, but expensive brown dress before piling her hair up, fastening it under a demure wide brimmed hat with two large hat pins.

Satisfied the hat concealed the evidence of her hurried morning ablutions, Bridget selected an extravagant necklace featuring a large, creamy coloured pearl surrounded by a ring of tiny diamonds. She matched this with a pair of drop pearl earrings and a small silver broach before slipping her feet into her favourite leather ankle-boots.

All the while she could hear William whistling impatiently in the next room.

The journey to breakfast was an awkward affair. They walked to the dining saloon on D Deck, descending the grand staircase arm-in-arm, smiling politely at the other guests as they passed. The steward escorted them to a vacant table then, having taken their request for a pot of tea he scurried away, leaving them alone. Bridget glanced around the room, deliberately avoiding making eye contact with her husband, who sat impassively opposite her. Neither spoke until the steward returned with the tea tray, which he placed centrally on the table. William ordered a cooked breakfast with all the usual trimmings for himself, and two slices of dry toast for Bridget, telling the steward she felt 'a little under the weather.'

Once the steward took his leave, William poured tea for them both. "I thought toast might be best for you, what with the sickness and all." His voice showed little of the emotions that Bridget believed must be tumbling around inside him.

"That is most thoughtful, my love." Bridget knew better than to disagree with him.

"How sweet those words would have sounded yesterday, yet today they have soured. I am no more your love than you mine. It is, with the honeymoon not yet over, a sad state of affairs, yet true." He placed Bridget's tea on the table then, interlacing his fingers, fixed her with a searching stare. "You see, I married you for your connections in America and because being unmarried, as I was at my age, warrants becoming the subject of idle tittle-tattle among the old women at society tea parties. And tittle-tattle is not conducive to being able to do business with those ladies' husbands. So you see, *my love,* you were a well-connected distraction, a young, beautiful and elegant distraction, but a distraction nonetheless."

Bridget took a sip of her tea, carefully placing the china cup back on its saucer. She thought she would feel guilt, a sense of self-loathing, of failure, but she didn't. As she sat opposite the violent bully she had promised to love, honour, and obey only a couple of months previously, she felt nothing as he revealed their marriage to be nothing but an astute business decision. In fact, if she felt anything at all, it was empowerment. William needed her. He needed her connections and her ability to charm his business associates, but most of all he needed not to have a scandalous divorce.

With a soft smile, she met her spouse's stare. She rapidly came to the conclusion that she no longer feared him or his riding crop, she was his equal. And best of all, he didn't know it. "My dear, William, I do not know how you found out about my pregnancy, but I do know it makes no difference. If I had told you next week I was pregnant and it was yours you would still have been angry, but none the wiser. You would have had to raise it as your own, and that still applies. I'm your wife and this, as far as anyone else is concerned, will be our child."

"I will not be party to raising a child, especially one whose parentage is in doubt." William hissed.

"Oh! There is no doubt. His father is at Yale, a dashingly handsome man who spent last Christmas in Boston as a guest of my father. The families are old friends, and I gave him a special gift on Christmas Eve, a gift a woman can never get back, a gift he accepted with great skill and enthusiasm." Bridget found it hard to keep the smirk from her lips as her husband's jawline tighten. Deep within his eyes, she saw the flickering flames of his anger as it threatened to consume him.

They sat in silence while William digested this information. His world, the accepted norms of his life, had just been turned on their head. He was rich, well respected, with a much-admired younger wife who, despite being a spirited filly, was subservient to his will, and had a mistress with whom he could indulge his love of opium and sexual deviance. Yet, his wife had whored herself out, and either by design or her own good fortune, now had him over a barrel.

William knew he could not divorce her; the scandal alone would be inconceivable, let alone the financial implications, and he needed to guarantee Bridget's silence or, at the very least, her complicity in their shameful wedlock. But the thought of looking at her every day knowing she had allowed another man to deflower her ... to fuck her, and then expect him to raise the offspring of that bastard union, was too much to bear. He may not want her sexually, but he would be damned if he would tolerate another man lying with her. For now, for the sake of appearances, he would have to accept the circumstances as they were. After all, pregnancy and childbirth were dangerous times for a woman. Anything could happen.

William relaxed a little and gave Bridget a forced smile as the steward returned with their breakfast. He waited while the man served their food, then when he had left them alone, spoke in a hushed, but confident tone. "It would appear we are both victims of circumstance." William decided to inflict some emotional damage of his own and in so doing, he hoped, strengthen his position. "I too have enjoyed the pleasures of the flesh with another, in fact, with your serving maid, Violet. She may not be a debutant of an exclusive finishing school, but she knows how to please a man in the boudoir."

Bridget nodded knowingly before replying, "So that was how you found out I'm with child, from your whore!" His revelation regarding the identity of his mistress didn't surprise her. She strangely had no say in Violet's employment as her maid, but Bridget would make sure she had a say in the bitch's dismissal.

"Yes, my dear. How does it feel to be betrayed by such a close confidante?" It was William's turn to smirk as he forked a large piece of bacon into his mouth.

"I wouldn't call her a confidante, it's just she's seen me naked more times than you have: a state of affairs that obviously applies in the reverse. But think on this, she has known of the pregnancy for a while, so why only tell you about it now? Maybe she has designs on your fortune, perhaps even, on being the next Mrs. Grafton. Now that would be ironic, as it

was only for your wealth and position that I married you." While she talked, she'd buttered her toast, adding a liberal spreading of marmalade, which she was about to eat when a thought struck her. "You only found out about the baby last night, mid-Atlantic. You've brought your Cyprian with you, haven't you? That's why you keep disappearing! You must have her stashed away in her own stateroom, you're too much of an English snob to visit her in second class, and *you* complain about *me* fraternizing with the hired help. Now *that's* ironic." Bridget threw her head back and laughed, her eyes sparkling in genuine merriment, the raucousness of her laughter disturbing the patrons at the nearby tables.

Far from making Bridget feel betrayed and undermined, William felt he had only succeeded in giving his wife a better bargaining position, and obviously, a good laugh at his expense, but he pushed on anyway.

"In the interest of avoiding an unseemly incident, I'm prepared to allow the child to be raised under my roof. However, I want to make it clear I will have nothing to do with it. In exchange, you allow me to continue my dalliance with Violet, thereby allowing us both to fulfill our desires."

No longer laughing, Bridget scowled at her husband. "She leaves our household. You want to fuck her you can do it somewhere else. Also, there will be no more riding crop, a real man doesn't need to beat a lady."

William gave a begrudging nod, then leaving his breakfast unfinished, he tossed his napkin onto the table and without uttering another word, stormed from the saloon.

Eighteen

Bernard, keen on finding his ticket into New York society, slipped out onto the ships exclusive first class promenade. Here, anybody who was anybody would step out for a constitutional stroll, or just sit on one of the ship's many deck chairs taking the chance to read or maybe just watch the ocean roll by.

It was late morning, and the weak April sun struggled to burn off the early morning mist that still surrounded the ship. The air was cold, the stiff breeze blowing from the northeast, colder still. Bernard wore his finest suit and a thick woollen overcoat that had, on close inspection, seen better days, and an old battered top hat. He spent a good while buffing the hat's well-worn silk so, at least from a distance, it looked the fine accessory of a well-to-do gentleman. In his pocket, he carried a silver case in which he kept gilt-edged cards announcing him as *Sir Bernard Astor.* The ugly, but not so gullible lady, bought it for him as a present, even having it engraved, before discovering he was nothing but a fraud. It became useful in completing his image as a slightly tarnished, even eccentric, but rich, well-to-do gentleman from the upper echelons of English society.

Bernard completed two leisurely lengths of the promenade and was nonchalantly turning for a third when he spotted a well-built middle-aged woman, dressed from head to foot in black, struggling with a parasol. A sudden gust of wind had turned the flimsy black material inside out and the woman in question appeared unsure of what to do. If she let go, it would be lost over the ship's side, but holding on to it only caused it to swing menacingly around her head, threatening to take someone's eye out. In her other hand, she held a large cumbersome handbag of the sort women used to carry knitting or sewing.

Bernard had seen enough. She was traveling first class; she was in mourning and was definitely in need of a perfect gentleman. He hurried to her aid; catching hold of the errant parasol with both hands, he quickly brought it under control, pushing the twisted spokes flat against the handle so he could fasten the canopy closed. He handed the parasol back to the relieved lady with a flourish and an exaggerated bow.

"Thank you so much. I thought it would be a good idea to bring some protection from the sun, but it looks like I was wrong on that score." She smiled at Bernard; her accent was American but not the soft, refined accent of well-to-do society. It was a harsh, shrill whine that sounded like a suckling pig being dragged through a mincer. Bernard immediately slipped into his bumbling country gent act giving her a gentle smile, the well-rehearsed smile which, over the years, had put so many unsuspecting women at ease.

"It can be so easy for one to misjudge the strength of the breeze from within one's cabin; however, I believe you were wise to furnish yourself with some protection from the sun. It's so easy to burn without feeling the sun's warmth, especially, if I may be so bold, with skin as delicate as yours." Bernard looked at his feet, feigning embarrassment. In his head, he counted to three then added, "Oh my! Please excuse my impertinence. I do not know what possessed me to make such a boorish utterance."

He made to walk away, but the woman caught his arm with her gloved hand. "It's been awhile since any man saw fit to pass me a compliment, boorish or otherwise, mister?" He turned to face her as she spoke and noticed, now that he looked at her up close, she was strikingly beautiful. Her hair, probably once so dark, was flecked through with strands of silver and pulled loosely up beneath the wide brim of her hat, while her eyes, a rich hazelnut in colour, had a disarming quality about them. The warm smile she gave him revealed near perfect teeth, the only blemish being a small gap right in the middle of her upper row, and she bore strikingly well-defined features, despite her advancing years.

Acting as though he had been caught off guard, Bernard flustered, aware she was waiting for him to introduce himself. "I'm so sorry, my manners have deserted me. I'm Sir Bernard Astor." He accepted the hand she graciously offered, touching it briefly to his lips before letting go.

"I'm pleased to meet you, Sir Bernard. I have no such fancy title and have to settle for Kathleen Black, but it is, nevertheless, a name that has served me well." Kathleen said in a shrill nasal twang.

Bernard resisted the urge to flinch with every syllable she uttered. He was well aware who she was. He had examined the passenger list in great detail, and he was also aware that her

husband had died a wealthy man, thanks to his investment in the American steel industry.

"It is a wonderful name that needs no fancy appendages," he replied before moving in for the kill with his next question. "Would you please allow me to escort you on your stroll?" He held his arm out, playfully waggling his bushy moustache.

Kathleen Black tried, for the sake of appearances, to look aloof and gracious as she politely accepted his arm. But that part of her, the part that remained forever a young girl dreaming of romance, was there for the trained eye to spot, and Sir Bernard Astor possessed such a trained eye. As they walked arm in arm along the promenade, he wore the smile of a prospector holding a nugget of pure gold.

Nineteen

Patrick entered the sparse cabin he shared with Bernard. Fate had thrown them together in this great adventure, and although he sensed they would become firm friends, he was relieved not to find the eccentric Englishman reclined on his bunk. Throwing his hat on to the top bunk he'd commandeered by boarding first, he sat on the hard padded bench occupying the opposite wall. Reaching into the storage space below, Patrick slid out the battered old valise. He removed a small paper bag from the pocket of his overcoat and set it down on the bench next to him before flicking the valise's brass catch open.

Patrick gently eased the valise open and peered into it. Pandora's confidence had grown, she still looked sad but no longer shied away, staring confidently, almost arrogantly, back at him. He made a clicking sound with his lips then said, "I've brought you some chicken, Pandora." Reaching into the paper bag he removed one of the pieces of meat, which he dropped into the valise. He watched with fascination as her small hands found the thumb-sized chunk of cold, white meat, which she inspected carefully for a moment before tearing it apart with sharp, pointed teeth. In just a few seconds, she had completely devoured his offering.

"You like that, eh? Here you go." He dropped another piece of the succulent meat into the bag, which the hungry monkey tore apart and consumed with equal ferocity. "Ah, Pandora, you're a strange one, make no mistake."

Laughing, Patrick reached into the paper bag for one last piece of chicken, his attention momentarily distracted from the valise at his feet. He located a suitable morsel of chicken and returned his attention to the open valise.

The eyes, that just a few moments before had portrayed such sadness now burned with an intense anger that surprised Patrick. A shrieking cackle filled the air as the diminutive monkey vaulted from the top of the valise onto Patrick's knee. He swung his arm at the splenetic primate as he struggled to get to his feet, but she was too quick for him. With one agile leap, the monkey's tiny hands latched onto his face.

Caught off balance, Patrick was helpless as the monkey's strong fingers clawed at his hair, her sharp nails scratching thin slits into his skin. He looked into Pandora's snarling mouth, briefly glimpsing her razor-like teeth before they tore into the tender flesh just below his left eye. Shocked at the sheer speed and ferocity of her violent assault, he took a few precious seconds to prise her hands away from his face. As soon as he broke the grip of her tiny fingers, he hurled the screaming Pandora into the corner. Stunned, she scurried under the lower bunk with a shrill cackle, a sliver of his skin still clamped in her deceptively strong jaws.

Patrick climbed shakily to his feet and inspected his bloodied facial wound in the small mirror bolted to the cabin wall. A three-inch long tear, surrounded by red swollen skin,

adorned his soft Celtic features. The wound bled profusely. A small flap of loose skin hung from the bottom edge of the jagged wound. He snatched a pillow from his bunk, quickly retreating to the far side of the room in case Pandora should attack again, and removed the white cotton case, wadding it into a makeshift bandage, which he pressed against the bite. Pain flashed through his cheek causing him to flinch, sucking air through his tightly clenched teeth.

He kicked the valise into the middle of the narrow aisle between the bench and the bunk beds. Throwing the remainder of the chicken into the bottom of the bag he hoped it would act as bait, allowing him to recapture his prized asset without risking further damage to either of them. All the while, he kept the pillowcase pressed tightly against his face trying to staunch the steady flow of blood seeping from the ripped flesh. Once done, he sat back down and waited, his eyes fixed on the space below the bunks where he could hear Pandora scurrying back and forth.

Only a few minutes had passed before the door swung open, and Bernard stepped into the cabin. He had a broad smile, clearly visible under his bushy moustache, and his eyes sparkled above his ruddy cheeks.

"I have a dinner engagement with the delightfully widowed, Mrs. Kathleen Black." He announced flamboyantly, then seeing Patrick's face he added, a concerned look pushing the smile from his countenance, "Oh! My dear boy, are you alright?"

Patrick couldn't help but smile at the older man's accent. It was a little too polished, too precise. "I'm fine. It looks worse than it is, but I will admit, it does sting a little." It was a lie; one Patrick sensed Bernard could see in his pained expression.

"How on earth did you acquire such a gruesome injury?" Bernard placed his hat on the top bunk and turned to push the door shut. A loud shriek heralded Pandora's bid for freedom as she scampered across Bernard's foot before slipping through the rapidly closing door.

The door shut, and Bernard turned to face Patrick, his left hand gripping his chest, a confused look on his face. "I think the sea air must be playing tricks on me. I believe I just saw a monkey leave our cabin."

"That was no trick, and the monkey you saw was the cause of my *gruesome* injury." He mimicked Bernard's exaggerated pronunciation.

"I trust you will protest in the strongest possible terms to the ship's bursar. It is quite unacceptable that on the maiden voyage of the world's most expensive cruise liner, you have your face savaged by a wild beast." Bernard's face had begun to turn purple he was so angry.

Patrick studied the old rogue's face, unsure whether he could trust him, but aware that as things stood, he had little choice in the matter. He looked ruefully at the rug partially covering the cabin's floor, and said, "I am afraid they will not be so understanding to my plight, as it was I who brought the wild beast aboard. I won him at cards from an old sea dog the night before we left Southampton."

Bernard's incandescent rage evaporated away and the large smile reappeared. "Ah, but the only other person privy to that particular piece of information is me, and I have no intention of telling. It will be our secret ticket to luxury."

Patrick remained silent as he considered the possibilities. He could see a voyage of luxury before him as he was in no doubt White Star Line would be eager to avoid any bad publicity on the *Titanic*'s glorious arrival in New York. It seemed unlikely anyone would discover their clever ruse, and even if they did, what could the authorities do? Hold them on board ship until they reached port then hand them over to the police? Even that seemed unlikely, as bringing charges would inevitably result in the story making it into print. A smile spread across Patrick's face, causing him to wince in pain as his torn facial muscles flexed.

Bernard, who had been patiently awaiting Patrick's response, started nodding his head, his eyes twinkling mischievously. "Do I take that smile to mean you are in agreement with my suggestion?"

"No sir, you may not." Patrick fixed him with a cold, emotionless stare. "I believe you to be a crook, a con man, and a charlatan, and that, dear boy, is why I am smiling."

The twinkle faded from Bernard's eyes and, for a brief moment, he looked slightly taken aback by the younger man's

impression of his upper-class English accent. Patrick lingered, savouring the moment before he continued.

"Those are also the reasons I'm agreeing with your suggestion. I think this could mark the start of a very profitable friendship." Bernard grasped the hand Patrick offered, and the two men laughed until Patrick winced in pain.

Twenty

Joseph Bell had previously served aboard the *Olympic*, and at the age of fifty-one, had already gained twenty-one years' experience as chief engineer and had, therefore, been the obvious choice to hold that position aboard the *Titanic*. A man of strong conviction and sound engineering sense, he was well-respected among the firemen, trimmers, and greasers that comprised most of the ship's unseen crew, buried as they were, deep in its dark, dusty bowels. He had already experienced the conflicting nature of the job. Mr. Ismay, on the day they left port, had pressed him to run the engines close to full speed on Monday, when the *Titanic* would be negotiating the North Atlantic's treacherous ice fields, in the hope of bringing them into harbour ahead of schedule.

Bell responded by saying he would only run the engines at the speed designated by the captain, a statement which had obviously infuriated Ismay. Bell had taken up his appointment aboard the *Titanic* while the vessel was still under construction and had every faith, when called on, the two huge Harland and Wolff engines could reach a top speed of 80 rpm, but he understood the captain's reluctance to push them so early in the maiden voyage, especially in such adverse conditions.

He checked the pressure gauges one last time and then, in line with the captain's instructions, ordered the engines increased to 70 rpm. He checked his pocket watch. It was noon, on the dot. With a satisfied smile, he marked the increase in the

engineering log then prepared to make his rounds with the third engineer, Mr. Hosking, who would be taking the next watch. Bell would allow himself to eat and grab a few precious hours sleep before returning to the engine room in preparation of lighting the remaining boiler. He would not put it past Captain Smith to accede to Mr. Ismay's wild demands, after all, it would be another feather in his cap and a fitting end to an already illustrious career. And Smith, like any other liner captain, had an eye for the theatrical. If that proved to be the case, he would need those boilers up to pressure by Sunday morning and that would mean putting further demands on the men under his command.

Joseph Bell wasn't the only person in the engine room feeling the pressure. Albert 'Hoggie' Hogarth was beginning to wish he had stayed down the Yorkshire coal pit like his father and grandfather and not signed up in search of a better life at sea. The stifling heat and the dry coal dust filled air were no different from the pits of Hell, and certainly no different from the pits of his home county. True, shovelling coal in the depths of the largest liner afloat, allowed him to work on his feet. A luxury not usually afforded by a coal seam, but there he could at least spend his evenings drinking beer under the stars while trying to snatch a kiss from one of the barmaids. Here he had just four hours between shifts, barely time to eat and sleep, and no chance of even seeing a woman, let alone snatching a kiss.

Driving his shovel into the coal bunker one last time, Hoggie hefted the coal up and into the intense heat of the boiler's fire then laid it aside, ready for the next watch's use. He wiped his brow with a thick muscular forearm, unaware he only succeeded in leaving a sweaty streak in the thick layer of coal blackening his face. Taking one of the narrow gangplanks, he walked stiffly to the door and out into the fireman's tunnel linking the boiler rooms with the living quarters. He began climbing the narrow, spiral staircase up to the forecastle above in search of fresh air and a leisurely smoke before his next shift.

He had not gone three steps when he thought he heard a soft scuttling sound from somewhere above him. He peered cautiously upward but couldn't see anything that would account for the noise. Probably just his ears playing tricks on him in the peace and quiet of the tunnel as opposed to the constant whining roar ever present in the boiler room.

"Bloody rats!" He muttered as he continued to climb the twisting staircase. The refrigerated food compartments were located close by as they required steam pumped from the engine room, and this acted as a magnate for the ship's rat population.

Hoggie clumped upwards, his downcast eyes focusing on his tired feet, willing them to lift one more time with each step. There! That sound again; only closer this time, much closer.

Hoggie lifted his head, and there, sitting level with his eyeline was a small monkey. It rested on its haunches using its nimble fingers to preen the tip of its long tail. It looked at the

sweat and coal-stained stoker with bright intelligent eyes which darted this way and that, taking in every detail of the much larger human, while its fingers continued to dig and scratch absentmindedly through the tail's matted fur.

It took a moment for Hoggie's tired brain to figure out exactly what it was he was looking at. He had never seen any primate in the flesh before, only in pictures. The fact his first experience of one should be in such a strange location, on a dark stairwell, on board a ship steaming across the mighty Atlantic Ocean, had dumbfounded him. He bent forward slightly and peered through the gloom, unsure whether his eyes were playing a cruel trick on him.

The monkey stared back at Hoggie through large brown eyes, its grooming regime now forgotten. The lighter fur around its neck and chest appeared wet and matted, the sticky clumps stained darker. Hoggie adjusted his feet slightly and leant to his right, craning his neck to get a better view.

"Where have you come from?" Hoggie muttered to himself, his face not more than three feet from the tiny primate. It just looked at him, head cocked to one side, and Hoggie thought it might be transfixed by his presence on the stairs, too scared of the giant human to move.

Twenty-one

Pandora was indeed transfixed, but not by the presence of a large, sweaty man squatting on the steps. What transfixed her was the small, rhythmic pulse beating enticingly close to the skin's surface just below the human's strong jawline. She could smell the stench humans gave off a mile away, and being this close the vile smell of stale sweat threatened to overpower her. This one smelled far worse than the others she'd encountered, but he had moved to one side exposing his bare, unprotected neck, and she could almost smell his rich, fresh blood.

It took her sensitive nose a few seconds to detect that sweet, warm aroma hidden in the myriad of smells present in this small corridor. The harsh, dusty smell of coal mingled with the sour sweat of man, and the burnt tang of cheap tobacco mixed with the crisp clean smell of machine grease, but through all that, Pandora picked up the sweet scent of fresh meat.

It was not just the pulsing of the blood that aroused her, it was the smell of the blood, the trail by which to hunt. As close as she was, Pandora could smell the richness of the liver, this one sweetened by a constant supply of rum, and the soft intestine, scented by a lifetime of country herbs and delicate spices.

She could almost feel the heart beating as every pulse surged through the engorged arteries of Hoggie's neck.

She had to feed.

Her appetite for flesh wasn't to be sated by a few measly scraps of boiled chicken and a mouthful of Irish face meat. She needed to consume, to devour constantly. The virus she had carried, dormant in her cells, since her birth in Africa, was awake and demanding food. It had taken over every cell in her tiny body and was now hunting for new hosts, looking for ways to spread. Her body ached in a way she didn't understand, but she knew feeding made it bearable, at least for a short while.

Without uttering a sound in warning, Pandora sprang, her strong, agile tail helping her balance; her small hands gripped the large man's course shirt, her arms pulling her in closer. Her feet, in turn, taking a firm hold as she coiled her tail around her victim's arm. Then she sank her powerful teeth into the soft flesh of Hoggie's neck.

She held on tightly as he screamed in anguish. He tried to pull her off, but she had too strong a grip. He resorted to unleashing a few wild, erratic punches, but even they failed to dislodge her. As he flailed his arms around wildly, he lost his footing on the step, toppling backwards. His body flipped over the curved rail sending him crashing head first to the deck below.

Still Pandora clung on, her teeth ripping into his soft skin. She increased the pressure, pushing home her advantage. Nature told her this would work. She tasted blood around her gums then; with a little *pop,* her mouth filled with its thick, sticky sweetness.

Hoggie's severed artery spurted blood, each heartbeat weaker than the one before. His vital life force gushed into Pandora's receptive gullet as he lay crumpled at the foot of the stairwell. He was dazed from the fall and too weak to put up much of a fight as Pandora thrust her strong fingers into his wound and ripped out his flesh. The last thing Albert Hogarth saw before he slipped away was Pandora pulling excitedly on his ruptured windpipe.

It was less than five minutes later when Joseph Bell discovered the body on his way for a quick smoke topside, before getting his head down for a well-earned kip. By that time, the body was unrecognizable as Hoggie. Even Bell, who had seen many gruesome sights in his travels around the world, could not look at the stoker's mangled face and ripped open chest cavity, without throwing up. Even when he had nothing left to vomit, his stomach twisted and contorted making him double over in pain as he heaved nothing but acidic bile, leaving a burning sensation at the back of his throat.

Several other engineers responded to Bell's shouts for help. Eventually they were able to drag Hoggie's lifeless body, draped in discarded coal sacks to hide his hideously disfigured face, into an unused refrigeration room while they awaited the ship's doctor and master-at-arms. Although there was no sign of whom, or what, attacked Hoggie, several of the men noticed that some of his wounds bore a striking resemblance to bite marks.

Twenty-two

As Patrick slowly climbed the polished wooden stairs leading to the ship's medical suite on C Deck, he was momentarily overcome by a feeling of nausea. He felt like the stairway had started spinning around him, leaving him confused and disorientated. The few passengers descending the stairs appeared to rush towards him; crowding around him, their voices blending into a disjointed clamour with no clear rhythm or coherence.

Then they were gone. Hurrying by on their way to lunch, eyeing the man with a bloodied pillowcase pressed to his face, with suspicion. Patrick had a firm hold of the bannister, a reflex act of self-preservation that had prevented him from tumbling backwards. He eased his grip, taking a few deep breaths to clear the fogginess in his head.

"Steady there. You might want to slow down a little. I expect you're experiencing some delayed shock." Bernard pressed his hand against the centre of Patrick's back, helping him preserve his balance and regain his composure.

Patrick's skin felt like it was ablaze, the sweat pouring from his brow had further soaked the pillowcase. Turning to thank his companion, he struggled to think of the right words.

His mouth opening and closing silently before, frustrated, he turned his attention back to the climb.

Bernard, thinking Patrick looked weary, tried to persuade him to rest for a minute, but Patrick was determined to push on. He was beginning to feel hungry, and he sensed he would find food at his destination.

"The medical suite is not far, and I'll be able to rest there," he insisted. The two men continued up the stairs, with Bernard providing the younger man with subtle, tactile support.

It had been Bernard who'd insisted Patrick visit the medical suite. "Let's start by getting you some medical attention, then maybe we should repair to one of the cafés to conjure a plan," he had suggested. They were intent on milking Patrick's injury for all it was worth, and to the wily old Englishman the logical first step should be to get official confirmation of the wound, and better still, its probable cause.

By the time they walked through the inviting doorway of the medical suite, Patrick's breathing had become laboured. Struggling to take a few deep breaths, he felt the unpleasant sensation of fluid bubbling in the base of his lungs, causing him to cough. Politely placing the back of his hand over his mouth, he coughed a fine spray of bright red blood across his fingers. Wiping it away with the already stained pillowcase, he noticed his skin had taken on a pale, almost translucent appearance, and his veins formed dark threads, like a rash spreading across his hands, and disappearing under his shirtsleeves.

"That's quite a cut you have there, sir." The nurse's tone was dour and unimaginative as she rose from her small desk. Her slate gray uniform, buttoned to the neck, hung to a point a quarter of an inch above the floor, the spotless white apron starched rigid. She bustled towards the two men, shooing Bernard away with a dismissive wave.

"This man can talk for himself. We don't need people loitering about spreading germs. Please go about your business elsewhere, and I shall send for you if needed." With that she ushered him out into the corridor, shutting the door before he had a chance to reply.

She turned her attention to Patrick, and with a dismissive air, indicated he should take a seat. She had treated many similar facial wounds, either caused by a bite or by a bottle, and the one thing they all had in common was drunkardness. It was the disease of the working class, and she didn't have time for it and even less time for those getting into fights because of it.

Addressing Patrick brusquely, she returned to her desk. "I am Sister O'Malley. Was that caused by a bottle, or did someone bite you?"

Patrick tried to answer her question but he didn't know how. He could visualize the words in his head; although if he were honest, he would have to admit he was unsure whether they were the right words. But try as he might, he couldn't remember how to speak. His lips twitched, and his jaw swung up and down, but even uttering the feeblest of sounds eluded him. The confusion this caused him was compounded by the nurse's impatient stare. She obviously thought he was wasting her precious time and made no attempt to disguise the fact.

Frustrated, he forced himself to walk towards the sturdy looking chair in front of the nurse's desk, hoping that, given a moment, his speech would return. But his legs felt heavy and unnatural, and he only managed to stagger a few short steps before his legs cramped up. A fierce burning pain seared through his calves and up into his thighs as each muscle, in turn, stiffened. His toes curled inwards, the cramps spreading into his feet. The intolerable pain caused his face to contort as he pitched forward with an inaudible cry of vexation and torment. He made a final desperate and undignified lunge towards the nurse, who, reading his intent, deftly sidestepped his outstretched arms.

As he crashed to the floor, Patrick felt a cold darkness encircling him. He heard the distant, muffled voice of the nurse calling for the doctor's help and was vaguely aware of approaching footsteps. A searing pain tore through his insides, every breath stabbed at his lungs as if he were inhaling fine shards of glass, and waves of crushing pressure swept through his head. The cramps that had so debilitated his legs spread up his body affecting his back and upper arms. His whole body burned with an intense fire which started deep within his chest and flowed through his arteries like a tide of molten steel.

And yet, Patrick still felt cold.

Sister O'Malley, aided by Doctor Sampson's arrival, pulled Patrick over onto his back. His body was stiff and unyielding, his limbs rigid. She noticed the skin around his wound had turned greenish-blue in colour, and the rash had spread to his face and neck. She leaned over him, staring down into his tired, bloodshot eyes. They were dull and lifeless, his stare focused on a point far in the distance. She had cared for British troops during the Boer War and knew that look only too well.

"Sir, can you hear me?" She shook his shoulder gently, but he made no response. She tried again, only with more urgency, her voice raised. "Sir, can you tell me your name?"

"Let me see!" Doctor Sampson said, crouching next to Patrick's body. He pulled open Patrick's eyelid and peered into the opaque iris, causing a droplet of blood nestled in the corner of the eye to trickle out across the mottled cheek. The spreading rash had gathered pace and now covered the entire face. It lay just below the skin's clammy surface, a spindly web creeping through the translucent tissue which oozed a thin, blood-like fluid forming droplets in the open pores and pooling in the body's natural crevices.

Placing his hand on Patrick's forehead, he continued, "He is feverish. We need to bring his temperature down." Then, feeling for a carotid pulse, he added, "And his pharynx has swollen. I doubt he will be able to breathe much longer."

The Sister, in response to the doctor's observation about the patient's fever, was on her way to fetch some wet towels but stopped as Patrick began a series of violent convulsions.

Gurgling, rasping gasps emanated from his throat as his body shook uncontrollably, smashing his head repeatedly onto the unforgiving, linoleum-covered deck. Then, as quick as it began, he lay still again.

Rivulets of blood crisscrossed Patrick's tired features, running from his nostrils, the corners of his mouth, and his wide, staring eyes. These focused on the doctor in a silent plea for help. The back of his head had become a soggy mass of hair, congealed blood, and torn skin. Doctor Sampson also noticed the convoluted twists of brain tissue pushing through the Irishman's smashed skull.

Patrick tried again to speak, a wet gurgle emanated from the back of his throat. Sampson, straining to hear what he knew would be his patient's final words, bent forward, placing his ear close to the dying man's lips.

Without warning, Patrick vomited a fountain of thick, warm blood vertically into the air. It gushed from his throat, hitting the unsuspecting doctor full in the face, before falling back on to his own prostrate form. As the torrent subsided, he let out a rattling cough, sending a fine mist of blood and mucus into the air, which unbeknown to her, Sister O'Malley inhaled as she rushed to the stricken doctor's aid.

Patrick McGowan let out a soft groan, his eyes rolling up into his head as he finally slipped into a colder, darker world. His body lay in a sticky pool of blood in a room he, only a few minutes before, walked into feeling only slightly unwell and a little disorientated. Such was the speed of his demise.

Twenty-three

Esme stretched her back upwards, rolling her head from side to side. She heard the tiny crinkling, crackling sound of the cartilage and muscles in her neck stretching this way then that, releasing the tension. She rolled her shoulders then rose, a little unsteadily, to her feet. She had spent the entire morning cleaning the silverware for the first class dining saloon, a punishment befitting her crimes according to Miss Wilson, who had taken great pleasure in overseeing her handiwork. She had regularly returned items she judged *unsatisfactory,* often after no more than a cursory glance.

Finally, and well past lunchtime, Esme had finished. Miss Wilson had disappeared to supervise cleaning the saloon following the lunch service, leaving a window of opportunity Esme couldn't pass up. She quickly slipped from the small pantry and hurried through the busy kitchen area before Miss Wilson had cause to notice she was missing. The Old Dragon would go mad when she discovered her absence, but Esme figured she couldn't possibly get in any more trouble than she already was, so what the hell. Besides, she had more important matters to attend to.

Esme was concerned for Bridget and needed to check on her. The last time she saw her upper class friend she left her in a room with her drunken ogre of a husband, who had been in the foulest of moods.

She made her way to the Grafton's suite and approached their door, intending to knock. Suddenly, it swung open. Esme turned, darting back around the corner. She carefully peeked back towards the open doorway just in time to see William step out into the corridor. He tugged at the bottom of his suit jacket, ensuring it fitted correctly at his sleeves, before pulling the door closed and striding purposefully down the corridor, away from Esme's crude hiding place.

She waited for him to round the corner at the far end of the corridor before hurrying to the door, where she knocked with a little more exuberance than necessary; such was her desire to check on her friend.

Bridget's voice, muffled by the door, commanded her to, "Enter!"

Upon entering the suite, Esme was relieved and a little surprised to see Bridget sitting at the Queen Anne style writing desk, obviously catching up with her correspondence. Bridget looked up as Esme closed the door; a thin nervous smile danced briefly on her lips, but soon vanished.

"Are you alright, Miss? I was so worried after I left you last night." Esme hurried towards Bridget, and once up close, noticed the faint bruising around the other woman's eye. Taking a moment to trace the bruise with her fingers, ensuring there was no swelling or evidence of a broken bone she added, "Did that bastard do this to you? Does it hurt?"

"He tried, but mercifully he'd consumed far too much liquor to connect with most of his blows." Bridget stood up and

taking Esme's hand, led her to the small couch. Once they were both sitting comfortably, she filled her in on the details of her breakfast with William. She explained about how he found out about the pregnancy, told her about Violet, and finished by telling her about their awkward agreement concerning her unborn child, Violet's tenuous employment status, and William's use of the riding crop.

"I may be no expert, but that ain't no way to conduct a marriage," Esme remarked when Bridget finished her tale. She looked at her friend, a troubled look on her face, as she asked, "Will he keep to his side of the deal?"

"Will he fuck!" Bridget's use of such coarse language surprised even her, and she giggled self-consciously.

"Mrs. Grafton!" Esme joined her in shocked giggles.

Bridget dabbed her eyes with a lace handkerchief before continuing, "The man is an insufferable snob who has probably never even heard of a suffragette. Even now, I suspect he is with his whore planning to beat the child from my loins." Her tears were no longer in response to mirth, and a mere dab of lace was not going to stem their flow.

Esme reached out and pulled the sobbing Bridget into her embrace while trying to offer some small words of comfort. Bridget's suggestion that William brought his mistress aboard this ship had taken her aback, and she resolved to question her further when a more suitable time arose. She stroked the distraught woman's hair, something that had always proved comforting to her young sister, Charlotte. At the thought of her

sister, she too began to fight the tears, aware her irresponsible actions would inevitably have dire consequences for them both. With the pretence of showing everything will be fine, Esme rubbed Bridget's back, seeking her own solace, and immediately felt Bridget flinch.

Bridget broke the embrace and sat upright, her hands planted demurely in her lap. After a few moments, where it was obvious to Esme Bridget was struggling to convey the right words, she said, "He took the crop to me again last night. He does it to teach me the proper way to behave as his wife, and to punish my misdeeds, but I also know it is, in part, simply to satisfy his own twisted needs. But I shall tolerate it no longer!"

"But what can you do? Surely he won't allow you to leave him; the scandal would be too much." Esme looked perplexed.

"I may have been a little foolhardy this morning. What was I thinking? He will most likely beat me to death in a drunken rage, cheered on, no doubt, by that treacherous harlot." Bridget's voice rose in pitch as she spoke, her eyes widened in panic. She stood up and paced to and fro in front of the couch, her hands clasped so tightly in front of her stomach, the whites of her knuckles showed.

"Oh, please calm down, ma'am. You will distress yourself and the baby." Esme worried for her friend, her rate of breathing had increased, the breaths short and sharp, and her eyes darted from side to side as if she were having a heated argument within her own head.

Trying to calm the rich American socialite, Esme grabbed her shoulders. Giving her a gentle shake to regain her attention, she said, "I doubt even he would believe he could get away with your murder, and at the very least, your antics at breakfast have given him something to think about. I suspect he will not resort to the crop again for fear of people discovering the truth about him. You are not a common street tart whose death would go unnoticed. You are a lady of privilege, wealth, and connections. If you were to disappear or even suffer injury, people would notice."

"But people have not noticed when he's beaten me in the past," responded Bridget. She had calmed slightly, her breathing, while still rapid, was deeper and more deliberate as if she were making a conscious effort to gain control.

"Because he has everyone fooled into thinking he is so wonderful and debonair, with his young, attractive wife. From the outside you are the perfect couple; it's a perfect smoke screen, and you have been too scared of what people will think of you to speak up. And that bastard knows it." Esme could tell her words were striking a chord with Bridget. She began nodding in tacit agreement and appeared much calmer. As a result, her next comment caught Esme off guard.

"I should kill him first." She looked straight into Esme's eyes as she spoke the words in a flat, measured tone, and Esme knew Bridget was affording the notion serious consideration.

"I think you should put away such thoughts. If you do murder Mr. Grafton, then they will hang you for sure." She tried to guide Bridget back to the couch, hoping this would draw the conversation to a close. But Bridget wouldn't be deterred.

"If I remain in this marriage then I would be putting myself and my child, especially my child, in mortal danger. As a mother, what else am I to do? I can't simply leave him, and he would never allow me a divorce. Suppose I did escape his clutches, then what? No one would want a woman with a bastard child, and I would get no financial help from William. I would be destitute, and likely as not, have to prostitute myself to put food on the table."

Esme noticed the sparkle in Bridget's eyes as she paused for a moment to regain her breath, before continuing excitedly. "So you see, I have to kill him because I would then inherit his wealth. After all, I did marry him for his money, it would be impossible to marry that man for love!"

Bridget's suggestion that she'd married William for money alone shocked Esme. Somewhere in the back of her mind she couldn't shake the notion his untimely death had featured strongly in his bride's wedding plans. Not that she cared one jot for the man. He was, without doubt, a violent bully, and she had personally witnessed his handiwork with the riding crop, not to mention his interference had cost her the position aboard ship. However, the Grafton's marriage was, at least as far as the gossip columns reported, a fairy tale, and she continued to be dumbfounded by the revelations she had become privy too.

Suddenly aware Bridget was looking at her expectantly, awaiting her to pass comment on the circumstances as she'd explained them, Esme said, her voice no more than a murmur, "But how? The police will not stop in their search for the killer of such an important man. You can't possibly expect to get away with it?"

"We need it to look like an accident," Bridget sounded distracted. She was silent for a few seconds, lost in thought then, as an idea began to take shape in her mind, she became more animated. When she again looked at Esme, her face had gained a natural glow. "An intruder possibly, set on some nefarious deed. I am sure, with our feminine wiles, we could find ourselves a suitable patsy." Then seeing the confused look on the young woman's face, Bridget added helpfully, "Someone we could trick into taking the blame."

Esme, on who Bridget's switch to the term *we* had not gone unnoticed, was not convinced. "I still say you are taking a great risk with your neck, besides, it would be wrong, evil even, to trick a fool into placing the noose around his own neck."

"That may be so, but as unconscionable as it is, the alternatives facing me are even more unpalatable. I accept it is a risky venture, but one I must embark on if I am to survive." Bridget's bravado slipped and she looked like a lost little girl as she asked quietly, "Please, will you help me?"

Twenty-four

Bernard slid into the first class Veranda café unchallenged. He had already secured a key to the metal grills separating the first and second class areas of the ship. It had always been his experience that everything and everyone had a price. The trick was finding it. In this endeavour, Bernard had received the invaluable help of Lady Luck the night before they left Southampton. Having taken a room in an old coaching inn situated little more than a stone's throw from the docks, he spent the evening enjoying a fine meal and experiencing the local ale. At the next table sat four men who spent most of the evening talking about their experiences working the Atlantic crossing. They compared amusing anecdotes and talked at length about their upcoming crossing on board the *Titanic*. Hearing this, Bernard asked the bartender to provide the table with another round of drinks while he introduced himself, claiming to be a reporter down from London to cover the ship's departure. He spent a couple of hours with the men, who turned out to be ship's stewards, observing them carefully.

Bernard prided himself on his ability to read people and wasn't surprised when two of the men made their excuses and left the table. He watched as they left the hostelry by a side door then, draining his own ale, he excused himself from the table, citing a call of nature as the reason. Then he casually sauntered to the side door and stepped out into the chill of the

evening, pulling his coat on as he looked up and down the narrow lane onto which he emerged.

To his left, the lane opened onto the main thoroughfare, and he could hear the voices and occasional laughter of revellers out enjoying the night. To his right, the lane led to a catacomb of small alleyways and crooked paths, servicing the shops and traders that provided for the dockworkers and their families.

Here and there, an occasional light cast an eerie glow, serving only to intensify the darkness of the surrounding shadows. It was in this direction that Bernard hastened, stepping lightly, the element of surprise being pivotal to his plan.

He followed the sidewall of the pub then cut across the courtyard towards the stables at the rear. He exercised caution at every turn so as not to stumble blindly into anything or anyone. Arriving at the end stable, he stood quietly in the shadows and watched as the two stewards fornicated in the straw.

Bernard had observed their sly glances, the gentle touch of hands and the almost imperceptible nod that passed between the men just before they left the bar. He waited a while, picking his moment, before stepping into the light. From then on it was only a little matter of blackmail, his stock-in-trade, and he had a key to pass freely through the dividing gates.

He looked around the café while waiting for a vacant table. It appeared, and the maître d' confirmed Mrs. Black had not yet arrived. He'd sent her a note, conveyed by one of the over-amorous stewards who were still eager to ensure his continued silence, inviting her to join him for a light lunch followed, perhaps, by a stroll on the promenade. Bernard was eager to reel his catch in before the ship docked in New York, and he lost the romantic advantage afforded him by the ship's grandeur.

Once seated at his table, he only had to wait a few minutes before the object of his financial desire strolled confidently into the café. As the maître d' escorted her to their table, Bernard took the opportunity to appraise Kathleen Black's classic good looks, deciding that, should he have to seal the deal in the boudoir, it would not be an unfortunate state of affairs. As she approached his table, he stood to receive her, subconsciously smoothing his bushy moustache as he did so.

"Sir Bernard, I do hope you have not been waiting long?" The shrillness of her voice caused several diners at the nearby tables to look up.

"I have myself, only just arrived," Bernard replied, touching his lips to the back of her hand. He waited for his guest to sit before taking his own seat, dispatching the waiter with a flourish to fetch them the finest champagne White Star had to offer.

"It was good of you to invite me to lunch. It can get so boring when traveling alone." Mrs. Black rearranged the cutlery as she spoke, glancing up coyly as she said the last word.

"It is my pleasure, Mrs. Black. I only hope you do not consider me to be, in any way, presumptuous. It is not every day a woman of your beauty crosses my path, and I couldn't bear the thought of you dining alone." Bernard had seen the coy look, and his insides were busy dancing a jig. This was going to be easier than he thought.

"It is only lunch. How can inviting a friend to lunch be presumptuous? And, please call me Kathleen. I hate all that formal nonsense. Why should friends call each other by their titles and surnames? It's all so pompous."

"I quite agree, Kathleen." Bernard gave her the benefit of one of his well-rehearsed smiles. He picked up the menu, perused it for a few seconds, then placed it back on the table. "I can recommend the fish. I had it yesterday, and it was divine."

"I shall heed your recommendation if you would be so kind as to order for me?" She smiled at him a little longer than was necessary, and Bernard felt his cynical old heart skip a beat.

They shared a fine meal during which Bernard found his smile was no longer that of a practiced con artist, but the true, warm smile of a man besotted with the elegant woman sitting opposite him. They talked about their upbringing, and although he lied about almost every aspect of his life, he discovered Kathleen's early life wasn't that much different from his own. It was when she married Theodore Black, an investment banker

who, more by good fortune than shrewd business acumen, invested in a steel company just before it won the contract to supply several New York construction companies, her life took a turn for the better. Theodore became a millionaire almost overnight, but society never accepted the new money rich, and after twenty years of marriage, a depressed Mr. Black took his own life, leaving his entire estate to Kathleen. She, only being in her mid-forties, set out to see the world and was now on the final, homeward leg of her journey. Even her abrasive New York accent didn't seem so bad when he was staring into her eyes.

After lunch, they took a stroll on the enclosed promenade before Bernard escorted her back to her suite. As they parted company, Bernard again kissed her hand, although this time he lingered over the contact, savouring the smell of her perfume, before hurrying away to find Patrick. They had much to discuss regarding their plan for blackmailing The White Star Line, and their ticket to the high life once in America. He was aware his burgeoning feelings for Kathleen Black threatened to set the cat among the pigeons and decided it would be better if he didn't mention that part of his day to his young companion.

Arriving back at their cabin, he found it unoccupied. Seeing no sign of Patrick's return, Bernard surmised he must either still be in the ship's hospital or down in one of the lounges, drinking off the effects of shock. Not wanting to encounter the hard-faced nurse again, Bernard wrote a quick note, which he left propped against Patrick's pillow should the

younger man return before him, then headed to the second class lounge in search of either his friend or a good card game.

Twenty-five

Nestled in a dark cavity and pressed up against a warm water pipe to escape the harsh chill of the sea air, Pandora again felt those familiar pangs. That craving that yearned for fulfilment. It was more than a hunger. It was that yearning for air experienced by a man trapped beneath the waves. Even knowing he will drown, the need is such he can't fight it any longer. Finally, he takes a breath hoping, perhaps, to find a blessed relief in death.

The feeling didn't originate in her stomach, or form from a notion in her brain, but emanated from every fibre of her being. It flowed around her body, carried by her blood, always increasing, always intensifying. It oozed from her pores, she tasted it on her breath, and it made her itch! That, coupled with the humming in her head, a constant drone that had been ever present since she woke in that hot, stuffy bag to feed on a bland, tasteless ounce of meat which lacked the nourishment of life's natural juices, was always there, unrelenting, and driving her mad.

Pandora knew what she needed to satisfy the yearning, at least for a short while. She needed fresh meat. She needed the warm, nourishing flesh and life-giving blood of man. She had acquired a taste for it, proving herself more than a match for any human. She already killed once for its raw, salty toughness, only for more men to disturb her feed before she could sate the desire.

The tiny monkey felt herself growing stronger and knew she would kill again, but she needed to bide her time and wait for the right moment. With a soft cackle, she closed her eyes and snuggled closer to the warmth of the pipe.

Twenty-six

"This is astonishing! I have never seen anything like this before. It's all rather confusing, to say the least."

Doctor Sampson stood next to Patrick's fresh corpse, the worry lines on his brow were etched deep as he surveyed the bloody scene before him. He'd joined the *Titanic* for two reasons, easy money and easier women, and neither involved young men violently bleeding to death on his floor. The description given to him by a friend, who himself applied for the position, suggested he would have an easy life. Nothing more taxing than treating the occasional elderly lady for a spot of seasickness while dining and dancing with an endless stream of rich young ladies, whose fathers would be ecstatically happy to see them marry a doctor.

Immediately following the man's untimely death, Sister O'Malley tried wiping away the blood dripping from Dr. Sampson's ruddy jowls and slightly bulbous nose, but the rich coppery smell and the violent images of the previous few minutes got the better of her constitution. Much to her professional embarrassment, and for the first time in her long career, Nurse O'Malley rushed to the hand basin and vomited.

The doctor removed his bloodstained tunic and used the cleaner patches to wipe himself down, while Sister O'Malley cleaned up around the sink before rinsing her face in refreshingly cold water.

"I'm so sorry, Doctor. I really am. I don't know what came over me," she muttered sheepishly. Embarrassed, her stomach had so spectacularly let her down in the presence of Doctor Sampson, a man for whom, despite his roguish reputation and her advancing middle age, she still carried a small, but hopeful, candle.

Doctor Sampson had given her a reassuring smile. "That's alright, Agatha. I think we just witnessed something extraordinary. Perhaps it would be best if we wrap the body, clean up this mess, and make no further mention of the events surrounding this man's dreadful demise, save those medical in nature?" He looked at Sister O'Malley, seeking her agreement.

"I think that would be a wise course of action, and one I will be eternally grateful for."

The look of discomfort on the nurse's face eased with the combined realization her indiscretion wasn't about to become common knowledge about the ship, and Doctor Sampson had used her Christian name.

Together, they loosely wrapped Patrick's limp body in a white linen sheet before lifting him onto the examination table in the doctor's office. While he wrote some brief notes detailing his observations of the patient's rapid decline, Sister O'Malley mopped the deck, trying to clean up the sticky pool of blood before it left an embarrassing stain on the new floor. Closing his journal, the doctor returned to stand next to the corpse, repeating absentmindedly as he gazed at the wrapped body, "Quite astonishing!"

His thoughts were interrupted by the hurried arrival of a dishevelled looking junior engineering officer. The young man was out of breath and appeared hot and flustered, so much so Sister O'Malley hurried forward to offer him some aid in case he should collapse. The officer waved away her offer of help but still took a few moments to gather his breath.

"Are you ill, sir?" The doctor asked with a note of impatience in his voice.

He sensed Patrick's death raised far more questions than it answered. Questions, he felt sure the captain and master-at-arms would want answered before their arrival in New York, and he was keen on getting the grisly business of examining the corpse completed.

"No, sir. Chief Engineer Bell ordered me to fetch you down to the cold store outside engineering, and to 'urry about it. It was farther than I expected, and I'm a little taken of breath." He spoke quicker as he got to the end of his last sentence, then started to cough.

Sampson rolled his eyes theatrically in Sister O'Malley's direction, who smiled and looked away, then waited for the young engineer to compose himself before asking, "Why does Chief Bell need me *fetched* to the cold store?"

"Tis a rum do, sir, no mistaking that. Hoggie, one of our stokers, and a giant of a man, we found 'im dead only minutes after completing 'is watch. The strangest thing, though, sir, was the bite marks, and 'is neck. Like a wild animal ripped it clean open."

Glancing self-consciously over his shoulder at the wrapped bundle on his examination table, Doctor Sampson replied, "Wild animal bites are not as unusual at sea as you would expect, young man, at least not today." Turning his full attention back to the Junior Officer, he said, "Now tell me. Did this Hoggie fellow show any sign of being unwell? Sickness, sweating, any strange markings or rash, particularly around, what we assume to be, the bite marks?"

The young officer thought for a brief moment, then shook his head. "I don't believe so, sir. That is, at least not to my knowledge."

Sister O'Malley finished mopping and stood next to the doctor, the little smile of just a few moments before long forgotten. Her eyes betrayed her growing unease at the developing events. She waited patiently for Doctor Sampson to ease her concerns about the presence of a fearsome beast loose about the ship, but she sensed this would not be forthcoming, at least not until he had inspected both bodies.

Doctor Sampson offered her a weak smile, hoping he appeared more confident than he felt. It had to be more than a coincidence. Two fit and healthy men die within minutes of each other following what, at least taken at face value, were animal attacks. One thing was for certain; the harbour authorities and the company would want answers. Answers he wouldn't find standing here.

"Nurse, can I leave you to arrange for our friend there," he nodded towards Patrick's corpse, "to be moved to the cold store? I would suggest you ask a couple of able seamen to do the transporting." Then, taking his hat from the hat stand by the door, he said to the engineering officer, "Lead on, my man."

It took the young engineering officer and the ship's doctor almost fifteen minutes to descend through the ship's intricate series of stairways and corridors, carefully avoiding the busier passenger areas so as not to arouse suspicion. Sampson had directed the younger man not to mention Hoggie or details of his wounds to anyone as it would in all likelihood cause undue panic, especially if the news spread to the passengers. He knew idle gossip and wayward speculation would hamper any investigation, and he couldn't rule out foul play, thinking it more likely than having a rogue wild animal stalking the ship; he was, therefore, keen to keep details close to his chest.

Chief Engineer Bell met them outside the cold store wearing a worn, worried look that gave him the appearance of a man ten years his senior. The two men exchanged greetings with a polite nod then, without a word of explanation, Bell pulled open the heavy storeroom door. A blast of cold air hit the doctor full in the face, causing him to inhale sharply. Taking a moment to congratulate himself on remembering to wear his hat, he stepped into the storeroom, his breath forming wild eddies of warm air as he looked around.

Bell pointed to the far corner and muttered gruffly, "Over there."

Doctor Sampson led the way as the two men approached the corpse. It lay along the back wall, and although dressed, the body was covered by carefully placed sacking. Removing the sacks, the doctor noticed the blood staining the man's dirty gray shirt and the gaping wound where the unfortunate man's throat should have been. He leant closer and noticed Hoggie's face and the back of his hands bore evidence of a struggle, and a fierce one at that. One finger appeared horribly misshapen and even without closer inspection, Doctor Sampson could tell it was broken, while the little finger on the right hand was missing, sheared off at the second knuckle. All that remained was a jagged piece of flesh and a splinter of bright white bone.

"If it's all the same with you, Doc, I think I'll leave you to it." Bell was already on his way back to the door as he spoke, leaving Sampson to his investigation.

Doctor Sampson knelt next to the body and examined the wounds carefully, taking special care to inspect the rough edges of the large tear opening the stoker's throat and the stub of the missing finger. Both appeared uneven and torn, the edges shredded and ripped. It was obvious to Doctor Sampson even the most amateur killer, with a half-decent knife, would make cleaner cuts. Most of the smaller facial wounds and those to the back of the hands bore a striking resemblance to scratches inflicted by a woman's nails. However, just above the man's wrist on the thick muscles of his forearm was a clear set of bite marks, small and oval in shape. Doctor Sampson judged them too small to have been inflicted by an adult, and he felt sure a man of Hoggie's size would easily be able to fend off even the most frenzied of attacks by a small child. He also noted a section of the man's throat was missing. He shivered, not entirely convinced it was due to the room's temperature alone.

He felt the man's skin and was not, given the ambient temperature, surprised to find it cold and lifeless. There were no, nor was he expecting any, signs of life, and the pale pallor of the skin supported the notion of him having bled substantially before dying some time ago. Remembering the strange dark rash pervading the skin surrounding the wounds inflicted on the unfortunate man now lying lifeless on his examination table, Sampson opened the giant stoker's shirt and inspected the man's upper chest and shoulders. There was no sign of a rash, although the area immediately surrounding the wound did have a slight, almost indistinguishable mottling. Sampson dismissed this as the result of the trauma inflicted on the thin, delicate area of the skin.

With a puzzled expression, the doctor walked thoughtfully back to the door and stepped out into the dimly lit corridor that separated the clean refrigerated stores and the dirty superheated engine room. The chief engineer looked at him expectantly but didn't speak. He could tell the doctor was troubled by what he had just witnessed. He couldn't blame him. Just being in the same room as Hoggie's body had given him a severe dose of the willies.

After a brief moment of contemplation, Sampson said, "Would you please arrange for someone to bring the body lying

on my examination table down here. I think, although there are differences in the exact manner of their deaths, the two victims are in some way intrinsically linked. I just don't know what that link may be."

Chief Bell nodded. "I hope you don't mind, but I thought it fitting to notify the master-at-arms."

"No, not at all, I was about to suggest that myself. I would also venture placing a guard at this door, at least until we know what we are dealing with."

Doctor Sampson removed his hat and dabbed the sweat from his brow with his handkerchief. He felt unusually warm this deep in the ship's bowels and was eager to return to his office and collect his bag along with a few other medical supplies pertinent to a more comprehensive investigation into the two men's deaths.

"I will arrange for one of my men to remain here until we find a more suitable solution, but for now I must return to engineering. I'll send two men to you within the hour to collect the deceased. I'll bid you, at least for now, good day."

Bell strode away, barking orders to his men, leaving Sampson to take a more leisurely stroll back up through the decks to his office. He had a feeling it was going to be a very long night.

Twenty-seven

The cabin was deliberately dark. The weak moonlight shining dimly through the small porthole behind the four-poster bed failed to cast sufficient light into the room. Bridget lay still, feigning sleep and listening to William trying to negotiate a passage through the reception room. She could tell he was drunk, and he had probably also smoked too much opium if she had learnt anything during their brief marriage.

A loud thud and a cry of pain, immediately followed by a curse that would turn a sailor's ears red, came from the other room. Bridget heard William *shush* himself theatrically, giggling like a naughty child.

Bridget waited. A tear stung the corner of her eye before rolling across her cheek, but she made no move to wipe it away. After a brief moment of disquieting silence from the reception room, the door to the bedchamber spilled open and William, his legs barely able to support his weight, entered the room. The overpowering, sickly-sweet smell of liquor and opium accompanied him. He belched loudly then stumbled awkwardly towards the bed, leaving the door wide open.

Bridget remained still, keeping up the pretence of sleep, her fist closing around the edge of her pillow, her delicate knuckles turning white as she struggled to hold back a renewed wave of tears. She had no doubt about where he had spent the evening.

The bed creaked as he sat down heavily, and she got a gentle scent of something new, yet something hauntingly familiar. The sweet aroma of perfume, the same perfume he bought her on their honeymoon in Paris. Yet he just came from his below stairs whore smelling of the same fragrance.

Bridget, determined not to make a sound, pushed her face into the pillow as her husband struggled with the laces of his expensive shoes. Finally defeated, he resorted to prising them off with his feet before kicking them noisily across the room. The exertion obviously getting the better of him, she heard him breathing heavily for a few seconds before he mumbled a few coarse words.

Then he swung his legs up onto the bed.

Bridget froze, resisting the urge to hold her breath, as William leant over her. His warm, vile smelling exhalations tickled her neck. His hands, the same hands she knew had, without a doubt, caressed his lover now embraced her, his fingers encircling her breast. She rolled over slightly as if his presence had momentarily disturbed her sleep, trapping his hand under her body.

William pulled it free with a frustrated sigh then, clearly unwilling to give up his drunken fumbling just yet, ran his hand roughly across her buttocks and down between her thighs.

Bridget forced her face deeper into the pillow, trying to stem the tears that streamed from her burning eyes. She felt humiliated. He did not even have the good grace to stay clear of his mistress for one day, and now, aroused by that sinful siren's song, he returned to the marital bed with a desire to violate her, his wife.

But then, as quickly as they had begun, William's clumsy attempts at seduction abruptly ended, and he slumped back on the bed with a loud groan. The smell of his breath almost brought Bridget to the point of gagging.

Bridget lay listening to the deep, guttural snoring of the monster she married only a few short months before. Her hands lovingly cradled her still small bump and she knew, the way a mother knows, her child wasn't safe; her child would never be safe.

Brazenly calling his bluff at breakfast, Bridget believed the threat of revealing his scandalous affair to the world would be enough to thwart his drunken womanizing and violent domestic chastisement, but she was wrong. He ran straight to his whore; how she must have revelled in the moment. Bridget knew with undying certainty, she and her child were in mortal danger.

William was a monster who believed his own ego and considered himself superior to all those around him. How dare she, a mere girl, fresh from her debutant ball, and a damned Yankee to boot, challenge his superiority? She must have been crazy to believe she could stand in the way of Captain William Grafton. He was the epitome of all that was wrong with the English establishment. He was arrogant, conceited, and in possession of too much wealth and privilege to behave any differently. She had known him long enough to know his Harrovian old boy network stretched its tentacles into every

facet of English life, from the judiciary to the Palace of Westminster and on down Birdcage Walk to the heart of Englishness, Buckingham Palace.

They would view her as a simple annoyance, a mere fly in his ointment, easily removed and disposed of, leaving him to grieve publicly the loss of his new wife while privately setting up his den of iniquity with Violet.

Before she knew it, Bridget had slipped from their bed to stand over her husband's slumbering form. Sprawled drunk across the crisp white linen, he still cut the dashing and handsome figure of the military gentleman who had swept her off her feet. Finding out he was wealthy to the point of obscenity made up for his advancing years and, in her eyes, sealed the deal.

She picked up her pillow which still held the warmth from where her head had rested; still damp from the tears she shed. Tears for his falsehoods, tears for her frustrations, then simply tears of fear. Tears that had watered the seeds of her revengeful deeds until finally, they had grown to fruition.

With shaking hands, she slowly lowered the pillow until it hovered a few inches above his face. She felt sick; the shaking spread throughout her body. With a sudden urgency, it was now or never, she covered his sleeping face, forcing the soft pillow down with all her strength.

There was no going back. Bridget knew she would live or die in the next few moments. For a second, maybe two, he

made no movement as if neither she nor the pillow even existed.

Then, with a muffled roar, he exploded into action. He tried lifting his head, but Bridget forced the pillow downward with all her might. He clawed at her hands, prising her fingers away one by one. Gradually loosening her grip, little bit by little bit. She realized with horror, that in a moment he would be free.

Free to extract his revenge in the only way he knew.

With an energetic leap, she brought her knees crashing down on his unprotected chest just as she lost her grip on the pillow. It slipped to the side revealing half his face. One accusing eye, catching the pale moonlight, stared up at her. The force of her knees landing on his chest drove the breath from his body, stunning him for what, to Bridget, were a valuable few seconds.

William struggled to gulp in the late-night air as Bridget pressed home her advantage. She pinned his arms with her bare knees, her silk gown riding up to expose her thighs, as she again forced the pillow over his shadowy features.

As a young girl, she learned to ride on a farm outside of Boston. She persuaded the stable hands, when her governess became engrossed in her embroidery, to teach her to ride like a gentleman instead of the more sedate and ladylike sidesaddle. She now put this skill to use riding his bucking torso, her knees pinning his arms to the bed, as she suffocated him with her soft, comfortable pillow.

His bucking became more frantic. His body pitched left and right, his knees slamming her in the back, as he fought for his life.

Bridget tightened her grip on the pillow and held on. Rolling her hips with each of his increasingly desperate thrusts, she kept downward pressure on the pillow. Each time his knee smashed into her back, the pain exploded across her shoulders and followed the line of every scar he left on her fair skin, renewing her resolve.

Bridget clung on. It was the ride of her life.

Finally, after what, to Bridget, had become an eternity, his knees stopped their insistent thumping on her back, his legs falling back on the bed. His movements grew ever more sporadic. His weak hands scrabbled frantically at the lily-white flesh of her thighs in a final desperate attempt to free himself. Then, with a shudder, his body fell still, his hands gently sliding back onto the pale sheets.

Still, she clung on. Her breath coming in short, staccato gasps, her body slick with sweat.

Bridget remained sitting on the pillow. The moonlight creeping through the porthole picked out the whiteness of her nightgown, turning it silver. She sat in the darkness astride her dead husband's body like a shimmering angel until her legs hurt. Until she was sure Captain William Grafton could hurt her no more.

Then Bridget slid from the bed, being careful not to dislodge the pillow from his face. She knew the sight of that one

dispraising eye, and its contemptuous, unblinking stare would haunt her to the grave, a destination, she feared, her actions had only hastened.

She kept her gaze fixed on his lifeless body while slowly backing across the room. Her outstretched arm searched the surrounding darkness for the dressing table, and the drawer containing the beastly riding crop that had caused her so much pain and anguish during her short marriage. Locating the drawer, her hands fumbled through its contents until her fingers brushed against the crop's smooth coldness.

Taking a deep breath, forcing her nervousness back into the pit of her stomach, Bridget picked up the whip. She took a few absentminded practice swings, the sound of it whipping through the air caused her to flinch involuntarily. Some deep-rooted and extraordinarily primal neurosis caused a burning sensation to sear through the scars on her back.

Her knuckles turned white as her pent-up anger and frustration boiled over. Until then, she had acted with cold, calculated premeditation. But now, released from the fear of failure, her rage consumed her. It wasn't just his adultery or the clockwork regularity of his beatings that propelled her across the room, her arm raised high above her head. It was his arrogance. William had, right up to his death, believed he could pursue whatever path he chose and no one, especially his wife, was worthy of consideration.

She beat his corpse with brisk, violent strokes. The unforgiving crop swishing and swooshing, back and forth as she

landed blow after blow, tearing his fine cotton shirt and flaying his torso until, exhausted and breathless, she sank to the floor. As she drifted off to sleep, lying next to the bed containing the shredded body of her husband, Bridget's lips wore the gentle curve of contentment.

Twenty-eight

The chambermaid knocked on the Grafton's door the following morning and, receiving no reply, entered the suite to change the bed linen and refresh the towels. Thinking the occupants had gone to breakfast or were, perhaps, enjoying a romantic early morning stroll on the promenade, she began by tidying up the reception room. It wasn't until she entered the inner room, the suite's bedroom, she discovered Mrs. Grafton lying, almost naked, on the floor.

The maid hurried to her aid, thinking she must have fallen from the bed during the night and had somehow injured herself. It wasn't until she stood beside the bed, above Bridget's prostrate form, that she discovered the full horror of the night's events.

The gentleman, a man the young chambermaid understood to be a person of not inconsiderable importance, was obviously dead, his torso torn and bloodstained, his face half covered by a pillow. His one visible eye was sunken and shot through with tiny veins giving it a blood red hue, while his skin appeared, even in the early morning light, to have taken on a blue tinge.

The maid drew breath to scream but only managed a choked gurgle as she wheeled away to deposit the contents of her stomach on the plush carpet. She was still retching and trying to wipe away the strands of vomit and spittle from her chin when she became aware of a figure standing next to her.

She looked up into the pale but concerned face of Mrs. Grafton and, thinking her to be a ghost, promptly fainted.

Bridget looked at the fresh-faced girl lying on her carpet for a moment, but then the smell of vomit assailed her nostrils, triggering her own bout of early morning nausea. She rushed to the bathroom, and having vomited and rinsed out her mouth, returned with a small glass of water which she set down on the carpet next to the chambermaid who was beginning to come around.

"I am so terribly sorry," said Bridget, as if waking next to a badly beaten dead body was a common occurrence for her, and one the chambermaid would, given time, get used too.

The fresh-faced young girl looked up, her brow furrowed, her eyes darting from the figure on the bed to Mrs. Grafton and then towards the door leading out into the ante-chamber.

Bridget placed her hand on the girl's arm. She stared back, a mixture of panic and terror filled her eyes. Bridget smiled, trying to soften her dishevelled appearance.

"Are you alright, I'm sure you must've had quite a shock, but I can assure you I am quite alive." She looked across at her husband's limp, lifeless body adding, "I fear, I cannot say the same for him."

The chambermaid climbed gingerly to her feet, never once taking her gaze from the bed. Bridget offered her hand, but the maid seemed not to have noticed, or simply refused to accept help from such a distinguished lady. Then in a faltering

voice, said, "We must alert the crew, whoever attacked you, killed your 'usband, they might not be finished." She made no effort to leave the room, choosing instead to stare at the wounds slashed across William's slightly flabby body.

"I need you to listen very carefully," Bridget said, taking the girl's hands in hers. "Do you know Esme, the maid who cleaned this suite before you?" The teenager nodded in confirmation. "I need you to find her and tell her Mrs. Graf, tell her, Bridget needs her." She eyed the young girl suspiciously, unsure whether to trust her. "Can you do that for me? Neither you nor I are in any danger, and it is of vital importance you tell no one about what you saw. I promise, when Esme gets here, I will tell you what happened."

The maid nodded again and Bridget led her to the door, reiterating the importance of her task. Once the door had shut, Bridget, aware her life rested in the hands of a girl barely old enough to sprout breasts, whispered quietly in a language more suited to the ranch hands who taught her to ride, than a lady of London society. "Holy fuckin' shit!"

Bridget stood by the door for a few moments using its frame for support. Both her heart and her mind were racing and she felt hemmed in, trapped in her own tale of horror.

Her knees buckled and she felt sick again, but by the grace of God, she remained upright. Fainting wasn't an option, she had far too much to organize if she were to avoid the hangman's noose and not much time to do it.

She stumbled towards the bedroom, devoting her entire concentration to the simple process of walking, to get dressed. If the chambermaid, who was undoubtedly running scared, were to tell the crew of William's death, and the master-at-arms arrested her, throwing her into the ship's brig, then Bridget was going to dress for the occasion. It would be extremely bad form to be arrested in one's nightgown, especially one splattered with the victim's blood.

Bridget stood naked in front of the mirror patting her body dry when the knock came. Before she could protect her modesty with the towel, the door swung open just long enough to admit Esme. She was alone and out of breath. The two women rushed to embrace each other. Bridget was so glad to see a friendly face she made no further effort to cover herself, the towel discarded on the floor.

Esme returned the intensity of the embrace, aware of the grave danger her friend had endured to rid herself of such a tyrannical beast. She was glad to see her safe and well. Over Bridget's bare shoulder, Esme saw William's cadaver lying on the bed. It wore an evening suit, although much of the front of the shirt was either shredded or coloured a deep coppery brown colour, and no shoes. The face, partially covered by a large pillow, was uppermost and a riding crop lay on the floor, close to the bed.

"Are you alright, Bridge? Did he harm you?" Esme gently stroked her friend's soft auburn hair as Bridget sobbed into her shoulder. She felt a tremor pass through the woman's body and the sobbing, momentarily, grew stronger. Esme pursed her lips, determined not to cry. Bridget needed her to be strong.

After a minute or so had passed, Bridget raised her head and looked directly into Esme's face. Her damp, puffy eyes, rimmed red, searched her friend's face as she carefully considered her words. When she spoke, her voice was barely more than a throaty snivel.

"He returned from his lover smelling of her perfume. Smelling of my perfume. Yet, he still expected me to perform my wifely duties. He groped me in a pathetic attempt to get me to acquiesce to his needs, while I pretended to be sleeping. His touch repulsed me, and it was all I could do not to be sick." Bridget shuddered at the memory, and Esme rushed to collect her robe. Pulling it on, Bridget continued in a stronger voice, her words spilling unchecked from her mouth. "Luckily, he had drunk to excess and soon passed out on the bed, how you see him now. I knew he would never change, and while he lived I would live my life in constant fear. A condition I'm not prepared to tolerate. So in that small moment, I seized the opportunity. Placing a pillow across his sleeping features, holding on, quite literally, for dear life until his struggles ceased, and I was sure he had breathed his last."

"But the blood? You said you killed him with a pillow, but that does not explain the blood?" Esme now stood next to the bed, staring down at William's flayed torso.

"I allowed rage to overcome good sense and took the riding crop to him. A stupid act of revenge which, in the harsher

light of day, I fear may lead to my downfall," lamented Bridget. Then, remembering the chambermaid she'd entrusted to find Esme, added, "Where is the other girl?"

"She is finishing my tasks, far too scared to come back, but she won't tell anyone. I'll speak to her later, but for now, we need a plan." Esme was thinking aloud. She knew that if they put a foot wrong now, Bridget would meet her end dangling from a hangman's rope.

"I did wonder if Mr. Moody would help. I believe he has something of a soft spot for me."

Esme shook her head. "He may have. But I doubt he would risk his position over the promise of a night between your thighs. Let alone the risk of a murder charge. Once you tell him what happened, he would be duty bound to tell both the captain and the police in New York." She began pacing, a faraway look etched on her face.

Bridget sat down in one of the imitation Queen Anne chairs and slumped forward, head in her hands. She watched Esme with admiration as she paced up and down, wrestling with her thoughts, one of life's survivors. She was too tired to even think straight and wanted nothing more than to pull William's body from the bed, then curl up and go to sleep.

"Get dressed and go to breakfast. If anyone asks, just tell them your husband is unwell, but remain vague in the details." Esme started laying clothes out on the other chair for Bridget to wear. "That deception will buy us some time, but it will be valuable time, allowing me to arrange your disappearance."

Bridget looked at Esme with some confusion. "Arrange for *me* to disappear? How do you plan to do that? Even Houdini himself would struggle to make someone disappear, even on a ship this big."

"It's just a case of smoke and mirrors or, in this case, my clothes and a fake suicide. You just go to breakfast and leave me to do some planning," Esme explained with a smile Bridget thought both confident, and if she were honest, slightly unnerving.

Twenty-nine

Bernard ate a hasty, but generous, breakfast in the second class dining saloon. He woke to find Patrick's bunk not only empty, but displaying no evidence of having been slept in, and this worried him. The last time he saw his traveling companion, a sour-faced and abrupt nurse had taken charge of him, guiding him to a chair. Patrick had looked terrified. Like a lost child, confused at what to do and unsure who to trust. The wound on his face had looked red and angry and the dark, thread-like rash, which appeared only minutes before, had already shown evidence of spreading throughout his body, darkening in colour as each second ticked by.

Leaving his delicately scented Earl Grey tea only half drunk, Bernard left the saloon, setting off at a brisk pace towards the ship's hospital. He wanted to satisfy his curiosity regarding Patrick's health and devise a story intriguing enough for the waiting New York press, yet plausible enough to convince White Star to make them a generous offer in exchange for their selective amnesia.

He arrived at the hospital to find the same nurse sitting behind the desk. She looked, to Bernard at least, far less intimidating than she did the previous day. Her eyes were dull and withdrawn and her skin pallid, while her movements were languid to the point of lethargic. She looked up with barely disguised indifference as he entered the room, then returned her attention to the papers on her desk leaving Bernard to

stand awkwardly midway between her desk and the few chairs laid out as a makeshift waiting room.

Bernard cleared his throat politely, but the nurse's only response was to wave a hand in the general direction of the chairs. She didn't even look up. He bristled at the woman's rudeness, taking a mental note to make a formal complaint, but headed for the waiting area anyway. Secretly, he was glad she had not already ushered him out of the room, and her unnecessarily surly attitude would only serve to add gravitas to their bogus complaint. He took a seat and busied himself by removing imaginary pieces of fluff from his suit trousers with his thumb and forefinger while he waited. After a short while, he tired of that and began tapping his foot impatiently, an action which was obviously proving to be an irritation to the nurse as she looked up several times, a dark scowl shadowing her features. Despite this, he didn't relent until the doctor, looking harassed and as pallid as the nurse, appeared from his office.

"I shall be in engineering if anyone has need of me," the doctor spoke softly to the nurse. Bernard rose from his seat to intercept him before he could leave.

"Excuse me, Doctor? I am Sir Bernard Astor, and I wish to enquire in to the health of a companion of mine." He physically blocked the doctor's path to the door. The medical man looked flustered for a moment but quickly regained his composure.

"I'm sorry, Sir Bernard, but I'm extremely busy at present." The doctor tried to sidestep Bernard's ample frame, but the older man was too quick and surprisingly light on his

feet, dancing slightly to his left, preventing his quick escape. With a frustrated look of resignation, the doctor glanced at his pocket watch adding with a sigh, "But I could spare you a few moments."

"I appreciate it, Doctor, and will endeavour to keep my enquiry brief. Yesterday, I myself delivered my companion to this very room. He was stricken with I know not what, following a nasty incident with a savage beast which inflicted on him a nasty bite just below his eye." Bernard was about to continue his lavishly embellished tale, but the doctor raised his hand signalling he had heard enough.

"I know whom you speak of," the doctor said quietly, his head bowed. "It pains me to be the one having to pass on this news, but he died within a few minutes of you leaving."

Bernard stared at him, his mouth gaping.

"It is too early to draw any definite conclusions, but it appears he bled to death." The doctor said the right words, but his delivery was cold to the point of dispassionate. Bernard understood the man was used to matters of death, yet still felt him to be unemotional, even blasé about his friend's passing.

"I don't understand. He wasn't bleeding, apart from the one wound to his cheek, and that was definitely not bleeding enough to kill him," Bernard said, struggling to grasp how Patrick may have bled to death in so short a time.

"I believed him to have bled internally. Possibly as a result of some infection, although it is not something I have seen before." The doctor moved towards the door, "Now, if you will

excuse me it is imperative I investigate further." With that he slipped past Bernard and out of the surgery, leaving Bernard alone with the nurse, who appeared too preoccupied with her work to notice.

Bernard wrestled with his conscience. He wasn't satisfied by the doctor's explanation, believing him to be privy to certain facts he wasn't yet ready to divulge. Yet he was unsure whether to pry too deeply lest his own fraudulent representations draw the unwanted attentions of the ship's crew, particularly those of the master-at-arms. After a moment of indecision, he mumbled a "Good day," to the nurse, who made no effort to acknowledge him, and followed the doctor out of the door. He hurried in the direction the doctor had taken moments before, eager to discover what further investigations the doctor needed to conduct with such urgency.

Doctor Sampson walked casually through the passenger decks, smiling politely at the few passengers he passed on their way to a late breakfast. He had not eaten since the night before, but unusually for him, he didn't feel hungry; although, his body did crave something. He felt the itch in his blood, but he had no idea what. He even tried lighting his pipe, taking a few enjoyable, but unfulfilling puffs while changing. His investigations into the connected deaths of two seemingly unconnected people, one a second class passenger, the other a crew member working in the strict confines of engineering, had kept him up most of the night. He'd concluded the two deaths

were very much linked. They both displayed evidence of bite marks, definitely not human; they were too small for that and the incisors too pronounced, but significantly not something small like a rat. But he had no doubt they caught an infection from these bites. The passenger, McGowan, died of the infection, while the stoker died of the attack, specifically having his throat torn out, but even after his death, the same infection had taken hold of his corpse. The death of the host had not inhibited the disease. If anything, it spread throughout the deceased body far quicker than it had in the live host.

Sampson did not mind admitting to himself, he was stumped. He had consulted his limited supply of medical texts and couldn't find anything that fit the disease's pathology, although a few tropical fevers did display some similarities. But how could these two men have contracted a disease only found on the Dark Continent? He felt the answer to that lay in the bite marks, not that proving this as fact helped him understand the infection any better, but at least it would give him something to tell the Captain. If there was something, some wild tropical animal, loose on the ship, it was someone else's job to find it. He chuckled aloud at his own ludicrous suggestion, a wild animal roaming undetected through the passageways of the world's largest ship indeed. How absurd will that sound when face-to-face with Captain Smith?

He turned down a short corridor set apart from the main passenger area, and after a few seconds, came to the plain doorway which opened on to the spiral staircase descending through the ship to engineering. Sampson allowed the door to swing shut then began his descent towards the cold store area where the bodies had laid overnight. He wanted to confirm his theory on the bite marks and inspect the bodies, and specifically the spread of the infection, one more time before facing the Captain.

Stepping out on to Lower Deck G, Doctor Sampson turned aft following the rat run designed to allow engineering crew access to and from their cabins without the need to venture into passenger areas. Although he was in a hurry to complete his task, the muscles in his legs ached with a deep pain causing him to stumble several times. He also had to exercise caution to prevent tripping on one of the raised bulkheads dividing the ships lower sections. Added to the general muscular malaise, he also felt a prickling, burning sensation in his lungs and a vague feeling of breathlessness and light-headedness. He made a note to himself to make use of the ship's gymnasium. As the ship's medical officer he should be setting an example, not stumbling into walls and puffing like an old steam engine after descending a few stairs.

He paused a moment to regain his breath and, placing two fingers on his wrist, took a quick measurement of his radial pulse expecting it to be galloping along in response to his breathlessness. He was surprised to find the strong rhythmic pulses beating at a rate far below normal. He moved his fingers and repeated the process, his eyes fixed on the minute hand of his pocket watch.

Fifteen seconds passed with nine beats of his heart. Doctor Sampson didn't need to do the calculation, his heart rate was half what he would expect in an athletic person twenty years his junior, and that shouldn't be the case. Perplexed, he stepped through the last bulkhead door into the large vaulted aft section housing the engineering workshops and the two refrigerated storerooms.

The sight that greeted him stunned him and made the concerns he had over his own health pale into insignificance. The storeroom's heavy door stood wide open and Sampson detected a chill in the air he hadn't noticed before, his warm breath forming little clouds of condensation with each slow, laboured exhalation. He took a few tentative steps forward, not sure why he was afraid, but aware of the gnawing, hollow sensation in the pit of his stomach.

"Hello?" The word escaped his tight throat with a creaking groan that was barely audible above the constant drone of the ship's massive engines. He cleared his throat, swallowed hard, and repeated his greeting with more conviction.

"Hello?"

He waited. His eyes searching the vessel's lower deck gloom trying to spot the guard Chief Engineer Bell posted the evening before. But Sampson saw no one and received no reply.

He inched closer to the open door, the temperature dropping with each shuffling step, until he could peer around its edge into the unlit, murky depths of the cold store. At first, he saw only darkness. Then shadowy shapes emerged as his eyesight grew accustomed to his new surroundings. In the corner, slumped against the far wall, was a body. From this distance, Sampson could not identify the person or discern whether they were dead or alive.

He slipped inside, his senses heightened. There was danger close by, he could almost smell it in the icy air as he stumbled past the empty shelves towards the darker recesses at the back of the room. He looked around nervously as he approached the crumpled form, but saw no evidence of another body or the guard. The air had a metallic odour he assumed, at first, came from the refrigerated air blasting into the room, but now he recognized it as the sickly-sweet tang of blood. He stepped next to the lifeless form, his foot making a soft splashing sound, and crouched down to stare into the face of the engineer assigned to guard the storeroom, or rather, what remained of his face.

The detail Doctor Sampson could see in the darkness surprised him. He had always had keen eyesight. As a child he used to watch the birds in the garden then draw them with colourful accuracy, but that was in daylight not in the badly lit depths of an ocean liner. And yet, he could make out every shocking detail of the engineer's chewed and ripped face. The missing nose, the empty eye socket, the exposed teeth and bone of the bottom jaw jutting through the torn flesh in a grotesque smile, and the neck, eaten away until the spine was visible. He also noticed the now familiar dark rash spreading

threadlike, outward from the wound, like it was putting down roots.

He looked down at the dead man's body and noted the traumatic amputation of the left leg just below the groin, the leg itself was missing. The tattered remains of the man's trousers stuck to the shredded muscles and torn sinews of his bloody stump. It was the blood pooled around this stump Doctor Sampson had stepped in, causing the soft splash. It also suggested the engineer was alive, his heart beating, when his attacker severed his leg.

Sampson stood up, now convinced a wild animal, possibly more than one and definitely bigger than a rat, judging by its ability to rip a man's leg off, was loose on the ship. He had seen similar rashes before, but those resulted from snakebites and were never on the same scale as the ones he had witnessed in the last few hours. He took a final look at the mangled corpse, aware he felt only one thing and it was not disgust or revulsion or even shock. He wasn't even concerned over the whereabouts of the two corpses he had inspected the day before. What he felt was hunger.

Thirty

Bernard ducked back into the shadows as Doctor Sampson staggered back along the Fireman's tunnel. He had followed him down from the hospital suite in his search for Patrick, holding back and peeking around the giant piston housing while the doctor spent almost five minutes within the dark confines of the cold store. Once he was sure the doctor was on his way back up the stairs, Bernard hurried over to the cold store door, aware his short digression into the restricted areas of the ship may soon be discovered. He stepped into the darkness and fumbled for the light switch. He was curious as to the doctor's reason for coming here and at a loss to understand how he could have seen anything? Everything beyond the first few feet of the cold store, which was illuminated by the outside lights, was in total darkness.

Finding a switch, Bernard flicked it down. The lights fizzed then flickered slowly into life like one of those new motion pictures, which were all the rage in America. The smell was acidic and unpleasant, and it caught in the back of his throat. Covering his mouth with a handkerchief, he resisted the urge to gag.

Bernard looked at the man lying propped up against the back wall, a trail of bloody footprints leading away from the body faded to nothing when they reached the door. Even from a distance, he immediately knew the person was dead. But not just dead; something had mutilated the body almost beyond

recognition. The corpse looked like a wild animal had savaged it. The features were unrecognizable, but Bernard doubted Pandora was responsible. She was too small to rip a man's leg off like she was tearing a chicken carcass.

Bernard didn't feel the need, and certainly lacked the desire, to get closer. He saw more than enough to know it wasn't Patrick just by the corpse's physical size and the one remaining boot. Rushing from the room, he bent double and vomited his generous breakfast over his own shoes.

It took several minutes for Bernard to be sure his retching had stopped and he felt composed enough to head back down the Fireman's tunnel and up the spiral staircase to the passenger areas. He felt sure the doctor knew more than he was prepared to share, or possibly allowed by White Star to say, and he was concerned things could get dangerous. The reason the doctor put forward for Patrick's wound being responsible for his death didn't sound likely. It was too small and on such an innocuous part of his body; however, Patrick, and at least one other man were already dead, a testament to the danger involved. Could there be something else loose on the ship, another larger animal perhaps, or maybe something less tangible, like a plague? At the very least, it could prove costly to his plans for a better life in America.

Bernard decided his search for Patrick's body would have to wait. He did not feel safe in the hot murky engineering levels of the ship and knew if he were discovered snooping about, he would have some uncomfortable questions to answer.

Esme rummaged about in her valise to find the dress she had worn the day she joined the ship. It was dark blue, subdued, and although it wasn't old, it didn't look new and was, therefore, absolutely perfect for the purpose she had in mind. She pulled it from the depths of her bag and held it up to the light. It had creases and no top button; she had meant to sew it on before this, but a little exposed neck had worked wonders on the generosity of the patrons in the Belvedere Arms, and that added to its perfection. She folded the dress as small as she could and placed it in a pile of dirty towels she had extracted from an unattended laundry cart on her way to her cabin before turning her attention to the choice of headwear. It was a simple choice to make. Esme, like most women her age and social standing, only owned two hats: one for the week and one for Sunday best. She had worn her Sunday best hat to board the *Titanic* so it was that one which joined the pile on her bunk. Making sure the towels covered the dress and hat, Esme scooped the pile up in her arms and headed towards the first class staterooms. She didn't want anyone to spot her carrying clothes into Bridget's cabin as that could put her whole plan at risk.

The walk up through the ship from her cramped bunk room in the bow section of E Deck to Bridget's palatial suite on A Deck was a nerve-wracking experience for Esme, and she felt relieved to arrive unchallenged. Although she was aware this was only the first, and by far the easiest, part of her plan, she

still had much work to do if she were to remove the burden of suspicion, and therefore, the threat of hanging, from around her friend's slender, well-to-do neck.

Esme knocked on the door to Bridget's cabin, and not waiting for an answer, swiftly stepped inside. Bridget was waiting for her, pacing to and fro and wringing her hands together so tightly her knuckles had turned bone white. Bridget's face also betrayed her apprehension. Her brow bore three distinct furrows, her eyebrows arched, and her eyes were downcast. The smile that fluttered across Bridget's face upon seeing Esme was shallow and false, and her eyes continued to look dull and distant.

"I do not like this one bit," Bridget said without formality.

"Neither do I, Mistress. But I fear we have no other course open to us." The use of the formal address earned Esme a disapproving look of reproof from her friend, and she added, "Sorry, Bridget."

Despite believing simply having wealth did not give you social standing, it was hard for the woman from Southampton docklands to break the subservient habit she had acquired hustling rich passengers for loose change while still only a girl. When Esme got a little older and her body developed, she found the gentlemen traveller to be rich pickings and a little subservience always helped raise the gift.

"What if I threw myself at the mercy of the court, claiming I acted out of self-preservation? His repeated beatings

and constant derogation of my spirit caused me to become temporarily unhinged, and fearing for my life, I suffocated him!"

Esme saw the false hope in Bridget's eyes even as she spoke. She knew no jury in the land would allow the murderer of such a rich and, sadly for his new widow, influential man to go unpunished. Both women were starkly aware of the punishment for murder.

"You would have to prove his vile actions against you, and I bet the prosecution will find ten, or even a hundred, witnesses to say what a kind, thoughtful, and caring man he was. They'll paint a vivid picture of him as a mild-mannered saint, seduced and killed by the attractive she-devil, simply for his money." Esme felt the anger rising within her as she laid out her clothes on the bed for Bridget to view. She brushed the long dress down to remove a few straggling threads and a fine layer of dust which all dresses gathered, no matter how well they are stored. Her right hand slapped against the fabric with enough force to sting and give her palm a warm, pink glow.

"Again, you speak with the sense of a woman much older than your years. If I am at liberty and in need of a lady with a resourceful and loyal disposition to run my house, and I fear Violet may have blotted her copy book to this regard, then I will do far worse than to keep you close." For the first time since Esme entered the room, Bridget smiled.

Esme looked up from the dress, stunned and confused by Bridget's words. "Ar … are you offering me a position in your

household?" She finally stammered as Bridget smiled at her from across the bed.

"If I escape with my liberty, then yes. But I think it would be better if I lived in America, well away from William's family. Would that suit you?"

For a moment, Esme smiled. Then her face fell. "I cannot. I must look after my sister, I'm all she has. Our mother is incapable and better left alone, but Charlotte needs me and, if truth be told, I her." At the thought of her younger sister, Esme's eyes dampened and her throat tightened, causing the final part of her sentence to be not much more than a high-pitched sob. She slumped onto the bed, her face buried in her hands, as her shoulders shook with each uncontrolled sob.

Bridget hurried around the bed to comfort her. She sat beside Esme drawing her into her embrace. "Hey, don't cry," she cooed, her own problems momentarily forgotten. "I would insist on her coming with you, why have one—what's your surname?" Bridget felt horrified and embarrassed at having to ask when Esme had put so much at risk in helping her.

"Jackson," Esme snivelled into Bridget's shoulder.

"Why have one resourceful Jackson sister around, when you can have two? If she's half as astute as you, we'll make a formidable trio." Bridget rubbed Esme's back in what she hoped was a soothing way.

"Charlotte's the feisty one, always fighting with the boys at school over something or nothing. If there's trouble to be found, she'll find it." Esme laughed softly, remembering her

sister. "In the Belvedere one day, because mother was too drunk to look after her, Charlotte took offence to one of my over-amorous suitors. She kicked him full in the shin then ran away with the disgruntled sailor hobbling comically after her."

"Then we shall have more fun and be more formidable." Bridget laughed. Turning her attention to the dress, she added, "Time I tried this on, I guess."

Thirty-one

Elizabeth sat in F Deck's main corridor playing with Betty, her shabby, well-worn, and well-loved rag doll. Her Papa had given her Betty the day he went away to find a new life for his family, and since that moment, they'd been inseparable. At six years old, and in her eyes almost a grown up, Elizabeth told all her important secrets to Betty, who listened with a fixed, woolly smile, never judging, never getting angry with her the way Mama sometimes did, and never ever telling.

Soon she and Mama would be in 'Merica, and she would see her Papa again; although, secretly she felt scared she wouldn't recognize him after so long. Betty knew this and didn't seem worried so she tried not to show she was scared. After all, she was so nearly all grown up.

But what if Betty was wrong? 'Merica was such a big place, Mama said so all the time. What if they couldn't find Papa? What if Papa had forgotten them? Elizabeth pulled her legs up to her chest, like at night when the darkness frightened her, and peered over her knees at the big brown eyes of her new friend.

"Do you think I'll ever see Papa again?" She rubbed the tear from her cheek with an angry sniff. Her new friend, no bigger than Betty, pulled back her ears, flattening them against her head, which she cocked to one side inquisitively at the sound of the little girl's voice. The cute little creature looked like it was carefully considering her question, its huge, chocolate

eyes staring right back at Elizabeth the way Mama's did when she thought of Papa.

"Well?" Patience was not one of Elizabeth's strong points. She wiped away another tear, this time with the hem of her dress, and stared back at the tiny bundle sitting frustratingly silent a few feet beyond Elizabeth's hunched-up knees. Elizabeth talked to Betty all the time, and Betty always replied, the words coming from deep inside Elizabeth's own head. But her new friend, the creature must be her friend because it chose to sit next to her, remained silent.

Elizabeth thought the animal looked sad, even a little bit frightened. She pushed out her bottom lip, turning it inside out. The tiny creature tried to copy her, its lips appearing larger and more pliable than hers. It pulled its lips back from the gums to reveal sharp looking teeth, four of which appeared longer and sharper than the rest.

Then the animal moved closer, no longer looking sad and frightened. It looked angry and frightening, its long tail arched and curled over its head as it crept towards Elizabeth, teeth bared.

Elizabeth buried her face in her knees, her arms hugging her shins, pulling herself into a tight, safe ball. She felt the tail swish against her hand. It was warm and soothing, yet strong, powerful and menacing. It curled around her fingers, flicked against her wrist then slowly wound around her small, lily-white forearm. She shook with fear, frozen to the spot. She felt her

urine trickle into her undergarments, soaking her thighs and pooling on the floor between her legs.

The tail uncoiled from her arm, and with a flick, was gone. A warm breath, and a soft throaty growl, filled the shell of her ear. Something warm and prickly, almost like Papa's thick, bushy beard, nuzzled her neck. Elizabeth wanted to scream, but when she opened her mouth, there was no sound, her throat tight and dry.

Then it was gone. Elizabeth remained huddled in a tight ball, unable to move, unable to scream, unable to look. Movement! And close, a puff of cold air blew across her legs. Something rustled next to her, and she heard a gentle sigh.

"Elizabeth!" The sound of her nanny's shrill voice, with its rough, abrasive East European-East London meld dragged her from her torpor. Elizabeth lifted her head from her knees and looked up into Nanny Catharina Kovac's dour, angular features. She stood with her feet together, hands firmly clasped below her breasts, a look of disappointment verging on mild frustration etched on her thin face, her eyes fixed on the pool of urine seeping from between her charge's legs.

Elizabeth shot a glance along the corridor in both directions. There was no sign of the tiny human-like animal that a moment earlier wanted to gobble her up.

"The creature ... it scared me," Elizabeth said feebly, aware Nanny Catharina's disappointed face usually led to far worse punishments than her angry face did.

"There was no creature. You are getting your imaginations to run away with you." Nanny Catharina's accent wasn't heavy, but Elizabeth thought her sentences never sounded quite right.

"But I saw it, Mistress Kovac. It was right here!" She slapped her palm on the thin carpeting as if to highlight her point.

"Get up, child." Her voice had grown stern in response to Elizabeth's petulance.

Elizabeth shook her head defiantly. What she saw was no childish imagination. She was nearly a grown up after all, even if the strange beast had frightened her. A middle-aged couple walked past, clucking their disapproval at her behaviour before whispering to each other as they continued down the corridor, occasionally looking back over their shoulders.

"I will not be telling you this again, Elizabeth. Get up!" Nanny Catharina's patience was wearing thin, and she spoke with slow deliberation, making her words clear and concise, leaving Elizabeth in no doubt refusal would lead to further punishment.

Elizabeth sat her ground, lips pursed, arms crossed.

"You are leaving me with no choices." Nanny Catharina's hand fastened around the child's upper arm, yanking her to her feet in one, well-practiced movement. Elizabeth's scream was part in pain, as her shoulder snapped upwards, and part in childish frustration at not getting her own way. Nanny Kovac lifted Elizabeth's arm so high she could barely keep her toes on

the floor as she was propelled into the nearby cabin, whereupon Catharina Kovac slammed the door shut with a flick of her heel.

Pandora remained perched on the pipe work running above F Deck's main corridor for a few minutes, then, accepting her prey had escaped, scampered away through the maze of ducts and vents in search of another meal. Her need to kill, to feed, grew with every passing minute, unabated by each fresh kill.

Thirty-two

Catharina Kovac had worked in service since she was fourteen, and her natural way with children led her into the nursery. She had worked as a servant and assistant to the family's nanny in two households before, only recently taking up her post as Elizabeth Robertson's nanny. A position made more attractive by the family's imminent immigration to America and the fact Miss Robertson was an only child; although, she thought that likely to change once Mr. and Mrs. Robertson were reunited. However, despite these two advantages, the position held one very obvious drawback, that of Elizabeth herself. Of all the children she had cared for, this precocious little bitch was by far the worst. Elizabeth acted like she was the lady of the manor, often ordering Catharina around like a servant. When Catharina didn't comply, Elizabeth would throw a sulk, refusing to cooperate until, eventually, Mrs. Robertson would acquiesce to her demand, ordering Catharina to do the child's bidding. This vastly undermined Catharina's position in the house, making her duties almost impossible to carry out.

Catharina didn't care about the awkwardness of her position at that moment. She had arranged to take a well-earned bath, a luxury she secured soon after boarding because of the limited number of baths available to third class passengers. So, having dropped her unruly charge in the care of another nanny at a nearby cabin, she entered one of the two

public bathrooms with her rolled up towel clutched under one arm.

The bathroom was ostentatiously large but sparsely decorated with an oversized enamel bath set in its centre. Catharina locked the door behind her and approached the bath, dropping her towel on the solitary chair as she passed. She opened the hot tap, letting the water run across her fingers until it began to warm, before pushing the plug home and returning to the chair where she began to undress. She removed each article of clothing, carefully folding it before placing it on the chair, forming a small neat pile, her cotton and lace undergarments on the top. Naked, she stretched, arching her back until her shoulder muscles ached in a delightfully refreshing way, and then gently removed the pins holding her dark curls in place, allowing her hair to tumble loosely onto her shoulders. She shook it free as she padded across the tiled floor to check on the temperature of her bath water.

This was her first free time since boarding, and she was determined to make the most of it. A warm bath followed by a spot of reading, but not Brontë's romanticism; she liked a darker streak to inhibit her dreams. She had recently read *Dracula* and become obsessed with the notion of vampirism, and to this end had engrossed herself in *Carmilla,* seeing herself as the powerful and enigmatic stranger. She trailed her hand absentmindedly through the bathwater then, remembering the task at hand, turned off the hot tap before continuing to fill the bath with water from the cold tap.

She waited for a few moments, allowing the cold water to mingle with the hot, her skin coming up in tiny goose bumps as the bathroom's cold air tingled her naked flesh. Her nipples hardened as she imagined the cause of the breeze being Stoker's handsome Count entering the room. Subconsciously, she tilted her head to the side, her eyes closed, her hair falling away to expose her delicate neck to her handsome visitor. Catharina felt his hands, strong yet gentle, momentarily caress her upper arms then one cupped her breast.

A soft, frustrated sigh escaped her lips as she banished her darkly delicious thoughts of giving herself to a vampire. She lifted her leg ready to climb into her waiting bath.

But the hand remained. The cold hand clamped to her breast, the strong fingers gouging into her sensitive skin and twisting the hard nub of her nipple causing her to catch her breath. Catharina's eyes snapped open, her watery stare focused on her own exposed chest. This was no imagined interloper. A man's hand, large and rough, the veins dark and bulging, twisted the pale mound of her right breast.

Terrified, Catharina drew breath to scream. Ready to beg for her virtue and scream for help, but a second hand quickly clamped across her gaping mouth, stifling any sound, before wrenching her neck violently to the left.

Catharina felt the fragile bones in her neck break with a soft crack, followed by the briefest moment of euphoric relief before death took her soul. Her lifeless body toppled into the bath's warm water, her neck so hideously twisted her face

stared back over her left shoulder, a thin trail of bubbles breaking the water's surface as her final breath escaped her body.

Thirty-three

Bernard turned and paced the small cabin for the hundredth time. A brief smile flickered across his face as he remembered their meeting only four days previously. Until recently he had shared this cabin, and the greater adventure, with Patrick, the kid from Dublin, who was astute and quick-witted. He would have made an excellent accomplice in the new world. The facts surrounding his friend's swift decline and subsequent death, and the doctor's role in the mystery, troubled him. He knew something was going on, but what? He turned and paced in the opposite direction.

Having returned to the cabin by way of one of the first class bars, whiskey was undoubtedly good for the nerves, Bernard spent most of the afternoon mulling over what little he knew. He concluded there was indeed something loose aboard the ship, something dangerous, and he needed to warn Kathleen about it. He was less sure whether this was out of some growing affection towards her as a woman or to protect his investment. Either way, he knew he had to be with her.

Snatching his hat from the bunk, he hurried from the cabin. If he was quick enough, and chose his words carefully, as he didn't want to appear too eager, he might persuade her to join him for a stroll, then perhaps dinner. His mind briefly considered a more base and carnal activity she could join him in after dinner, but he shook his head, dismissing the thought. She was too much of a lady to consider such a suggestion.

He made his way through the second class corridors and slipped quickly through into the first class area. One of the ship's officers nodded respectfully as they approached each other on the grand staircase.

"Good afternoon, Sir Bernard," Officer Moody said.

"Good afternoon to you too, Mr. Moody. I trust everything is shipshape?" The two men laughed politely at Bernard's feeble joke and continued their respected journeys. Although Bernard thought he noticed an uncomfortable twitch at the corner of Officer Moody's right eye as they passed each other, he picked up the pace slightly, his desire to share his evening with the delightful Mrs. Black all the stronger. It was not until he reached the top of the stairs and turned into the plush corridor serving her suite that he realized he had not thought about her financial wealth for some time. He studied his reflection in one of the mirrors lining the walls, adjusting the clumsy knot of his tie, he said aloud, "Well dear boy, this is a new experience." He removed some stray fluff from his shoulder then mumbled under his breath, "Just don't fuck it up."

He strode confidently down the corridor and knocked sharply on the door of Kathleen Black's suite. It opened immediately, a startled looking servant standing in the doorway.

"Oh! Sorry, sir, you gave me quite a fright. Is Mistress Black expecting you?"

"I don't believe her to be, but it would give me great comfort if she was," Bernard said, clutching a hand to his heart.

The chambermaid flashed a knowing smile and held the door open for Bernard to enter. "Madame has seemed happier of recent days, and I daresay there is a chance she might receive you." She closed the door and ushered Bernard towards a small couch in the suite's outer room, saying, "Please make yourself comfortable, and I will speak with Madame."

"That won't be necessary, Matilda. Please fetch the tea and set an extra cup for Sir Bernard." Kathleen's voice shredded the hushed respectability of the room, her usual high-pitched nasal twang rising even higher in her ill-concealed excitement at seeing Bernard. She bustled across the room as Bernard rose to greet her, but instead of offering her hand as he expected she embraced him, pulling him in and holding his body tight against her bosom.

"I do not feel the need to stand on pompous ceremony when we are alone. We are both too old to waste time dancing tactfully around the situation. I feel alive again in your presence, something I thought I had lost forever, and believe you feel the same about me. Let's give ourselves a chance at happiness and not waste another second on stuffy formalities."

"Not that I'm opposed to this course of action," Bernard replied, his face alight with joy. "But will it not sully your reputation so openly cavorting with another man so soon after your husband's death?"

Releasing Bernard from her tight embrace, she spoke with a mischievous sparkle in her eye, "I doubt very much that I have a reputation worth sullying, and as for cavorting? You

need to hold your horses there awhile, Sir Bernard. I made no mention of cavorting, openly or otherwise."

Bernard laughed sheepishly as she took a seat next to him on the small couch, her body turned towards him so her knees pressed against his.

"I did not mean to infer we should be cavorting, I simply voiced my concern for your reputation, nothing more."

"To hell with my reputation! I have money enough not to care about idle gossip, but enough of this tactful, verbal dancing. Was there a reason you came to visit me without first seeking an invite?"

It was only then that Bernard remembered the true reason for his visit, so excited was he by Kathleen's amorous overtones, his joyous mood evaporated and was replaced by a gut-wrenching malaise.

"I actually came to warn you about a danger on board this ship. But strangely, I can't tell you the exact nature of the danger or even if the danger is real and not just my own fears manifested."

"A danger to me?" Kathleen asked, a fearful look haunting her eyes.

"I don't believe so. But there are things going on that I have no answers for, and in finding the answers, we will undoubtedly uncover the danger." As Bernard spoke, a frown line creased his forehead.

"Speaking in riddles has only served to heap confusion on my fear, Bernard." Her soft hands sought out his, holding them

tightly, she asked, "Please offer some explanation for your reasoning? Have you seen something?"

"In a manner of speaking, yes; I have, but that is where the confusion begins." Bernard explained about Patrick's strange death, leaving out the details surrounding the monkey's ownership and the nature of their relationship, referring only to him as a business partner. Then he continued, talking first about the doctor's strange behaviour then moving on to discuss the mystery surrounding Patrick's missing body.

Kathleen listened earnestly to every word, then when he finished, she sat in silent contemplation. When she finally spoke, her voice was quiet and reassuring, her brash accent toned down as if to fit the subdued mood. "I think I should change before letting you escort me to dinner. Black is such a depressing colour, don't you think?"

Thirty-four

Officer Moody stepped off the grand staircase and crossed the first class dining saloon's small, but exquisite, lobby. His instinct told him there was more than met the eye with Sir Bernard, but he couldn't put his finger on it and didn't have the time or inclination to press the matter further. Especially with the captain summoning all the officers to the bridge for an impromptu, and yet, given the lack of notice, urgent meeting.

Moody walked briskly around the saloon, acknowledging each of the stewards in turn as they prepared the tables for the evening service, before entering the frantic chaos of the ship's main galley, which served both first and second class passengers. He raised his hand towards the head chef, who simply nodded in return. With only an hour or so to go before starting the dinner service, the head chef was far too busy to engage in small talk with Sixth Officer Moody. The captain himself would have struggled to get more than a few begrudging words from him this close to dinner. Moody hurried on intent on completing his rounds before the meeting with the captain, not wishing to be found wanting should a senior officer ask him about the ship's current readiness.

He knocked on Miss Wilson's door and politely waited for her to answer before entering. Frankly, Old Dragon, as the chambermaids somewhat less than fondly called her, scared the shit out of him. And worse still, she knew it, even revelled in it.

"What can I do for you, Mr. Moody?" She eyed him suspiciously from her lair on the other side of her imposing desk.

"I'm Duty Officer, and I'm completing the afternoon inspections prior to attending the captain's officer meeting."

"What meeting?" The head housekeeper demanded, cutting him short.

Realizing the wrinkly Old Dragon knew nothing about the meeting, and therefore, had not received an invite, Moody decided to have some fun.

"I'm not at liberty to say, ma'am." He also had no idea about the intended subject matter of the meeting, but seeing the Old Dragon almost breathe fire at the suggestion something important was about to happen, something important she knew nothing about, was a priceless moment he would cherish.

"I see. I shall take the matter up with the captain, myself." The scornful look she gave him lingered long after her words died away, seeming to suggest he would be in for an awkward, even painful, return journey should he be in any way lying.

After a long pause during which Moody savoured his brief victory, he asked, "Is there anything you need to bring to my attention?"

"As a matter of fact, there is, young man." Her refusal to address him by rank, almost dismissing him as a child, was a calculated move to undermine him on Miss Wilson's part.

Moody ignored her snub, and through a polite smile, asked. "And what would that be?" He fought the urge to add the phrase, *you Old Dragon.*

"Esme Jackson! She was taken on as a chambermaid in Southampton; although I am truly baffled about how, has constantly neglected her duties. I am also led to believe she has struck up an overfamiliar friendship with Mrs. Grafton. It is the sort of friendship which will surely result in the Grafton's embarrassment and tarnish the reputation of both White Star and the *Titanic*. I have already served her with her notice, but would be obliged if you undertake the delicate matter of speaking with the Graftons concerning our handling of this matter." Miss Wilson glared at Moody over her spectacles, appraising him with the thinly veiled look of disdain the elderly reserve for anyone under thirty.

Moody fidgeted under the intensity of her gaze but remained silent, unwilling to interrupt the hoary woman, lest she turn her dissatisfaction in his direction. Finally, she pushed her spectacles firmly back onto the bridge of her nose and added, "I suggest you address the issue with Captain Grafton. He is a gentleman with an understanding of such matters. I fear his young bride exhibits a more naive attitude towards matters of class—she is American, after all." A wry smile twitched at the corners of her mouth.

"I shall endeavour to speak with him during dinner tonight. Will that be all, Miss Wilson?" Officer Moody had the feeling the Old Dragon had warmed to him and was astute

enough to know her experience earned the captain's ear. A little polite deference and subtle discretion would do his promotional prospects no harm at all.

"That is all for now, Mr. Moody." Her reinstatement of his name caused Moody to suppress a smile. Then she added, "But don't think I haven't noticed the stupid expression that crossed your face at the mere mention of Mrs. Grafton's name. I suggest you get any notion you may have in that respect, out of your head this instance. Is that clear?"

Moody felt a warm flush prickle his skin, and he was barely able to mumble, "Yes, ma'am" as he scampered out of Miss Wilson's office feeling like a naughty schoolchild, unaware he would never get to deliver her message to Captain Grafton.

Thirty-five

Patrick's corpse looked down at Catharina's still twitching body. His gaze scanned across her shapely legs, lingering on the gentle curve of her buttocks before moving up the smooth alabaster skin of her back and hideously twisted neck and into the serene beauty of her face. The bathwater still sloshed from side to side in the wake of her violent passing, her swirling hair gradually fanning out around her angelic countenance like the twisting snakes of Medusa's living locks. Driven by an unquenchable need, he knelt beside the bath, running his hand over the firmness of her muscle before leaning over her half-submerged body to rip a strip of tender flesh from her soft, slightly pinked buttock with his teeth.

It tasted divine, better than any steak the previously living Patrick had ever tasted. He pushed his fingers into the open gash and ripped more of the fatty flesh free of the dead nanny's rump. He stuffed the slippery morsel in his mouth, not bothering to finish the first mouthful, and chewed the still warm flesh, oblivious to the water soaking the sleeves of his tunic and running in tiny rivulets from his elbows. He didn't notice the bathwater turning a dark, dirty brown as Catharina's torpid blood gently seeped from the tear, and he was unconcerned by her beauty or the allure of her firm curves. He just needed to feed, to consume without consequence, without conscience, and without compassion.

Once he satisfied his hunger, Patrick rose from the bath-side, dropping Catharina's torn and chewed remains back into the bath's murky Hungarian nanny goulash, and staggered to the door. He fumbled clumsily with the door's handle before finally freeing himself into the corridor beyond, where he stumbled into a scruffily dressed passenger walking towards him, a knowing smile plastered on his bearded face, his eyes twinkling impishly.

"I bet you fucked her good. I saw that seductive bitch follow you in there." The words died in his throat as he saw fresh blood smeared around Patrick's mouth and across his strangely marked cheeks. The unsuspecting passenger's eyes moved slowly down the darkly stained jacket, which hung at a rakish angle caused by several missing buttons, to look at Patrick's bloodied hands, his mind struggling to understand how the stranger had gained such severe injuries.

The bearded man took a step back. Confused, he glanced over Patrick's shoulder into the bathroom the Irishman had just left. The pale, lifeless face of the young nanny stared back at him over the edge of the bathtub, and although he could only see her face from where he stood, it was enough for him to know she was dead.

"Sweet Jesus!"

Emitting a deep, throaty growl, Patrick lunged at the young passenger. Before the man had time to react, Patrick was on him. His actions and reactions heightened, his speed and strength increased. Patrick bit into the man's lower lip, tearing

away a large chunk of sticky, wet flesh, leaving the man gasping in pain, too shocked to respond. Then, lifting him with one hand, Patrick slammed his head against a protruding iron girder. The scruffily dressed stranger went limp; the dead Irishman dropped him on the deck without a second thought.

Patrick had sated his appetite for flesh with Catharina, and having no need to feed on the bearded passenger's body, quickly stepped over his prone form and disappeared into the comfortable darkness of a nearby laundry cupboard. Here he hoped to sleep off the drowsy effects of gorging himself on prime Hungarian rump, firm flank, and one succulent, juicy breast.

Thirty-six

Captain Smith watched as his officers walked onto the bridge one by one. Chief Engineer Bell and the master-at-arms, Mr. Thomas King, had already arrived and taken up their position to the rear of the room just forward of the wheelhouse. Smith had sailed with almost all of them before and was instrumental in their appointments to the *Titanic*. It always gave him a feeling of pride to see them all assembled in the one place. Doctor Sampson shuffled in behind the line of officers looking as if he had just got out of his bunk. His hair was lank and appeared not to have seen a comb in days, and his creased uniform had several disgusting looking stains on both his jacket and shirt, while Sampson himself looked pale and lethargic.

Sniffing the air for the telltale odour of alcohol, Smith frowned at the doctor. "For future reference, Doctor Sampson, when you come onto my bridge, you will dress appropriately. That means a clean, pressed uniform." After an awkward pause, he added, "And make some effort with your appearance, you're a disgrace to the crew, and this fine ship. Do I make myself clear?"

Sampson nodded, but barely lifted his head, avoiding the captain's piercing stare. Exasperated, Captain Smith continued by thanking everyone for coming; he would deal with Sampson later, he had other issues to discuss, issues too pressing for further delay.

"Gentlemen, I expect you are all aware of the unfortunate death of both a passenger and a stoker yesterday. These types of incidents have an unfortunate habit of becoming common knowledge long before we have a chance to properly address them." He paused while a general murmur of agreement rippled through the assembled officers. "It is," he continued, "with great embarrassment that I must first confirm these deaths and second, reveal both bodies have since disappeared. Furthermore, their disappearance coincided with the discovery of a third body, an engineer assigned to watch the deceased overnight." His gaze moved along the line of officers scrutinizing their reactions. He was aware they had probably all heard the news on the grapevine, but the stoic faces staring back at him gave him some reassurance they would deal with this in the same quiet, professional manner they went about their everyday duties.

Chief Engineer Bell broke the silence, his northern accent somehow more pronounced in the relative quiet of the bridge surrounded by the ship's officers, as opposed to the industrial hustle and bustle of the Engine Room. "That's two good men I've lost in under a day."

"The doctor inspected the bodies and noted they all died in similar circumstances. He understands they died because of an attack by a wild animal. All three showed evidence of bite marks." The captain paused to consult the doctor's hastily compiled report then continued, "The first victim died following one bite, the second and third suffered multiple bite wounds. In

fact, the master-at-arms, who secured the third victim's body, described it as having had his face and the stump of his severed leg eaten away. Is that a fair assessment of what you told me, Thomas?"

Thomas King looked as if he was about to reply, but the shock of what he witnessed was still clearly raw on his nerves. After a brief pause, he simply nodded.

"The first one, McGowan, the passenger, the bite didn't kill him, it was too superficial. He died … he died because of the poison," Doctor Sampson spoke in rapid bursts, his breath short, raspy.

The captain stared at the doctor in surprise. "What do you mean by 'the poison?'"

"All three had a dark rash. It followed the route of their venous system. Like a snakebite, only worse, far worse. This rash continues to spread, creeping through their body, even after death. Like it is consuming the victim from within." The doctor's words trailed away into a fit of coughing. He held a handkerchief to his mouth but waved away offers of help.

"I think you should return to your quarters, Doctor. You are obviously unwell." Captain Smith felt a twinge of guilt at having assumed Sampson to be drunk. "Before you go, are you sure the poison enters their system at the point of the bite? It couldn't come from some other source?"

Doctor Sampson met the captain's stare with bloodshot eyes. His answer, when it came, was firm and decisive. "Quite sure, sir, there was no other source. The third victim, sir! His

wounds weren't inflicted by an animal, his were human bite marks."

The remaining men watched Doctor Sampson, as he shuffled from the bridge, in stunned silence. The shock and revulsion caused by Doctor Sampson's observation left Officer Moody with an uneasy feeling at the bottom of his stomach and a few pressing questions, such as how could someone bite another human being's face off? It wasn't just the physicality of the act, but the sheer mental derangement someone would need to suffer in order to eat another human being. The prospect was all the more terrifying when the perpetrator of such an unimaginable act was aboard your ship in the middle of the Atlantic. This lead to the more important questions; what was the identity of this deranged lunatic, and would he strike again? Glancing at the stern faces of the other officers told him he was not alone in his concerns.

Gauging the unease among his most trusted advisors, Captain Smith cleared his throat and addressed the group. "That's mere conjecture. The doctor is not an expert in animal bites and has only made the most cursory of examinations of each body."

"Aye, but he is an expert in anatomy. If he says they're human bites, then like as not, they're human bites." First Officer Murdoch's broad Scottish accent filled the bridge, such was its resonance. "If he is right about the poison, I'll wager he is right about the bites."

Captain Smith looked thoughtful for a moment. When he spoke, his voice was calm, his words measured. "It appears we have an animal on board with the ability to poison, or at least infect, its victims. This coupled with a man, I cannot fathom this to be a woman, with an insane taste in human meat." He fell silent, clearly searching for the right words with which to continue. Then, raising his finger as if to accentuate his point, he concluded, "I find it incongruous to believe these are not, in some awful way, linked."

"Could it be that, somehow, the poison drives those infected mad and in this delirious state, these previously mild manner gentlemen, taking leave of their senses, viciously lash out against those they meet?" Chief Engineer Bell put his theory forward tentatively, exploring the possibility in his mind's eye, even as he spoke.

"That's a possibility," Captain Smith replied with a brief nod. "However, the doctor assures me both victims were deceased when the third man was attacked ..." If he was about to go on, Bell's outburst cut him short.

"Fuck that! With respect, sir, both bodies are missing, and I doubt anyone just happened by the cold store and stole them. If they were deceased, then they're not now. I'm not a superstitious man, but something queer's going on, like voodoo, they bring back the dead." Bell was getting increasingly agitated at the captain's refusal to accept what he increasingly considered to be the obvious, however bizarre it appeared.

"I think we need to remain calm, gentlemen." Captain Smith looked pointedly at the red-faced Bell, who raised a hand in apology, but who was still clearly on edge. "Nor do I hold with the notion of voodoo or any other mumbo jumbo, for that matter. But, I'm obviously concerned about the loss of life, and more so about preventing further loss of life. We need to find the missing bodies, and this may prove more difficult, the source of this infection; the animal that caused the death of passenger McGowan. And gentlemen! We need to do this without causing a panic."

Master-at-Arms King stepped forward, inspecting the faces of each man present. Finally, he announced, "We will split into pairs and conduct a search of the ship. The pairings and search areas are on here." He handed a page torn from his notebook to Officer Moody. "Please conduct your search discreetly when in passenger areas. Anyone asks, it's just routine. If you find anything, contact the bridge, and we'll get help to you. Is that clear?" The officers nodded, each, in turn, checking their assignment. "In the meantime, ship's routine continues as normal. Captain Smith will brief Mr. Ismay then dine with the passengers as normal, duty watch to remain on bridge."

"Thank you, Thomas. Gentlemen, you have your assignments." With that, Captain Smith marched from the bridge to prepare for dinner and an awkward meeting with the vessel's owner.

Thirty-seven

Esme left Bridget to try on the clothes she had given her and went to the pantry in search of something to eat. Her rendezvous with the odious Doctor Sampson was looming, and while she was dreading every minute she would have to spend in his lecherous company, she knew she had to do it. Not just in the hope he would put in a good word for her and prevent Miss Wilson putting her ashore in New York, but because Bridget needed her too. It was a vital part of her plan to remove the suspicion of murder from around the American socialite's neck, a part she was fortuitously placed to carry out with only a slight risk of discovery.

Carefully avoiding going too close to Miss Wilson's office, she entered the pantry servicing the second class saloon where she found a tray of cold meats left over from the buffet style luncheon. Hastily stuffing some white chicken meat into her mouth, she eased open the door into the saloon itself. Miss Wilson was inspecting the cutlery on the far side of the room so, not wishing to be caught by the Old Dragon, Esme eased the door closed again and slipped out through the busy galley. She picked up a silver salver laid out for one of the first class passengers to dine in their room and walked confidently out behind two other chambermaids. She couldn't risk one of the stewards questioning her about why, at such a busy time, she was leaving the kitchen empty-handed.

The two chambermaids, who were some years older than Esme and had obviously worked the liners for several years, were whispering conspiratorially about a discovery of a third dead body. One of them, a plain looking woman who spoke with a Welsh lilt to her words, said the victim's face looked like chewed meat and his body had a strange black rash as if it were rotting from the inside. She also said two bodies, quite dead the night before, were missing and they carried the same strange rash.

Esme strained to listen as she followed them from the ship's galley out into the first class corridor. Her thoughts were of the strange body she had seen on the waste ground the night before they left Southampton. That man, a foreign sailor she believed, also had a strange rash, and she thought him dead, decomposing even, and yet inexplicably, his body disappeared in just a few minutes. The memories sent a shiver down her spine and a swirling pit of uneasiness gripped her stomach. Whatever this rash was, whatever caused it, if you believed the gossip, involved in the death of four people.

Esme's mind raced. The dark, twisted images of what she'd seen on that muddy patch of waste ground, mixed with snippets of the chambermaids' conversation and a cold fear gripped her heart. Her thoughts turned to Charlotte. Was there something horrifyingly loose in the shadowy alleys and passageways of the docks? Was there someone, or something, spreading its foul disease or, worse still, if that were possible, chewing the flesh from the faces of its victims?

Esme felt helpless. The despair rolled over her like the powerful Atlantic waves that crashed against the *Titanic's* giant hull, each one dragging her deeper. Her chest tightened, her breath coming in short gasps as tears of hopeless frustration ran down her face, soaking the starched collar of her uniform. Stumbling into a service stairwell, she left the two women to continue their mindless gossiping while she wiped her face with her sleeve and took several large, deep breaths.

In through the nose, out through the mouth.

She kept repeating the words like a mantra until her breathing returned to normal. This was not the time to panic; she could do nothing to help Charlotte anyway. She needed to focus on ensuring Bridget escaped punishment for killing her husband, seemingly in cold blood. No jury in the land would understand her reasons while sitting in the emotive atmosphere of a courtroom.

The pressure was beginning to get to Esme, a pressure that had been slowly, but steadily, building since her stupid decision to fuck with the Old Dragon on her first day. She remembered that brief moment of power when she became aware of how much Miss Wilson despised her for her youth and looks; it seemed a distant memory now. Only Bridget had shown her any genuine kindness. Even Doc Sampson's offer of help came with a terrible price most women would never consider. But then, most women weren't in her predicament. Leaving the silver salver on a table pushed against the wallpapered wall, she headed down to C Deck and her inauspicious fraternization with the detestable Doctor Sampson.

Wilbur Jenkins was, since his earliest memory, a keen swimmer. He excelled at college, just failing by a fingernail, and no doubt an Ivy League education, to represent the U.S. at the 1908 Olympics. He was travelling home after spending the spring as a guest of the American ambassador in Rome. He had gone to college with the ambassador's son, also a member of the college swim team, with whom he had shared a room, and during their last year a bed. The decision to return to America was hard. Europe seemed so much more liberal in its attitude, but his parents insisted, even lining up a job on Wall Street at his father's firm. His mother even had a suitable young woman in mind for him to meet. By this, he knew she really meant to marry, despite her knowing about his sexuality since literally catching him and their gardener with their trousers down. She had, to her credit, promptly left the room and never spoken of the matter either to him or, he had to assume, his father, but he always noticed a distant sadness in her eyes after that. The gardener left their employ the next day to take up a position in Baltimore, and Wilbur never saw him again.

The decision to swim so close to dinner looked to have proved a good one. The changing rooms were empty. Wilbur quickly changed into his woollen swimming costume and walked through to the poolside where he left his towel on the peg provided. At the far end of the darkened pool, he noticed a man in rough looking work clothes kneeling over the pale, bloated body of a half-naked man who lay on his back beside the water's edge. The fully clothed man, to Wilbur's well-practiced eye, looked muscular and athletic. Wilbur, who had always had a soft spot for the rougher, menial type, watched with growing excitement as the man, his head bent low over the other man's crotch, continued bobbing up and down. There was a soft, gentle moan and the other man's head rolled over to look straight at Wilbur who gasped, aware his incidental voyeuristic act had been discovered.

The athletic man's frantic movement stopped, and he quickly began to stand. The fat, bloated man didn't move, just stared, almost invitingly, in Wilbur's direction, as his companion strode confidently along the poolside towards the intruder.

Wilbur smiled, his college lover all but forgotten. This was more than he could have hoped for. The stranger rounded the corner of the pool, wiping his mouth with the back of his hand, his long stride swiftly closing the distance between them.

Excitedly, Wilbur glanced round contemplating a retreat into the safer surroundings of the changing room's darkened cubicles, aware discovery would lead to a devastating scandal. He knew many gentlemen in both New York and Boston society who preferred the forbidden intimacy offered by another man. Indeed, some were quite open about their preferences, at least within their close circle of friends. But to be caught in flagrante delicto with a man of such obvious working class origins would be unforgivable.

The heavyset man was nearly on him. Wilbur abandoned the idea of the safe, dark changing rooms in exchange for spontaneous, raw passion. He also felt he owed the half-naked gentleman a chance to watch him enjoy the delights of the muscular labourer. It was only fair and maybe a prelude to them getting together later. Besides, if events heated up they could always move to a cubicle for the more intimate moment of their union. He felt his arousal pushing urgently against his bathing suit as his new lover reached out, drawing him urgently into his strong arms. The light fleetingly caught the handsome stranger's face. The tattooed lines on his neck and face caused Wilbur's heart to skip a beat. This was a fantasy come true, not since the gardener of his inexperienced youth had he experienced the illicit pleasure of a lover from the wrong side of town.

Following that single skipped beat, Wilbur's heart only beat twice more before Hoggie's mighty hands ripped his head from his shoulders in one violent twist. He would feed from Wilbur's severed neck later, but now he returned to his already disembowelled meal with a soft, satisfied groan, dipping his face into the open cavity to pull at the delicious intestines within.

Thirty-eight

Violet sprawled on the soft eiderdown, her needlepoint carelessly discarded on the floor beside her bed. She sighed, puffing her cheeks out in an exaggerated fashion before taking her book from the bedside table and opening it with a resigned shrug. William had missed their afternoon tryst, and she had grown bored with her luxurious prison cell. He had been most explicit about her never leaving the room for fear of her coming face-to-face with Mrs. Grafton, an instruction she was more than happy to acquiesce to. Provided, of course, William made regular visits to relieve her tedious existence.

The book failed to hold her attention, and she soon tossed it back on the table. Violet lay on her back staring at the ceiling, her thoughts once again turning to William. It was he who had taught her to read; not that she had been completely illiterate, but he helped her develop, helped her understand the meaning of the words and in so doing, taught her to enjoy reading. She would often lay naked next to him, reading passages from the books he bought for her while he helped her with pronunciation, or explained the meaning of a word she had not encountered before. Violet often thought, back then, he would ask her to marry him. To make a lady of her, why else would he bother to teach her to read, if not to make her pass for a young lady of repute? He never spent his time, or money, with any of the other girls, only her.

Then he met that bitch Bridget, the fucking pretty American whore with all the right connections. It was really obvious he didn't love Bridget. It was his idea for Violet to leave the security of Madame Beauchamp's Belgravia house and become his wife's servant. It would allow them to be close, allow him to continue his peccadillo, his penchant for the abnormal. William had told her the marriage was just business; Bridget was useful to him.

But she heard them … fornicating! And what about the baby, surely that would change things if she wasn't careful? What if, faced with the prospect of fatherhood, William mellowed, embracing the respectability that came with having a family?

Violet jumped from the bed and began to pace. Her dress rustled with each forceful stride. Her blood thumped loudly in her ears as a hot flush rose through her body and tiny beads of perspiration formed on her furrowed brow. She curled her fingers into fists. The skin, stretched tight across her knuckles, shone pale as the blood drained from her hands.

Was that why he hadn't come to visit that afternoon? Was he busy playing the happy father-to-be, the newlywed husband who couldn't keep his hands of his beautiful young bride? Society was so fickle.

As a single man of means, he could do as he pleased. It was no secret gentlemen longed to be him and the ladies, many of them already married, desired him, and all would turn a blind eye to his philandering. But now he had taken a wife, and she was at risk of becoming a scandalous dalliance, a cheap indiscretion at the heart of the Grafton household. An indiscretion, she knew, he could easily dispense with, especially if the young Mrs. Grafton were to be receptive to the more unusual aspects of his advances in the boudoir.

Violet's rage consumed her from within. It burned from her heart and radiated throughout her body. She loved William, not for his money or his power, but because they were kindred spirits born into absurdly different worlds. She saw a side to him few others even knew he possessed and in return, he respected her, not just for her body and youthful exuberance, but for her mind. She was clever, astute and deviously cunning and he'd nurtured that. When he ran into difficulty over rights to expand a mine under a neighbouring estate, it was her idea that she should meet the landowner, a local member of Parliament. William still had the letter of entitlement, allowing him to expand his companies' mining operations, secured in his safe, with the two photographic plates showing the esteemed politician asleep in Violet's arms.

Violet was a fighter, and she wasn't ready to give up on her future just yet. She may be only a lowly chambermaid now, but one day she would be Mrs. Grafton, even Lady Grafton. She would find a way of removing the threat posed by that Yankee bitch, and she would start tonight by giving William an evening he wouldn't forget, even if that meant leaving the cabin and going in search of him. She would start by taking some time to free her mind, then she would find something suitable to wear,

and with it, something to disguise her features, should she encounter his loathsome bride. Then, if he still had not visited her, or at least sent word giving details of their next rendezvous, she would dine in the first class saloon as her ticket entitled her to, ensuring she sat close to the Grafton's table. The thrill of the event, expecting discovery at any moment, and the expression on William's face, when she revealed herself to him, would all make for an intoxicating, if not arousing, evening.

Drawing a warm bath, Violet took an ornately carved bamboo pipe and a small china pot, brightly decorated with a hand-painted Chinese dragon, from the top drawer of the dresser. She carefully lifted the lid and took out a small tablet of opium, which she burned on a metal plate balanced above the electric lamp. After a few minutes, she reclined on the bed and began inhaling the relaxing, psychotropic vapours through the pipe.

Once she had slipped into a comfortable groove, where the walls rippled and twisted, contorting into strange shapes and spinning spirals, and the portraits spoke to her in strange tongues, she stumbled through to the suite's compact bathroom. She quickly shed the silk stockings and nightgown she had worn all day in expectation of William's visit, leaving them forgotten on the floor. Slipping into the water's welcoming warmth she sank into a tranquil, if bizarre, daydream as the opium eased her troubled mind, while the effects of the bathwater soothed the tension in her muscles.

Thirty-nine

Sixth Officer Moody led the second search party and had been assigned the task of searching the first class areas of Upper Deck E. The main corridor, dubbed *Park Lane* by the crew, housed forty-five staterooms, and as the captain made clear, the passengers should not be disturbed. They only searched the corridor itself before moving on to the main second class reception area and the central stairwell. They had just descended to Middle Deck F and were entering the swimming pool and Turkish baths on the starboard side of the ship.

Moody walked into the swimming pool's outer room expecting to find one of the two stewards usually on duty but it was empty, the counter deserted. "Officer on deck!" His voice was loud enough to carry into the tiny back office but, he hoped, not loud enough to disturb any passengers who may still be dressing following a few quick lengths before dinner.

There was no reply. Moody nodded towards one of the two able seamen accompanying him. "Mr. Davis, if you would be so good to check the office."

"Yes, sir!" Davis lifted the hinged section of the counter and disappeared into the room beyond only to reappear a few seconds later. "There's no one here, sir."

"Probably nipped off for a crafty smoke when everyone left for dinner," said his shipmate, a jovial Liverpudlian who'd joined the ship in Southampton from her sister the *Olympic*.

"I do hope not, Mr. Baines," Moody replied with a frown. As an officer, Moody was aware of the practice of slipping away for a quick smoke and would often turn a blind eye, provided the relevant stations were properly manned.

The three men moved through into the changing room area. The lights were off, the room dark and uninviting, the dark oak lockers only serving to deepen the shadows along the far wall. Davis flicked a switch just inside the doorway, and a weak light filled the unoccupied room.

"Maybe everyone's gone to dinner, sir," said Davis, hoping his superior would get the hint. Moody inspected the lockers, opening each in turn until he reached the second from last in the row. This one would not open.

"Perhaps so, Mr. Davis, but someone has left their property in the locker, and I doubt they would leave their clothes here and return to their cabin in just their swimming costume." He needed to inspect the pool beyond the inner door as there were two stewards yet unaccounted for and possibly a passenger. "We'll conduct a brief sweep of the pool area, and if we find nothing, Mr. Davis, you can check the duty logs to find out who should be here. Then find them."

"Aye, aye, sir," Davis said respectfully. Dinner was going to have to wait. He wasn't even sure what, or who, they were searching for, but it was obviously important. He knew from the general gossip among the ship's crew at least two people, one a passenger, died, and according to rumour, someone had stolen the bodies, so he guessed this search had something to do with

that. But the ship's officers were, as one would expect, keeping things close to their chest. If news of this got out, it would damage the reputation of the White Star, the ship, and all aboard her, from Captain Smith down to the lowest trimmer. It wasn't uncommon for people to die at sea, no one would disagree over that; even three deaths, although unfortunate, was not unheard of. With more than three thousand people on a weeklong voyage, one could argue it was almost unavoidable. But the seeming theft of the bodies was totally unacceptable.

Davis assumed them stolen; after all, dead bodies did not just walk off on their own accord. What puzzled him was, why? Why would someone want to steal one body, let alone two? And how, on God's earth, were they planning to smuggle the bodies ashore in New York?

He was still pondering this question as he followed Baines through the swing doors out onto the dimly lit poolside. His more senior colleague stopped abruptly just inside the doorway causing Davis to bump into him with a soft sigh of annoyance.

"What the …?" He exclaimed, pushing himself away from Baines before they tripped over one another's legs in the gloom.

"S … Sir?" Baines called over his shoulder, his usual unflappable calmness dispelled, replaced by a palpable fear and apprehension, causing the word to come out as a faltering whisper.

Davis stepped to the side to allow Officer Moody to follow them through the door, at the same time catching his

first look at the reason for Baines' reticence. Lying before them, wearing only a dark coloured bathing suit, was what he assumed to be the body of the missing passenger. Identifying that to be the case would take a while, as the dead man's torso ended in a bloody, ragged stump where his head should have sat.

In that moment, Davis couldn't see the missing head. He stood transfixed by the hideously grotesque neck stump, unable to tear his eyes away from it until, with barely a sound, he doubled over and vomited. He took a few deep breaths then wiped the back of his hand across his mouth before straightening up. He glanced at Baines, who had remained silent, unsure his friend had even noticed the warm, sticky puke that spewed from his gullet.

Moody came around from behind the two men and stood beside them. Davis watched the officer's normally ruddy complexion turn deathly pale as, in a shocking moment of comprehension, he took in the scene before him. He heard the quiet intake of breath as the young officer struggled to control his emotions, the long sigh as he cleared his lungs, his cheeks puffing as the air forced its way out through pursed lips. Finally, almost inaudible to his two subordinates, he muttered, "Who the fuck can do that to another human being?"

It was not clear whether Moody's question was rhetorical or if he wanted an answer. It didn't really matter, as neither man had one.

There was a long moment of silence, during which time the three men looked from one to another, an unspoken pact forming between them. They were witnessing, firsthand, the brutality of this beast, and the fear gripping their souls and twisting their guts was written clear in their eyes. It was a brutality no one would believe unless they, too, witnessed the beast's handiwork, and a fear only understood by those who thought the beast was coming for them. A fear that chilled even the most hardened mariners to the core. A fear they wished never to disclose to another living soul for fear of ridicule.

Finally, Baines spoke, his voice creaking as he struggled to keep his emotions under control. "I think there may be another body in there." He raised a shaky hand to point towards the shadows at the far end of the pool where the darker outline of a human form floated face down, arms akimbo. A dark, cloudy circle had formed around the body which was, ever so slowly, spreading outwards.

Davis wretched again, his stomach empty.

Moody took a deep breath. It wouldn't do for him to hurl his guts in front of the two crewmen; this was a time for strong stomachs and stronger leadership. Whatever was loose on board the ship had now killed at least five men in, if the headless corps was anything to go by, the most barbaric of circumstances.

"Mr. Baines, would you please fish that body out of the water?"

"Aye, aye, sir." The sailor's response was barely audible as he unhooked a long-handled boat hook from the wall. Standing at the edge of the pool, he extended the hook out across the water. On the second try, he latched into the floating corpse's bloated flesh, towing him gently towards the poolside. Once the body bumped softly against the pool's tiled wall, he extracted the hook from the skin with a deft flick of his wrist, before kneeling down to haul the water-laden body from the pool.

Davis, who watched the proceedings with a gaunt, pale expression, his hand clasped firmly over his mouth, finally hurried forward to aid his colleague. Moody stood a few yards away, supervising the men's efforts. Although it was a concern he didn't dare voice aloud, he wanted to keep watch in case the killer returned or, worse still, was lurking close by awaiting his chance to kill again.

Davis was still a few slippery yards from Baines when the previously thought deceased reared up from the pools murky water, his insides tumbling from a huge cavity torn through his abdomen. Several yards of sloppy entrails floated in the dirty water beneath him as his fat, fleshy fingers tore at Baines' throat before he found the purchase he was after. Gripping the able seaman firmly, the man from the pool pulled him down so their faces were only inches apart.

Baines gurgled what might have been a terrified scream had not the corpse had such a firm hold of his larynx. Perplexed by the speed of the attack, Moody and Davis remained rooted where they stood, frozen with fear. The dead man bared his teeth in what Moody briefly thought a macabre grin, before biting deep into Baines' unprotected face, ripping his nose away with the first frenzied bite. The pair toppled into the water, the deceased spinning his victim so he dragged him under the water in one smooth motion, his gnashing teeth closing in on Baines' neck as they disappeared into the foaming darkness.

Davis stared down into the churning water as his shipmate fought for his life. His attacker was clearly dead. If he lived to be a hundred, Davis knew he would never forget that grinning face.

But the attacker was clearly dead. Floating face down, his innards trailing in the water, the man was clearly dead. Wracked with indecision and confused by the speed of events in the last few seconds, Davis didn't know whether to go to Baines' aid or run for his life.

Moody was first to react. Grabbing the young seaman by the collar, he dragged him away from the water's edge. "Fuckin' move, Davis! Come on!" he screamed hysterically as he continued to half carry, half drag the man towards the changing rooms.

"What 'bout Baines? We can't just leave 'im," Davis mumbled, his face pale and bloodless.

"You saw what he … that thing did to the other one. Baines is already dead, and we'll join 'im if we don't move!" Moody did not break stride as he propelled Davis through the door. The two sailors almost tumbled as they ran through the tight changing room before recovering their balance to stumble past the office door before crashing out into the corridor.

Davis was breathing heavily, bent over, hands on knees, "What in the name of God was that because it certainly wasn't right! You saw 'im, he was fuckin' dead, 'is guts was floating in the pool."

"Quiet, Davis. The captain was specific about the surreptitious nature of this investigation. I doubt he will take kindly to you running your mouth so publicly," Moody hissed, pulling the door closed.

"Pardon me, sir, but if you still think you can keep this quiet, you're a bigger fool than he." Moody noticed the able seaman was shaking as he spoke, the full horror of what he had just witnessed finally sinking in and sending him into shock. Moody slapped Davis on the shoulder in what he hoped was a confident and encouraging manner, although he too was aware of the futility of their situation. Piecing together the information from the captain's briefing, coupled with the events of the last few minutes, he reluctantly concluded that, in some extraordinary way, the dead themselves were responsible for the killings. If that were true, the number of killers was only going to rise and the ship, as vast as she was, was only so big, and at least two days at full steam from any port.

"Listen to me, sailor. The last thing we need now is pandemonium. If word of these killings gets out, then confusion and chaos will reign, and that will result in many more deaths. Do you understand me?" Moody deliberately kept his voice low

and casual. He needed Davis to be with him, and right now, the poor man was holding on by his fingertips.

Davis took a deep breath, flashing a hesitant smile in Moody's direction, he nodded.

"Sir!" The loud address in an American accent came from the far end of the short transverse corridor in which they stood. Moody looked up to see able seaman Callahan walking swiftly towards him.

"Mr. Callahan, it would be lax of me not to mention how glad I am to see you."

Callahan made no effort to return the officer's attempted good-humoured greeting. Instead, and with some degree of urgency noticeable in his voice, he said, "The master-at-arms asks for your immediate help in steerage, sir. There has been an incident."

"An incident?" questioned Moody. "What do you mean by incident?"

"The first search party was attacked, sir." Callahan gave Moody a confused look, before adding, "By the dead, sir."

Forty

Esme arrived outside Sampson's private cabin just after the shrill, brass tones of the ship's bugle had called the first class passengers to the 19:30 dinner service. A fine sheen of perspiration coated her face as she felt the telltale tingle of embarrassment flush through her cheeks. She took a deep breath and dabbed her brow with her handkerchief before running her hands down her dress, smoothing out the creases.

She wanted to turn and walk away. More than anything else in the world she wanted to forget all about Doctor Sampson and his disgusting proposition, but the die was cast and events already set in motion. Both her return to Southampton to her sister, Charlotte, and the future liberty of Mrs. Grafton depended on her actions in the next hour or so.

She tapped the door gently with the knuckle of her forefinger and waited.

There was no reply, although she thought she heard a muffled movement from within the cabin. Feeling exposed and self-conscious, she knocked again. This time, driven by urgency, her knock was louder and more confident. She knew if she didn't do this now she never would, and she didn't want her visit to become common knowledge. The doctor had a well-known reputation, and should she be seen calling on him it would not tax people's imagination about why. She could do without the sniggering whispers of the other maids and didn't want to give the insufferable Miss Wilson any more

ammunition. The cow already believed her a whore and would, no doubt, enjoy throwing her unceremoniously off the ship in New York.

She listened intently for a moment and was just about to turn on her heel and scarper back to the relative safety of the ship's galley when she heard the doctor mumbling. She couldn't make out the exact wording of his reply, possibly because of the thickness of the door, but she got the general drift. Esme placed her hand on the door and gave it a push, hastily stepping into the cabin beyond before swinging the door shut behind her.

Doctor Sampson lay on his bunk in a pair of scruffy trousers and a filthy shirt, open to reveal an equally grubby vest stretched tight over his barrel-like stomach. The cabin itself stank, an unpleasant mix of manly sweat and something not unlike rotting meat, causing Esme to balk at venturing further into the dimly lit room. She remained by the door, appalled by the doctor's unkempt appearance and repulsed by the air's foul odour. Surely, he could have had the good grace to remain sober.

She reserved her feelings of abhorrent disgust for herself. Even in her darkest musings about this moment, he remained a gentleman of breeding, polite and well-mannered; he at least kept up the pretence of seduction. But in reality, and away from prying eyes, he was a vile slob who'd preyed on her vulnerability.

On seeing her, the doctor groaned loudly and tried to get up from the bed. He flailed his arms and legs like a stranded

beetle as he tried to gather enough strength to roll over, before finally flipping himself off the bed where, momentarily confused, he remained face down.

Esme slid her hand behind her, feeling for the reassuring hardness of the doorknob which she gripped with relief. She couldn't do it. Whatever Miss Wilson did to her would never be as bad as letting this loathsome man touch her. She would find another way back to her sister, and she and Bridget would have to think of another plan, one that didn't involve the contents of the doctor's trousers.

Then she saw them!

They were sitting on the nightstand next to the bed. The doctor's heavy looking bunch of keys, which would include the key that unlocked the gates dividing steerage from the first class areas of the vessel. The key would allow Bridget, dressed in Esme's clothes, to disappear into the masses huddled in steerage. Once they reached port she could safely reappear claiming she had feared for her life after discovering her loving husband's murdered body. Meanwhile, Esme would find his mistress Violet and lure her on deck with the promise of a moonlight tryst with Captain Grafton. Once there, she would push the adulteress overboard before leaving a hastily written, tear-stained confession and suicide note in Violet's cabin.

Esme would then raise the alarm, claiming she saw Bridget jump overboard. The delay in raising the alarm would allow the sea to claim Violet's body and a search of the cabins would not find Bridget Grafton, leaving the crew to believe Esme's deliberately vague identification.

On the discovery of Violet's note, it would be assumed she killed Captain Grafton in a fit of passion before taking her own life, leaving Bridget to emerge as a grieving widow, who fearing for her life, took refuge among the immigrants. The discovery of her husband's adultery with their servant, while obviously scandalous and shocking, would pale against the revelation she was pregnant with her dead husband's first child, and heir to his considerable fortune. Esme hoped this would garner public sympathy, and coupled with the confusion surrounding William's death and the role Violet played in it, would completely exonerate Bridget.

She had it all planned. No court in England would convict a lady of such good stock, with no tangible evidence and so much reasonable doubt. *Chambermaid confessed! Lady Grafton feared for her life!* The headlines almost wrote themselves.

She needed that key, but the grossly bloated and foul smelling lump of lard that masqueraded as the ship's physician stood in her way. Doctor Sampson, his back to Esme, climbed unsteadily to his feet using the furniture to support his considerable frame, while he groaned and moaned with the exertion.

Disgusted, Esme looked at the bed, a small hollow in the mattress still noticeable where he'd lain, and almost gagged. She clamped her hand across her mouth as her stomach lurched. The mattress and sheet were both heavily stained with

what she immediately thought to be a foul mixture of blood and faecal matter. The bottom of the hollow had filled with a thick, sticky reddish-brown liquid, and it was from this the cabin's putrefying smell emanated. Several flies were flitting around the tiny pool, occasionally alighting on its surface before darting away.

Esme began frantically fumbling with the doorknob behind her. All thoughts of the key, of the plan, banished from her mind. All she could think of was getting out of there. Something was terribly wrong, but in the confusion, her mind couldn't piece it together. Her hands shook, the palms so damp with a nervous sweat she couldn't get sufficient grip on the smooth brass to twist it far enough to free the latch from its retaining plate.

Doctor Sampson turned towards her. It was then she recognized the true horror of her circumstance. His deathly pale face, round and podgy at the best of times, was engorged, the skin pulled taught. Droplets of yellowish fluid seeped from the open pores, an intricate web of darkness creeping across his features. His mouth gapped open with the bulbous, green lump of flesh that must have once been his tongue lolling from the open cavity, the tip of this oral appendage had turned black and necrotic. Esme, who'd seen plenty of injured seamen with badly treated wounds, recognized the onset of gangrene; although, she'd never seen it develop at such a rapid pace.

But what really induced the cold, vice-like hands of fear to grip her heart, draining the blood from her face and almost causing her to urinate where she stood, were the doctor's eyes. Where they were once filled with mischief, dancing and twinkling whenever he spoke, they were now just dark sunken hollows housing eyes as black as coals, the vibrancy of life drained from them to leave the ill-defined stare of death.

Esme had no doubts the doctor was dead, and yet, unless her eyes were playing the cruellest of tricks, he was standing, although a little unsteadily, in front of her. His soulless eyes gazed languidly through her and yet somehow still regarded her with the utmost scrutiny.

She realized with a sickening jolt that her frantic attempts to open the door had ceased. Crippled with fear, her wide-eyed stare focused on Doctor Sampson's hideously marked face.

He shuffled closer. His monstrous mouth twisting into a chilling leer, as if he'd remembered the purpose of her visit. Esme watched his approach. She felt her skin tighten as though a thousand tiny spiders had crawled across its pale surface; a cold sweat chilled her forehead and wetted her back.

She inhaled, almost gagging on the putrid smell of decay, and forced her legs to move. Edging to her left, using her outstretched hand to guide her, not daring to tear her eyes away from the dead man lurching towards her, she encountered a solid barrier. Furniture, a chest of drawers, she guessed.

Sampson's leering face loomed closer. His hands, swollen and yellowing, the fingers blackening at the tips, reached towards her. She ducked, scrabbling under his raised arm, trying

to get to the other side of the heavy furniture hoping to use it as a defensive barrier within the tight confines of the well-organized cabin.

As she straightened, her forward motion stopped and she toppled backward. Twisting her body, she managed to stay on her feet, but her scalp blazed with a burning pain as the doctor, his strong fingers entwined in her hair, pulled her back. She beat at his arms with her fists, each blow preceded by a wild windmilling of her arms as she desperately tried to break his hold.

But it was no use. He dragged her forcibly towards the bed.

"Get off me, you fuckin' bastard!" Esme screamed, her voice sounding loud inside her own head, taking her by surprise. Tears filled her eyes. She felt the needle prick pain as his tightening grip tore the hair from her scalp. She lashed out at his right shin with her left foot, but she kicked across her body, and although she made contact, it was weak and merely scuffed the edge of his calf instead of crunching against the sensitive bone. The swinging momentum of the kick toppled her off balance and she lost her footing. With a final violent twist of her hair, the decaying carcass of Doctor Sampson threw her against the filthy bed.

Esme's knees hit the unforgiving wooden floor with a jaw-jolting crack, her hips slamming into the bed's metal frame, doubling her over so her face splashed into the fetid liquid fluid pooled in the hollow of the saturated mattress. For an agonizing few seconds, she could do nothing, stunned and winded by the force of her landing and blinded by a combination of her own tears and his foul-smelling excretions.

Then she inhaled.

The vile putrid soup filled her throat and stung the sensitive membranes in her nose. Esme raised her head in panic as the fluid pervaded her lungs. She coughed violently several times, then, as it swarmed back up into her throat, she gagged, adding a mouthful of vomit to the mess on the already ruined mattress. Frantically pulling at her now filthy apron, she wiped the glutinous mess from her face in time to see Doctor Sampson's corpse standing over her, a lecherous leer playing on his cracked scabby lips as he tugged at his belt.

Even in his state of walking decay, he seemed to remember the reason for her visit. As far as he was concerned, she had come to fulfill his sexual desire in exchange for him putting in a good word with the Old Dragon. It was one of his oldest and most successful ploys. He had never put in a good word for the young women he seduced this way. Miss Wilson's demeanour terrified him and he rarely spoke to her, certainly nothing more than a polite acknowledgment. As for the young women, they were always too ashamed ever to mention their rendezvous with the doctor. Who would believe the wild accusations of a chambermaid over the word of such a learned gentleman and ship's doctor?

But now his corpse was simply acting on a thread of memory ingrained in its being, in the same way a gramophone

plays a tune ingrained on a record. The doctor, in life, had spent so much of his existence preying on young girls, that in death the primary desire that drove his rotting flesh on was not that of food, but sex. But then, like a spider, he could always feast on her voluptuous young body afterward.

The doctor's trousers, free from the restraint of his belt, slid down his legs to crumple around his ankles. His legs were mottled in hues of green and blue, while his veins, prominent and black, spread branch-like through his vile, damp epidermis.

The sight spurred Esme to life. Still spitting the foul mix of vomit, blood, and faecal matter from her mouth, she climbed to her feet, grabbing the keys from the nightstand with her left hand. Then, moving with a swiftness that surprised even herself, she reached down and seized a handful of the dead man's bunched up trousers before pushing herself away, her legs driving her upwards as she tugged violently on the thick material.

For one terrifying moment, she faltered. Her legs wobbled, her body threatening to sink back into the stinking mire on the mattress. She clutched the nightstand for support, the keys digging deep into the palm of her hand. Regaining her balance, Esme pitched her weight to the left yanking hard on the material twisted in her right hand, dragging the doctor's rotund corpse off its feet. Doctor Sampson's body crashed to the floor, his unprotected head striking the corner of his neat desk, whipping it to the side with the force of the impact.

Briefly, Esme slumped to the floor, back against the bed, her loose hair tumbling across her face while the remains of her once pristine bun rested haphazardly against the nape of her neck. Her lungs prickled with every faltering breath. Her scalp stung with the intensity of a hundred bee stings and tiny rivulets of blood trickled from between the fingers of her hand still clenched tightly around the large bunch of keys. Doctor Sampson's broken body lay a few feet away, his lifeless eyes staring, almost accusingly, in her direction while his limbs still twitched sporadically in a macabre death dance.

Summoning all her remaining strength, Esme struggled to her feet. Lifting the bedside table high in the air, she brought it down with a sickening dull thud on the unprotected head of Doctor Sampson. Then she did it again and again until his skull completely caved in.

It was only then Esme began to cry a gentle self-pitying sob as she looked in the small mirror above the sink, fixing her hair and wiping the sticky mess from her face with a clean towel. Satisfied she would at least pass a casual glance without drawing attention to herself, she carefully inched past the doctor's crumpled body before quietly opening the cabin door.

Stepping out into the corridor, Esme came face-to-face with the jealous corpse of Sister O'Malley.

Forty-one

Violet struggled to find a foothold in reality. She only occasionally dabbled with the opium flower, and then only to free her inhibitions when in William's company. But over the last few days, restricted to the confines of her room, she had used it to excess, partly to relieve her boredom and partly to escape the reality of her existence. She was a rich man's plaything, nothing more, and with the Graftons' baby on the way, she understood that was unlikely to change. Even taking Mrs. Grafton out of the equation, she doubted William Grafton would debase himself so much to marry a housemaid, however skilled she was in the bedroom. She went out on deck hoping the brisk, refreshing sea air would unscramble the jumble of thoughts that tumbled through her mind with no coherent pattern or meaning, but to no use. The coldness of the evening served only to narrow her arteries, effectively forcing the drug into her brain, intensifying its effect.

She stood at the rail on the first class promenade deck sucking in fresh, clean air and looking out across the dark expanse of the Atlantic Ocean. Although dressed in an expensive evening gown, a thick fur shawl to keep away the chill, and a wide brimmed hat to conceal her features, she still felt displaced and vulnerable. This feeling was not helped by the knowledge that none of the clothes actually belonged to her. They were all Mrs. Grafton's; Violet had borrowed them for the trip and would have to ensure she returned them to her

mistress's wardrobe when she arrived back in England. William had thoughtfully booked her a second class cabin for her return trip the following week, arranging for her to stay at a hotel during the interim. There was no doubt he would visit her during her stay so they could engage in the sexual activities his prim and proper wife would find abhorrent.

William had not visited her as promised today, so she decided to defy his instruction for her not to leave the cabin. She would, of course, not be so stupid to go near his cabin for fear of running into Bridget, but if she exercised care, she could at least get to eat in the saloon. That would be a treat beyond words, but if William were there! She could only imagine the look of shock on his face as she boldly introduced herself.

But what if he were dining with Bridget? She realized she had not thought of this most likely scenario. Then, a thought so wicked crossed her opium ravaged mind, and she started to laugh aloud. If her lover was dining with his wife, she would take a seat at a table behind Bridget so she could catch his eye. Violet would then leave immediately and wait for him in her cabin where he would be sure to show before the evening was out, no doubt aroused by excitement and anger.

Buoyed by the expectation of an evening of delight, Violet pulled the shawl tight against the chill and strolled down the almost deserted promenade towards the entrance to the grand staircase. She would, for once, enter a dining room as a lady, dressed in all her finery and not skulk in as a servant to collect the dirty dishes.

Bernard collected Kathleen from her cabin and, as promised, she had exchanged her dowdy black mourning dress for one in emerald green, which he thought, accentuated her ample curves in all the right places. He escorted her to dinner, taking a short excursion out onto the covered walkway to show her the early evening sky's canopy of twinkling stars. Long ago, Bernard had perfected the secret craft of romancing a lady and was going to ensure he used it to maximum effect on Kathleen. His cynical old heart, the heart of a trickster and charlatan, had never skipped so many beats as it did when he was with her. He convinced himself ... well almost, her vast fortune had nothing to do with what, to him at least, was a strange phenomenon.

He found her to be attractive, witty, and surprisingly intelligent with a direct, flirtatious, and carefree attitude he found refreshing. She was like no one else he had ever met in the stuffy country houses attended by the inbred upper class of English society. He felt his determination not to let her slip through his fingers coursing through every fibre of his being, and he knew this could be his one true chance of happiness.

Bernard escorted Kathleen down the grand staircase to the accompaniment of Brahms, expertly played on the piano in reception by a member of the ship's orchestra. A young woman descended the stairs before them, and although well-dressed, Bernard noticed she didn't carry herself in the way expected of a young lady. As she reached the bottom step, she hesitated and threw a nervous glance towards the saloon, as though having second thoughts about entering. He spent so long being someone else that he grew accustomed to spotting individuals who did not fit the picture they were trying to portray. He guessed, because she was dining alone, her gentleman friend was otherwise engaged this evening, probably with his wife.

"Good evening," his jovial greeting caught the young woman unawares. She swung round, a startled look on her face, but quickly regained her composure when seeing Bernard and Kathleen a few steps above her.

"Good evening. Sir, madame."

"Good evening. That is a lovely dress; you must tell me where you bought it," Kathleen gushed as she glided down the last few stairs. A look of terror filled the young woman's eyes. When she decided to attend dinner, she obviously had not anticipated having to engage in conversation with other passengers.

Seeing her fear, Kathleen came to her rescue, "It is such a daunting prospect, is it not, entering a restaurant on your own, especially one filled with so many pompous, old farts."

"I hope you're not including me in that statement," said Bernard with mock indignation.

The young woman smiled nervously. "I must confess, I do feel somewhat out of my depth. Maybe it would be better if I dined in my room ..."

"Nonsense!" Kathleen interrupted with a dismissive wave of her gloved hand. "You shall dine as our guest, and that's all there is to it."

"No, sorry, that's such a kind offer, but I couldn't possibly impose."

"It will be no imposition, I can assure you. We would be glad of the company and any scandalous gossip you may have. Let me introduce ourselves, I'm Kathleen Black and this is Sir Bernard Astor."

"I'm pleased to meet you. I'm Violet … um … Holmes," replied Violet, clearly flustered at having to introduce herself.

"Don't worry, Miss Um Holmes. We'll take a seat at a discreet table, and if you should see anyone whom you would prefer did not see you, then just keep your head down and stay close to us." Bernard winked at Violet before striding over to the maître d'.

Violet looked at Kathleen apologetically, "Is it that obvious?"

Kathleen smiled, "Like a beacon, dear. Who is it you wish to avoid? Is it your master or your lover?"

"They are one and the same," confessed Violet, suddenly too ashamed to meet Kathleen's eye. "And I don't expect it's considered good form to bump into his wife either."

"Oh … extremely bad form indeed I would think," laughed Kathleen as she took Violet by the arm, following in Bernard's wake as a steward showed them to their table.

Forty-two

Guggenheim watched them from his table and briefly wondered whether the frightful Mrs. Black was actually fucking the phoney English knight. It seemed a fool and her husband's money were easily parted. He smiled at the thought as he turned his attention to the wine list. He had left instructions with the maître d' to invite Captain and Mrs. Grafton to join him for dinner. Not that he wanted to spend his evening with the insufferable William Grafton, but in the stuffy world of high society, Bridget was a breath of fresh air, and a beautiful one at that. Her intelligence and flirtatious nature obviously infuriated her pompous husband, but he found it engaging and exciting, making her exceptionally good company.

After a few minutes, during which the saloon started filling up with smartly suited gentlemen and ladies dressed in the latest European fashions and sporting ostentatious items of jewellery, which had no purpose save for the open flaunting of wealth, Bridget entered the saloon alone. The maître d', as directed, and lavishly tipped, escorted her through the bustling crowd to the billionaire's secluded table.

Rising politely from his chair, Guggenheim greeted Bridget with a smile. "I'm honoured you accepted my invitation to join me. Will Captain Grafton be joining us?" It was clear by his tone where his preferences lay.

"I'm afraid he will not, Mr. Guggenheim. He is feeling a little under the weather so you have me all to yourself tonight," Bridgett replied with a coy smile.

"If you will excuse my boldness, it is a privilege to be entrusted with one so beautiful, Mrs. Grafton." He wasn't sure if she was deliberately flirting with him, but he was prepared to find out. He waited for Bridget to take her seat before retaking his.

"I will excuse your boldness, Mr. Guggenheim, because you are American and therefore know no better." Bridget spoke in her finest finishing school English, a haughty, almost dismissive expression set on her graceful features, the mere suggestion of a smile tugging at the corners of her mouth.

"But, madam, do I need to remind you of your own heritage?"

"No, you do not!" This time the American twang was very much evident in her accent. "That's another reason I will excuse your boldness. I believe it is our boldness, as a nation, that sets us apart." She fixed him with a firm stare, "It is also a fact that no woman on earth will demand an apology from a man for calling her beautiful."

Guggenheim now felt sure she was flirting with him. "Please pass on my best wishes to your husband. It is nothing serious I hope?" Even he thought his lie obvious.

Bridget fidgeted in her seat and looked about the saloon nervously before answering, her mind replaying those moments when she rode his chest, forcing the pillow across his face. "No, just something he couldn't get off his chest. I'm sure he'll be fine."

Bridget fell quiet as the wine steward appeared; Guggenheim ordered champagne, then studied his guest in silence for a short while. She appeared, at least to him, to have something on her mind and yet, by the same token, to be freer in her words and attitudes than at any other time he had seen her on the voyage. He could only surmise it had something to do with her husband, but he wasn't one to pry. Perhaps they had argued and in a childish spat, William refused to join her for dinner. If that were so, it was his loss.

The waiter returned with the champagne, which he uncorked with an expert hand, catching the cork before it sailed across the room. He poured the sparkling liquid first into Guggenheim's flute glass then, on Guggenheim's nod, into Bridget's. They looked at each other in silence, Guggenheim waiting for the waiter to leave before speaking.

"It's with regret that I have to announce I will not have you to myself. I have also invited Captain Smith, Bruce Ismay, and Thomas Andrews to join me, as I'm fascinated by this impressive vessel and her abilities. I'm afraid Madame Aubart does not share my fascination and chose to dine in her room this evening."

"What more could a lady want than to have four men of such importance all to herself. I'm sure I will be able to more than make up for Madame Aubart's absence."

Bridget deliberately left the sentence hanging in the air between them. If Esme's plan was to work, Bridget would need the testimony of Benjamin Guggenheim and a little flirting would certainly ensure he remembered their time together. And if she needed to go further then, with her life and her husband's wealth at stake, she would.

"Ah, I believe my other guests have arrived." Guggenheim's attention switched to the saloon's entrance. Bridget took a moment to check the positioning of her hat and that her hair was in place before the other men arrived. Then she took a generous swig of champagne to settle her skittish nerves.

For a brief moment, she thought about Esme and wondered how she was getting on with her attempts at securing a key to the gates separating steerage from the rest of the ship. Then Guggenheim's guests arrived and she spread a smile across her face and plunged into the role of a doting wife.

Forty-three

Sister O'Malley stood swaying gently in the corridor, blocking Esme's escape from the dead doctor's cabin. If she was surprised to see Esme leaving Doctor Sampson's cabin, her decaying features didn't show it. Her mottled skin looked bloated with a road map of blackened veins spreading across her face, branching out from the thick tracks on her neck. Her lips, and the tongue bulging out from behind them, were purple, and their once delicate surfaces dry and cracked with several dark, weeping sores. Thick, green mucus dribbled from her lips to land on her chest with a soft plop.

Esme recoiled in shock. Covering her mouth and nose with her hand, she tried to block out the reeking stench of rotting, putrid meat accompanying the nurse, to no avail. Esme gagged, her stomach knotting and twisting as it forced the warm, acidic bile up into her throat and propelled it out through her nose and mouth. It burned the sensitive membranes in her nostrils, blurring her vision as salty tears welled in the corners of her eyes.

The rotting figure of the ship's nurse opened her mouth to speak, but the loud splattering sound of her decomposing bowels falling to the floor beneath her uniform drowned out anything she may have uttered. Sister O'Malley looked down at the mass of congealed body tissue seeping out from below her full-length skirt with confusion, as if some latent knowledge of human physiology told her she should be dead, not standing

outside Doctor Sampson's cabin face-to-face with another of his young harlots. She shuffled towards Esme who retreated into the cabin, sobbing in terror.

Esme's foot brushed against the doctor's body and she fought the urge to scream. She didn't want to draw attention to herself. The situation she found herself in would be hard to explain away, and this was the second rotting member of the Devil's crew she had encountered. How many more would come if she screamed? She eyed the open doorway behind the lumbering nurse and knew if she were to escape her deadly clutches and avoid being dragged into Hell, then she could afford to delay no longer.

Esme charged at the approaching O'Malley, evading her outstretched arms and smashing her shoulder into her soft, plump body, driving her out of the cabin and slamming her into the wall. The force of the impact caused thick, vile smelling sanguineous fluid to spray from the dead woman's open cavities. Her now ill-fitting uniform left a glistening dark smear down the wall as she slid to the floor. Esme, knocked off her feet by the initial impact, scrabbled across the deck to evade the stunned nurse's flailing arms before regaining her feet and hurrying towards the stairway at the end of the corridor.

As she passed the suite that formed the ship's hospital, she heard a loud crash. Checking over her shoulder she witnessed O'Malley, still lying on the ground, eating her own intestines. Content she was not being pursued, Esme ducked

inside the hospital suite intent on warning whoever had come in search of medical attention about ...

Esme stopped in her tracks. She had to warn them about what? That the doctor was dead and his assistant, Nurse Stench, had resorted to crawling around on the deck eating her own innards. Who, outside the walls of Bethlem Hospital, would believe such a farfetched story? But still, she reasoned, whoever was in the suite may still be in need of help and she should at least warn them of the dangers lurking in the corridors.

She approached the swing door to the treatment area and, standing on tiptoes, peeked through the small round observation window. A narrow bed covered in a blood-soaked sheet occupied the centre of the room, and next to it Esme saw an overturned trolley, its contents scattered across the floor. The far wall consisted of a row of glass-fronted cabinets in front of which stood the hunched figure of a man, his back to her.

Easing the door open an inch, Esme called out softly, "Hello, are you hurt?"

The man turned to face her, his features obscured by the spider web of ruptured veins below his skin. Blood caked his clothes and matted his hair and when he began to walk towards her, his movements, although swift, appeared unnatural and ungainly.

Esme let the door swing shut and ran towards the stairs like she should have done as soon as she escaped the nurse's vile clutches. Whatever had happened to these people appeared to have started on the lower decks and was now

spreading up through the ship. She needed to get to Bridget's cabin; it was obvious they would have to rethink their plans, as it would not be safe for Bridget to hideout in steerage.

Forty-four

Callahan opened the gate separating the first and second class areas of the ship from steerage then stepped back to allow Officer Moody to enter. At first, this part of the ship seemed quiet, almost deserted. They locked the gate behind them and walked side by side down the stairs. Davis, whom they couldn't persuade, *'not for all the tea in China,'* as he succinctly put it, to stay at the swimming pool, brought up the rear.

As they neared the bottom of the stairs, they heard a commotion from farther down the corridor; a door slammed, raised voices followed by a scuffle. Moody lengthened his stride and Callahan had to break into a trot to catch him before placing his hand on the officer's arm, physically holding him back.

"I don't think you should be too hasty. If there is something on this ship killing people, rotting their bodies from the inside and leaving their husks to feed off the living, I would not be too quick to encounter it."

"We must offer our aid to the living; besides, how many of these living corpses can there be?" Moody shrugged the American's restraining hand away and continued to walk purposefully towards the disturbance. Reaching a corner he looked down the shorter transverse corridor. He stopped so quickly that Davis, glancing over his shoulder at the safety of the stairs behind them, failed to notice and walked into him at full tilt.

"I'm so sorry, sir." His words were instinctive, and he fully expected a dressing-down from Moody, but his superior hardly noticed the collision, so intense was his focus on the crossway. Able seaman Davis looked in the direction of Moody's shocked stare.

"What … the … fuck …" His words trailed away as he tried to make some sense of the melee of people filling the short passageway. After the incident in the swimming pool, he thought he had seen enough disturbing sights to last him a lifetime, now he realized that was a mere sample of the horrors to come.

The corridor contained thirty or so people, all of whom appeared dead, their bodies in varying states of decomposition and most dressed in the plain, practical working class clothes of the immigrants travelling steerage. One wore the remains of a White Star seaman's uniform although it, like its wearer, only had one arm, the hat set jauntily on a head missing half its face.

Most had gathered in two groups, their attention focused on shapeless bundles lying on the ground. From the nearest of these two groups, a pair of legs protruded from beneath the general melee. They were smartly dressed in the same White Star uniform the half-faced corpse wore and the shoes were unmistakably well polished.

Then briefly, as if allowing the crewmen a glimpse of what was in store for them, the throng parted to reveal the eviscerated remains of a member of the search party sent to investigate this section of the vessel. The assembled throng had

torn open the man's abdomen, ripping his organs from the exposed cavity before leaving his entrails pooled in a sticky-looking heap on the blood-soaked deck. Such was the extent of his traumatic death that his identity would have to remain a mystery. A young woman with wild, curly hair the colour of marmalade sat feasting from the ragged neck wound, dipping her fingers into the throat's open bore then licking them clean, like she was stealing from a honey pot.

Farther down the corridor, two men tussled over a human leg ripped forcibly from its original owner, several tendons and the straggling remains of its arteries dangled from the jagged stump. Blood still dripped from the severed end, spraying both the walls and those standing nearby, as the feuding monsters swung it back and forth. The others didn't seem to mind, one even opened his mouth trying to catch the flying droplets on his swollen black tongue.

Davis sank to his knees and stared at the remains of his fellow crew member with unseeing eyes, his senses shutting down to protect his fragile mind from the atrocity he was witnessing.

It was Callahan who reacted first. He grabbed Moody by his shoulder and dragged him back from the corner. Out of the corner of his eye, he detected movement. The undead, which were no longer huddled masses gathered around their fresh kill, were beginning to move towards the three sailors. Only two or three at first, but more were leaving the throng to join them with each passing second. Individually, their movements were

ungainly and awkward, but as a pack, they moved with inexhaustible determination, like wolves running down their prey. Determined, relentless and focused solely on the kill.

"Sir!" Callahan's voice had risen in pitch, his gestures becoming more frantic as the pack closed in.

Moody looked at the American tugging urgently on his arm, a moment of confusion clouding his features. Then, comprehending the approaching danger, his expression turned to one of gratitude as the two men stumbled away from the seething mass of death and decay.

It was only as they reached the relative safety of the stairs they discovered able seaman Davis had not followed them. Pausing, Moody looked back ready to encourage one of the most experienced seafarers under his command to make a final bid for safety. The words died in his throat as he watched Davis, still kneeling in a catatonic stupor, being engulfed by the first wave of diseased corpses. For a fleeting moment, Davis turned towards his fleeing comrades as if pleading for their help.

Then he was gone.

Moody watched the feeding frenzy for a few seconds. He didn't know if it was because he felt he owed it to Davis or whether it was as penance to absolve his own guilt at abandoning a man, although not deliberately, to certain death. If it was the latter, it did not work. With a heavy heart burdened with the guilt only a survivor knows, he turned and followed Callahan up the stairs. They locked the gate behind them hoping

to contain the rotting core of the deadly plague before it threatened the entire ship.

In silence, they hurried to tell the captain of their discovery, their search for the missing bodies all but forgotten. Neither man dared put his fears into words, but both knew the plague had already spread throughout the ship and no amount of locked gates would keep them alive until they docked in New York.

Forty-five

Captain Smith was seated at a table in the ostentatious surroundings of the first class saloon. The conversation centred largely on the *Titanic* herself with Guggenheim firing questions at the three White Star men like an excited child while Andrews and Ismay revelled in the attention. They talked in detail about specifications and costs and regaled the industrialist and the delightful Mrs. Grafton with humorous anecdotes about the vessel's design and construction even hinting, for the captain's benefit, about how soon they could be in New York if they lit all the boilers.

Captain Smith noticed Mrs. Grafton followed the conversation with her eyes and laughed at all the right moments but appeared distant, even checking the time on several occasions. He wondered, absentmindedly, why she, still barely out of her wedding dress, had chosen to dine with the well-known philanderer, Guggenheim, as it would not go unnoticed in the tight circles of high society. A scandal would probably only enhance the industrialist's reputation; the same wouldn't be true for the Grafton's. Still, it wasn't his concern what the rich and famous got up to. He had his own problems, not least a potential scandal that could ruin White Star's glowing reputation.

He thought maybe that was what everything came down to, reputation. What would happen to him as captain of the liner where not only people died, but the deceased bodies then

went missing? Perhaps he should have retired when his wife first suggested it. He could be pruning the roses in a cottage garden in Dorset now, not walking the political tightrope of trans-Atlantic steam commerce while searching for an unknown killer.

"The lamb is absolutely divine, don't you agree, Captain?"

Jerked uncomfortably from his private train of thought, he felt slightly embarrassed to find Mrs. Grafton looking at him expectantly. The three other men were still deep in conversation about the price of coal and the effect it was having on the industry and were oblivious to either her question or his confusion.

"I'm so sorry Mrs. Grafton, I was miles away. Please go on."

The attractive socialite gave him an understanding smile and nodded towards his plate. "The lamb," she repeated, "divine."

"It most certainly is, Mrs. Grafton. But one would expect nothing less from the chefs on this, or for that matter, any other White Star vessel." He returned her smile, grateful she did not take umbrage at his brief lapse of manners.

"They are to be congratulated," she raised her wine glass in toast, "as are you, Captain. This is a splendid ship. I'm sure you're very proud of her."

"I am, but also humble enough to know the ship's splendour is down to Mr. Ismay and Mr. Andrews; I cannot take

credit for that." He too raised his glass, and with a twinkle in his eye added, "To the *Titanic*, and all who sail her."

"And to the lamb, that she died not in vain," replied Mrs. Grafton with a polite, but genuine, laugh before taking a generous sip from her glass.

Captain Smith, out of politeness rather than interest, was just about to ask why her husband had chosen not to dine with them when a steward appeared at his side brandishing a folded piece of paper. "From Mr. Moody, sir. He was incredibly insistent on the urgency of this matter."

"My dear, Mrs. Grafton, if you would excuse me for a moment, duty calls." He took the piece of paper and read the note, aware the other men at the table had stopped their discussion and were looking on expectantly. Ignoring them he quietly asked the steward, "Where is Mr. Moody now?"

"He, and Mr. Callahan, are waiting in the pantry, sir." From his calm demeanour, Smith guessed he had not taken the time to read Moody's scribbled note.

"Thank you, that'll be all." The steward left the table as unobtrusively as he had arrived. "Mrs. Grafton. Gentleman. I'm afraid I must attend to a few matters, if you will excuse me?" Captain Smith rose from the table, gesturing for the others to remain seated.

Bruce Ismay eyed the captain suspiciously. He had known him long enough to know when something was amiss, and it was out of character for him to interrupt a meal, especially with

someone as important as Guggenheim. "Is everything as it should be, Captain?"

Captain Smith chose to ignore Ismay's tone, his suggestion being if anything delayed their arrival in New York, he would place the blame squarely on the captain's shoulders.

"Everything is on course as expected," replied Smith with a confident air. "I have a small matter I need to attend to with one of my officers, which, I am afraid, cannot wait." With that, he hurried away before Ismay could ask any further questions. If what he had read in the note was true, then nothing was as it should be.

Captain Smith strode into the pantry. He could feel his anger rising and hoped he misunderstood the note from Officer Moody. One look at his Sixth Officer's ashen face as he hunched over the table sipping tea from a china cup, told him he had understood it perfectly. Smith looked around the small pantry, ensuring nobody else was present. Callahan stood with his back against the wall, just staring at the ground. Neither man acknowledged his arrival.

"How bad is it, Mr. Moody?"

It took Moody a few moments to answer, and then he mumbled, "The worst kind of bad."

The captain, his mood already fractious from the day's events, found his patience wearing thin. The two men were obviously in shock but he had a job to do, and they were professional seaman. It was he who shouldered the responsibility for every man, woman, and child aboard ship and

he needed answers: proper, informative answers. He raised his voice slightly, hoping his impatience didn't come through too strongly in his tone, and repeated the question.

Officer Moody looked him full in the eye, his features dour and emotionless, and said, "They're all dead."

"Who's dead, for God's sake man, make sense!"

"Baines, Davis, the search party in steerage, and probably everybody else down there by now. There are people, no, dead people, a lot of dead people, sir … and they're eating the living."

"Don't be ridiculous, Mr. Moody. How can the dead eat the living? That is simply the most preposterous thing I have ever heard."

Smith's simmering rage threatened to boil over. How could one of his officers believe, let alone report, such supernatural mumbo jumbo? A few people die, granted in circumstances that did not, on face value, appear normal and he had to accept those bodies were misplaced, possibly stolen. But to believe the dead had risen to claim further victims was insane. Mr. Moody must, he thought, be suffering from some form of hysteria brought on, no doubt, by the stress of the job.

"He speaks true." Callahan's voice was quiet, calm, his stare still fixed on a point just in front of his own toes. "We witnessed both Baines and Davis die in the most gruesome of ways, one that, should I live to be a hundred and given what I witnessed, I think that unlikely, will never leave me. The dead just tore them apart before our eyes, a similar fate had already befallen those in the search party. I saw the arm of a friend of

mine hanging from the jaws of a passenger who in turn, was missing his left ear and half his neck. A man would be hard pushed to survive such an injury let alone summon the strength to tear another man's arm from his body." The American finally looked up, his eyes sunken into his sallow complexion. "The devil has designs on this ship, and we can do naught to thwart his advances, and that, sir, is the uncomfortable truth."

The captain looked from his junior officer to the able seaman and back again, weighing the information. The doctor's earlier words about the third victim's bites being human in nature provided some credence to their story, but then, Moody had attended that same meeting. Could that have clouded his judgment, fuelled the hysteria? He decided he needed to see things for himself, especially if, as Callahan believed, the entire ship and the lives of everyone on board were at stake.

Finally, he said, "Will you two gentlemen be so good as to escort me down to steerage so I can see all this for myself."

They looked at each other in silence. Both had a faraway look in their eyes as if reliving the anguish and trauma of their last horrifying jaunt into the depths of the ship. As if by some unspoken bond, both men nodded their acceptance of his request.

"But I'm going to finish my tea first," said Moody, adding chillingly, "No point in leaving it, I doubt I'll be back."

"Come now, Mr. Moody, we will only venture to the dividing gates. What harm could possibly occur?"

The captain hoped his voice sounded as confident and calm as he intended. His unflappable, cool exterior, a trait he had become well renowned for among the sailors who served under him, was in danger of slipping away. The evidence pointed to a phenomenon even half a century of trans-world sea travel couldn't prepare him for, and if there was one thing Captain Edward Smith hated, it was being ill prepared.

Moody continued sipping his tea while Callahan stared uncomfortably at his boots, neither man prepared to offer an answer to the captain's question, all too aware of the harm that could befall them. Moody offered up a silent prayer for a swift and decisive death, one that wouldn't see him rise again in search of human flesh.

Forty-six

Bridget ate little of the lamb, divine as it was. She had little appetite and much on her mind. Her thoughts revolved around Esme, William's body, which still lay stretched across their bed, and the plight of her unborn child. What would become of it if they caught her and tried her for murder? There were so many things that could go wrong with Esme's plan, it seemed unlikely to succeed. But, she told herself, it was their only plan so it had to work, somehow. She could at least go to the gallows secure in the knowledge her child would live free of the evil William Grafton, that in itself was some recompense.

"Mrs. Grafton, perhaps tomorrow I could escort you and your husband on a tour of the bridge?" Bruce Ismay sat across the table, his plate already empty and a stiff-backed steward silently recharging his glass.

"I do not presume to speak for my husband, but I will be sure to tell him of your kind offer, while I myself would be delighted," she said enthusiastically. Bridget could think of nothing that would bore her more than men talking about levers, knobs, and dials, but she needed to make an impression, to preserve the ruse that William was alive and well.

Whatever Mr. Ismay said next, Bridget didn't hear. Seated at a table not twenty feet away were a middle-aged couple and a young woman. The couple were of little consequence to Bridget, it was the young woman who captured her sole

attention, causing her to rudely ignore her dinner companions in favour of staring brazenly at the diners at the other table.

"Is something the matter, Mrs. Grafton?" Guggenheim asked, although Bridget barely heard his question as she continued to stare at Violet in stunned disbelief. She could not believe the sheer audacity of the woman. She knew her husband's below stairs whore was aboard ship, but never expected to see her brazenly dining in first class and wearing one of her dresses in the bargain.

"Mrs. Grafton? Bridget, are you alright, you seem a little pale?" Guggenheim raised his voice, breaking the spell Violet's appearance had cast over her.

Bridget turned her attention back to the rich philanthropist. He wore a concerned expression and had already started to rise from the table, possibly expecting her to faint, or something worse.

"Sorry. Yes, I'm quite all right, just a little tired." She smiled weakly at the gentlemen sitting around the table. "Maybe one of you would be so good to order me a tea, after which I shall retire for the night."

While Guggenheim called a steward and Ismay and Andrews perused the menu in search of pudding, Bridget stole a furtive glance in Violet's direction.

Violet, her attention caught by Guggenheim's raised voice, stared back at her from below the brim of Bridget's own hat. For a moment the two women sat in quiet contemplation, their eyes locked in an unspoken battle of wills. Each daring the

other to reveal their hand, each equally wishing the moment would slip quietly by.

The moment did indeed slip by, but it did not go quietly. Frenzied screams filled the air as the carefree diners became embroiled in a frantic battle for their lives as the minions of Hell, spawned deep in the bowels of the ship and forced upwards in search of sustenance, spewed into the saloon with but one dish on their menu.

Forty-seven

The corridor skirting the two dining saloons was eerily quiet, and Esme's footsteps sounded loud on the exquisitely polished decking. She kept her head down, walking as briskly as she dared towards the huge galley's service entrance, hoping she did not encounter one of the eagle-eyed chefs or worse, Miss Wilson. Particularly while wearing a uniform soaked in the blood of half the ship's medical department. Behind the wall, she heard the muffled hubbub of dinner service, the usual hundred conversations and the constant clatter of cutlery all set against the gentle melodies of a chamber orchestra.

But tonight it sounded different. It was louder, more frantic, chaotic even.

Reaching a discreet set of double doors, Esme paused, her hand resting lightly on the polished brass plate. She gently pushed the door open a few inches. The general hubbub grew louder. She strained to listen, trying to distinguish individual voices above the maelstrom of sounds swirling past her ears, but could not pick anything out clearly. There was nothing to suggest someone might be standing close to the door, so she pushed it a little wider, just enough to slide quietly through before the powerful springs pulled it shut behind her.

The service pantry, as usual at this time of the evening, was empty. Esme, aware she had not taken a single breath since reaching the double doors, let the air escape her lungs, causing a soft moan to roll up from her throat. She darted across the

small room to the doorway through to the main kitchen and peered through the small porthole-like window cut into the door. At the far end of the vast kitchen a few chefs were crowded together but otherwise, the usually busy kitchen was strangely empty.

She pushed open the door. The noise from the dining room grew louder and Esme felt sure she heard individual screams punctuating the general din. Not wanting to draw attention, she strode sedately towards the far end of the kitchen where she hoped to pick up a freshly laundered apron to cover her blood-soaked uniform. Walking past the long trestle table on which the chefs prepared passenger meals before service, she noticed abandoned, partially prepared food scattered across the smooth oak surface. A colander containing boiled potatoes and a saucepan of garden peas sat next to an empty plate and farther down the table a large slab of raw meat, probably lamb going by the evening menu, lay on a large platter. She paused to study the succulent meat, curious about why someone should require their meat served in such a way.

Esme looked towards the few chefs still working, but they had their backs to her, engrossed in their task, so she returned her attention to the table. The meat had gone, leaving a bloody outline on the large gilt-edged platter. While she pondered the possible whereabouts of the lamb, she chewed absentmindedly on the soft, tender steak in her hand while its sweet juices trickled down her chin.

As she raised the raw meat to take a second bite she abruptly realized what she was doing. Her stomach lurched, and she cried out in disgust, throwing the uneaten portion to the floor. She hunched over, spitting the well-chewed meat onto the floor next to the uneaten portion. Even as her digestive system recoiled at the texture and taste of the uncooked food, something deep inside her wanted it. No, the feeling was stronger. She craved it. Something inside Esme craved the juicy, raw cut of dead bovine.

Feeling her stomach twist and contract, she bent forward and hurled a stream of bright, red blood. It splattered on the deck, speckling her shoes with fine ruby droplets. A cold shiver passed through her body bringing a second wave of nausea and leaving her weak and disorientated. Her knees buckled, forcing her to cling defiantly to the table while she waited for the room to stop spinning. Footsteps, originally distant, were now getting louder, getting closer.

She turned her head towards the approaching sound, her neck stiff and painful, each joint popping and creaking with every movement.

Squinting slightly to focus, Esme recognized the chefs, resplendent in their pressed white tunics stained with the fresh blood that still dripped from their gaping jaws. She saw the intense, cold stare of death in their eyes, the mottled skin, and thick, dark tracks crisscrossing their features. But most of all, she saw the severed human leg swinging back-and-forth in the swollen, purple hand of the nearest chef.

She edged away and tried climbing to her feet, but her heels snagged in the dismembered remains of a waiter. His head, torn from his shoulders, lay next to his half-eaten body, a serene look of peaceful acceptance evident on his face as if, at the end, he had welcomed death as the better alternative.

Esme made one last desperate effort to get to her feet, but the chefs quickly closed in on her as she stumbled. Unsteady and disorientated, she practically fell into their waiting arms. The vile smelling creatures pulled her down into their icy grip, their cold hands tearing at her uniform as they prepared her for their main course.

Esme tried screaming for help as she stared into their gaping mouths, drooling with fetid saliva, lips drawn back to reveal bloodstained teeth which threatened to rip into her flesh at any moment. Deep down, she knew help would never come, that this was it. A sharp ripping sound filled the air as one of her assailants pulled a sleeve free from the bodice of her dress, exposing the mottled flesh below. She closed her eyes not wanting to witness the frenzied expressions on her killer's faces as they tore her apart.

Then they stopped.

They simply let go of her, and Esme fell to the floor like a child's unwanted old rag doll. Exhausted, she lay on the rough flooring unable to move, expecting, at any second, a final blow, one terminal slash that would cleave her head from her torso.

But it never came. Instead, the chefs began feasting on the dead waiter's ragged neck stump, pulling at the tender, soft

flesh with their bare hands before eagerly shovelling it into their mouths like excited children with a birthday cake.

Esme started to move. Slowly, inch by inch, so as not to draw the unwanted attentions of the ravenous cooks, she edged away from the headless corpse. Every part of her body hurt, either from the attack or from the fire raging inside her. She gently rolled onto her knees and crawled a few more feet before hauling herself to her feet, using the table for support. She felt dizzy, confused, and had the mother of all headaches, but she was not going to let these bastards beat her, not the dead doctor, not a rotting nurse, and certainly not a bunch of cannibalistic chefs.

She inspected her exposed arm. Her soft, pale skin looked swollen and blotchy. The delicate wispy blue veins replaced by angry raised tracks that started as hair-thin lines in her fingers and grew larger as they travelled up her arm, forming disgusting, thick lesions as they disappeared under the ripped shoulder of her dress. Esme now knew why the dead chefs left her alone. Why they had simply stopped? She understood the burning pain flowing through every organ in her body as though her blood was ablaze, the desire to eat raw meat, and her suddenly slower, clumsier movements.

She had become one of *them.*

They had already beaten her, and she never even knew it. They no longer viewed her as an appetizing *hors d'oeuvre* for them to feast on; her body was in decay, rotting where she stood. Esme wanted to cry but her tears were too thick, too

congealed to flow, and the despairing wail that welled within her chest as the true horror of her condition dawned on her, died in her throat. Without the air rushing from her lungs to vibrate her vocal chords all she managed was a low guttural gurgle.

Esme stood in silent shock for a moment trying to think, trying to apply some reason to her predicament where none existed, but her faculties were failing. The pain in her head had gone, replaced by a dense fog. The images her mind produced became random, disorganized, and horrific featuring mutilated bodies and festering corpses. Among them, her sister, Charlotte, her innards torn from her stomach, laid out like a suckling pig at a banquet.

And all the time she endured the agonizing craving for fresh, raw meat. It consumed her, and it was what finally drove Esme to move. She was ravenous, and her hunger needed to be sated. Slowly, purposefully, she walked towards the double swing doors leading through into the commotion of the first class saloon. Her abilities to think and reason were slowly diminishing while her senses were sharpening, becoming more acute. Her vision had become tunnelled, the peripheries dark and blurred while the images in the centre were sharper and more focused than they ever were in life, and she could hear every individual heartbeat of her prey. She had the urge to hunt, and the ability to kill.

Pushing open both doors, Esme walked through to the saloon. As they swung shut behind her, she surveyed the

opulence of the room and its furnishings with disinterest. It was something she had seen before and tonight she was looking for something special, something warm.

Something alive.

Forty-eight

Bridget stared at her servant in disbelief. The sheer audacity of the below-stairs strumpet had left her momentarily speechless. How dare she presume she could dine in luxury in full view of her lover's wife without getting her comeuppance? A comeuppance Bridget would gladly administer personally. However, as the two women stared at each other in an unspoken battle of wills, the rich and famous clientele around them dissolved into hysteria as the infected masses overran the saloon. They could no longer huddle below decks, the infection had spread rapidly in the cramped conditions of steerage, meaning fresh meat was scarce, and the demand for it was growing.

Guggenheim reacted first. As the first of the undead swarmed towards their table, he used his chair to ward off their advances, thrusting the stout wooden legs into their faces.

"Mrs. Grafton ... Bridget!" The urgency in his voice drew her attention away from Violet's confident, almost arrogant, stare.

"Oh my! What ..." Bridget's words were cut short as Guggenheim physically pulled her from her seat with one arm while pinning a scruffy urchin with bloodstained teeth under his chair with the other.

"Please excuse the overfamiliarity, Mrs. Grafton, but our exclusive little soiree appears to have reached its conclusion."

He used his body to shield her from the approaching horde as he led her briskly from the table, making his way in a roundabout fashion towards the entrance with a terrified looking Andrews and Ismay bringing up the rear.

"That's perfectly alright, Mr. Guggenheim," she paused a moment to catch her breath, then added with a forced smile, "Propriety, at moments like this, seems a trifle redundant."

"Quite so, Mrs. Grafton," he replied, swinging a champagne bottle like a baseball bat into the face of a man in dirty overalls and large hobnailed boots. The bottle struck the assailant square on the chin with a resounding crack but did little more than turn the man's head and dislodge a large flap of skin which stuck to the front of his overalls. He advanced another stride, his lifeless eyes staring past them, and yet, seemingly taking in every move they made. Bridget hiked her skirts up past her knees, gathering the material in a loose bundle at her waist, and swung a low, vicious kick into the side of the man's knee. His leg broke with a sharp crack, sending him to the ground where he continued to scrabble after them, but more in hope than menace.

"Rough childhood," she shrugged in response to the men's astonished expressions. Stealing a glance to where Violet had been sitting, but there was no sign of her. The older couple whom she'd accompanied to dinner were engaged in a violent struggle with one of the plague-carrying invaders. Its teeth were embedded in the man's arm and he and his lady friend were frantically beating it about the head with their napkins. As

Bridget watched, several more of the gruesome attackers joined the fray, swiftly overpowering the helpless couple and dragging them to the floor where they began to dismember them as the two lovers clung to each other in one final embrace. Bridget heard their bloodcurdling cries above the tumultuous melee of screams echoing about the room as the hungry mob tore them apart.

"I fear we must make haste if we are to survive this evening; lingering here will certainly result in our demise." Guggenheim had to shout to make his voice heard, although he preserved his gentlemanly poise.

"I couldn't agree more!" Ismay shouted, ducking away from a rotting crewman before disappearing into the crowd at a sprint.

"The man's a coward," said Guggenheim firmly. "Let's get you to safety, Mrs. Grafton. I have no doubt the captain will have devised a plan to ensure the safety of those passengers not infected by this terrible menace, and if the situation appears lost, he will authorize launching the lifeboats."

With that, he took a firm grip of Bridget's wrist and led her swiftly across the room using his free arm to push and punch anyone or anything that got in their way. He pulled Bridget behind him until they reached the relative calm of the lobby.

"Go to your room, Mrs. Grafton. You will, at least for the time being, be safe there." He turned and strode back towards the pandemonium of the saloon.

"But what about you, Benjamin?" Bridget asked, although, in her heart, she already knew.

"Tell my wife in New York that I have done my best in doing my duty." With that he vanished into the fracas with his fists raised like a prize fighter.

Forty-nine

Violet watched Bridget's emotional farewell with her fellow American from her vantage point on the grand staircase above the lobby. Once she witnessed the look in her mistress's eyes at the dining table, she knew the only way she would ever have William was to remove Bridget from the scene, and it was at that very moment the Devil himself intervened to provide her with the perfect opportunity. As Guggenheim heroically pulled Bridget from her seat, Violet and her companions, Sir Bernard and Mrs. Black, were attacked by the deranged hobbledehoy from below deck. Sir Bernard had, after a firm shove in the middle of his back from Violet, taken the brunt of the assault, providing her with the time she needed to slip away, abandoning her new friends to their violent deaths.

As Bridget hurried across the lobby, intent on following Guggenheim's advice and locking herself in her suite, her late husband's lover darted, unseen, up the last few stairs. She slipped quietly into a doorway, planning to take advantage of the melee downstairs to finally rid her life of William's undeserving wife.

Bridget climbed the stairs steadily, but with little haste. It was getting late and the pregnancy was beginning to tell on her. She felt tired, her back ached, and her legs felt weak, leaving her to pull herself up each step with the help of the expertly crafted bannister rail. She kept looking behind her, expecting to see one of those ghastly creatures nimbly climbing the stairs in

pursuit, but they were too busy feasting on the diners too slow to escape. A young couple broke from the doorway and sprinted across the lobby, the gentleman almost dragging the woman off her feet, such was his urgency to escape. They ran past her without acknowledgment; it had become every man for himself.

Bridget stepped into the plush corridor of A Deck and took a moment to gather herself, hand on the small of her back, deep breaths in through her nose. With startling realization, she remembered William's body still lay on the bed in her suite's bedchamber. But what if he was no longer dead? What if he were one of those undead demons from Hell, waiting for her return? She stood in the corridor looking first one way, then the other, suddenly feeling very alone and frightened, unsure of what to do.

A movement to her left caught her eye but before she could react, strong feminine hands pushed her backward towards the bannister and the long drop beyond. She fought back frantically, but her attacker, with the element of surprise, had already gained the ascendancy. The bannister pushed against the small of her back and she began to rock backward, her head swinging out over the deadly void, one hand clutching at the bannister the other raking her assailant's face and hair desperately trying to fend them off.

Bridget smelt familiar perfume, her perfume; the flowery scent of opium, a smell she now realized had long lingered about William. She twisted her fingers into the woman's hair,

pulling it free from the pins holding it in place under the wide-brimmed hat, and yanked hard unveiling Violet's face.

"William's mine, you stuck up cow!" Violet's words came out as a high-pitched screech as Bridget frantically clung to her hair to stop herself toppling to her death.

"Too fucking late, you bitch. He's already dead!" Bridget spat in her adversary's face, a final defiant gesture as she rocked backward uncontrollably, her feet lifting from the floor as her own body weight began to tip her over the rail.

Violet screamed, her face just inches from Bridget's. It was not the ecstatic cry of victory as her nemesis fell to her death, but a cry of shock and pain as Esme's teeth clamped down on her unprotected throat. Esme's incisors ripped a large hole, tearing through the vital veins and arteries of the young woman's neck. Blood sprayed through Violet's fingers as she frantically tried to stem the flow, her attempts to push her lover's wife to her death forgotten.

Bridget felt a firm hand pull her back from the brink of death and found herself staring into Esme's lifeless eyes. Her face had become pale, almost gangrenous, and the fire that once burned so bright in her eyes was gone, replaced by a vacant stare. The telltale black web-like rash had spread across her face; it grew from dark trunks at her neck and gave her bloodstained lips a deep purple tinge. Her expression was one of sadness as she stood before her still living friend, one hand still holding Violet's body which twitched sporadically as her life slowly ebbed away through her trembling fingers.

The fear held Bridget motionless. These abominations were tearing people apart to gorge on their innards in the saloon below, and Esme herself, if she could still be called by a Christian name, had so nonchalantly and brutally dispatched Violet. Bridget believed she was next. That this foul ghoul with the lifeless features of the once vibrant chambermaid would, at any moment, slay her like a deer before feasting on her young succulent flesh.

Esme reached towards Bridget's face. The American heiress closed her eyes, mumbling The Lord's Prayer through quivering lips, the smell of death and decay overpowering her senses as icy fingers caressed her cheek. Helpless, sheer terror gripping her heart and twisting her stomach, Bridget waited for the end. Praying it would be quick and final, she didn't want to become one of them!

Then the fingers fell away from her face. She flinched, unsure what to expect. The harsh sound of material ripping briefly filled the air. Bridget cautiously opened her eyes to see Esme sink her teeth into Violet's exposed breast, pulling the soft, milky white skin apart to leave a deep gash from which she continued to feed.

Realizing some flicker of humanity within the living carcass now devouring her husband's lover still recognized their friendship enough to not only spare, but actually save her life, Bridget gingerly edged away. She hurried down the corridor away from the screams of terror and death reverberating up the

staircase and away from the sickening sound of Esme gnawing and slurping on her kill.

Rounding the corner, Bridget took a final look back and whispered a silent *'thank you'* to her loyal friend as Esme pulled Violet's intestines from her open abdomen like a magician pulling knotted scarves from a top hat.

Fifty

Captain Smith was about to lead Callahan and Moody, who had reluctantly abandoned his tea, down towards steerage in search of the undead hoards that killed the master-at-arms, and the other members of the search party, when the undead hoards came searching for them. The infected corpses that already swarmed the lower decks had climbed into the first and second class dining saloons before the three men even made it to the stairwell.

But Captain Smith had seen enough to know the lives of everyone aboard his ship were in grave danger. "Moody, take Callahan and close as many bulkhead doors as you can. It may buy us some time. Then get up on deck." He paused, unwilling to articulate the inconceivable, before finally adding with a weary sigh, "It may become necessary to abandon ship."

"Aye, aye, sir!" Moody hurried away with Callahan beside him as the captain turned and headed for the bridge.

Once out of the Captain's earshot, it was Callahan who voiced concerns at the plan. "There is little we can do to slow them now, they've already broken through to D Deck and there are no bulkheads above the waterline that we can close. Those creatures will have free roam about the upper decks. Our only chance is to get everyone to the upper deck and defend the lifeboats."

Officer Moody assessed the situation. Callahan was right. With the gates separating steerage from the upper decks already breached, there was little that could be done.

"Let's close all doors leading to access to the lower decks. At least it will force them to come up via the dining saloons and the grand staircase, creating a funnel. Maybe it will slow them down?"

Callahan sensed the question was rhetorical but felt the need to mumble an unconvincing, "Maybe." He knew, as well as Officer Moody, the situation was hopeless. There were too many people huddled in steerage for the infection not to have spread, and with more either becoming infected or dying every minute, the odds were heavily in the pitiful creatures' favour. He looked Officer Moody in the eye and could see the unspoken fear. They were both young men with their whole lives ahead of them, yet deep down, they knew those lives would only number a few more hours.

"Sir. If I, you know, turn into one of those … things. Will you end my misery?"

"I trust you'll do the same for me," replied Moody. It was a statement of fact, not a question. They briefly shook hands, each secretly drawing strength from their comradeship. They were entrusting each other with something far more important than their lives—they were entrusting each other with their deaths.

The two men hurried to complete their task, closing the two doors that gave access for the catering staff to the crew

quarter's three decks below. As they moved down the passageway towards the larger passenger doors, they were confronted by a small group of the infected feeding on a lifeless body in what remained of an evening suit. Moody signalled to Callahan for them to retrace their steps and try the next passage. That too was blocked, although the infected souls were not lucky enough to have found food and the sight of fresh meat had them scurrying after the two crewmen with surprising agility.

"I think," said Moody as they scrambled back the way they'd come, "we can safely assume this deck lost and delaying will only lead us into trouble."

"I wholeheartedly agree with your assessment of the situation, Mr. Moody." Callahan was hot on his superior's heels as they headed towards the second class area of the ship. "We can access the boat deck from the rear deck just for'ard of the rear mast."

The American's breath was coming in short gasps as they sprinted past the second class dining saloon, his voice raised to make himself heard above the clamour coming from within.

Crashing through a set of swing doors, the two men barrelled into a shuffling corpse, knocking it from its feet. The ensuing tangle of limbs brought Callahan tumbling to his knees. He powered on, pushing himself forward using his momentum to stay clear of the creatures grappling hands and gaping maw, as Moody hauled him unceremoniously to his feet by his collar.

"Keep fuckin' moving!" yelled Moody.

Able seaman Callahan, never one to disobey orders, kept fuckin' moving; staggering upright, he followed the sixth officer towards the outer door and fresh air. They hadn't noticed it until then, but the air inside the ship's mid-decks had turned stale, rancid even. The odour of decay filled their nostrils with each breath they took and the taste of death lined their throats with every laboured gasp.

Fifty-one

As he strode authoritatively onto the bridge, Captain Smith was also aware of the prevailing stench of death. He pulled the door shut behind him, trying to block it out, but it clung to every fibre of his smartly pressed uniform and lingered in the air around him.

"Mr. Murdoch," he addressed the officer on watch. "As you're aware, we have a medical crisis on board that has already claimed the lives of many of the ship's compliment and a far larger number of passengers."

"Aye, sir," Murdoch's expression remained professionally impassive.

"I'm of the opinion this plague should not reach New York. I have, therefore, ordered Mr. Moody to secure the boat deck for the eventual evacuation of survivors." He moved to the window and stared out into the darkness, lost, for a moment, in thoughts of the retirement he would never get to enjoy with his precious Eleanor.

"Sir?" Murdoch moved to stand at the captain's elbow, "Am I to understand you propose to abandon ship in the hope of isolating the infected on board?"

"No, William." Smith spoke quietly, preferring to address his friend informally, the weight of his decision lying heavy on his heart. "I propose to sink this unsinkable vessel to prevent this plague ever rearing its ugly head again. To simply abandon her would inevitably lead to rescue ships or salvage vessels

becoming infected, leading to more unnecessary deaths and the plague's onward transmission. I cannot be responsible for that."

After a few moments contemplating the captain's words, Murdoch turned away.

"Please set a course forty degrees starboard."

"Forty degrees. Starboard. Aye, aye, sir." The order relayed without question and a moment later the huge vessel gradually began to swing north, heading into the northern route's treacherous ice flows.

"Speed twenty-two knots."

"Speed twenty-two knots," confirmed the helmsman.

Captain Smith inspected his pocket watch. The hands ticked towards 11:20. With a weak smile, he addressed the first officer. "Thank you, Mr. Murdoch. I shall be in my cabin."

His voice trailed off as if he were going to say more, but thought better of it. After a brief moment, where the two experienced sailors looked at each other with knowing looks, he strode confidently from the bridge.

Once in his cabin, Captain Smith removed his officer's peaked cap and sat with his head in his hands. This was not how he envisioned his glorious career ending: sinking his own ship and sending hundreds of innocent people to their deaths at the bottom of the unforgiving ocean, but that's what it had come to. His only hope was some people would survive and history would show his actions, and those of his crew, to be just. He didn't want to be a hero, but he could not bear the thought of

Eleanor and the family believing he made a fatal mistake, or worse, went insane and tried to murder everyone on board.

At 11:35 Captain Edward John Smith wrote a brief note in his personal journal before making a detailed report of his orders to Mr. Murdoch. He was just adding his initials when the vessel swung hard to starboard. Several quiet seconds passed then the largest ship ever to set sail began juddering; a strange and distant groaning sound accompanied the tremors as they passed through the massive steel hull. This lasted all of ten seconds, but to those who knew what it meant, it felt like a lifetime. When it finally stopped, it left a chilling silence in its wake that would haunt the survivors in the darkest hours of the night for the rest of their lives.

Fifty-two

Frederick Ives, shovelling coal in boiler room six, heard the creaking groan as the massive wall of ice scraped the length of the *Titanic*'s side. The massive rivets holding the hull plates together popped like champagne corks as the sheer pressure of the ice buckled the metal. He looked up in time to see the double skinned wall above his head ripped asunder. He didn't even have time to flinch as the mighty wall of water cascaded in. It plucked him from his feet and carried him tumbling and somersaulting in its icy wave, until barely a second later it slammed him mercilessly into a bulkhead, the force of the water crushing the life from his broken body in an instant.

Frederick was the first victim of the ship's collision with the iceberg, but the rest of the crew working in boiler room six swiftly joined him. Those who survived the initial surge of water did not have time to escape through one of the bulkhead doors such was the force of the water and the speed at which the room flooded.

Death savagely squashed Frederick's soul from his body before the young stoker even understood his time was up. Others were not so lucky. Harry Blackman, working on the far side of the room, was denied a quick and painless death. Instead, he suffered the horrifying experience of drowning. He frantically fought against the tumultuous torrents of churning seawater, only to find the doors to the adjoining compartments shut. Unable to hold his breath any longer, he inhaled. Water

rushed into his lungs, its coldness shocking his respiratory system, causing him to choke. He frantically clawed at the darkness knowing death was just a heartbeat away. Panicked spasms racked Harry's body until finally, his suffering was over, his lifeless body floating silently in the darkness, suspended for eternity in an icy tomb.

Back on the bridge, unaware of the damage caused below the waterline, Murdoch issued well-drilled orders. "Full stop. Close bulkhead doors!" Then after a brief hesitation added, "Belay that. Bulkhead doors to remain open."

He repeated the order for the benefit of the helmsman. If they were to sink the unsinkable *Titanic* they would need to allow the seawater free access to as many compartments as it could flood. He offered up a silent prayer for the men down in engineering who would drown as a result of his order. It was an order he would have to live with for the rest of his mercifully short life. He thought it fitting he would be joining those brave men before the night was out.

As he prayed, Murdoch watched as the massive wall of ice, towering a hundred feet from the water, continued to slide slowly, almost majestically past the ship. Large chunks of ice, dislodged by the collision, rained down on the ship's deck and crashed into the ship's superstructure like massive cannonballs.

"Report please, Mr. Murdoch?" Captain Smith's commanding figure arrived on the bridge.

"We struck an iceberg, starboard side. Engines stopped. Bulkhead doors remaining open, sir," Murdoch replied without the slightest hint of alarm in his voice.

"Damage?" Smith asked, staring through the windows at the bows, expecting to see the damage for himself, but darkness enveloped the forward half of the vessel.

"Unknown at present, sir. Suggest we sound the ship." Murdoch's thoughts immediately turned to assembling an inspection party to ascertain the damage caused to the hull by the collision, but the captain's reply stopped him.

"No, Mr. Murdoch, that won't be necessary. We've lost too many good men to this damned plague to send any more to their deaths. Let's concentrate on assembling the survivors on deck and launching the lifeboats. With luck, she will sink before the night is out."

"Aye, aye, sir." Murdoch picked up the phone connecting him to the helm. "Steady as she goes, quartermaster. Preparing to launch lifeboats."

He listened for the reply then replaced the receiver with slow deliberation. As an officer, he knew his responsibilities were to the passengers; the old and chivalrous adage of women and children first would mean there would be no place in the lifeboats for him. Stoically, he accepted the simple truth that he had undoubtedly seen his last sunrise.

Fifty-three

In the melee and confusion of the dining saloon, where hungry, infected immigrants and the overfed, unsullied elite fought one another for survival, they barely noticed the collision. The clean, metallic smell of fresh blood mixed with the rotting stench of death and decay to produce a piquancy that chafed the throat and turned the stomach of those lucky enough to still feel repulsed by such things. Many had succumbed to the hoard, some dying in a pool of their own blood, either physically unable or not quick-witted enough to escape. Some stayed their ground, believing their social standing alone would be enough to secure their safety: that these rabid animals, driven insane by bloodlust, would listen to reason if delivered in a courteous but firm tone.

Benjamin Guggenheim was under no such illusion. He and a few other gentlemen who shared his noble, humanitarian attitude were taking the fight to the diseased, intending to establish safe passage for as many ladies as could be rescued. Guggenheim himself was in the centre of the fray, brandishing a bottle of VSOP Cognac, the contents of which he drank straight from the bottle as he punched and kicked his way across the room. Their positive approach had taken the infected by surprise, although significantly outnumbered, they had already furnished aid to several damsels in distress and incapacitated, at least for a short while, several of the inhuman beings.

Guggenheim struck one of the creatures so violently about the head with a broken chair leg he heard the skull break away from the neck. The creature's decayed flesh sheared away as the head, teeth bared in expectation, bounced across a nearby table. Guggenheim put his foot in the bloody remains of the poor soul's dinner and looked down to see the charlatan, Lord Bernard's death-mask face looking up, wide-eyed and leering. His pale hand still clasped Katherine Black's hand to his empty chest cavity, their fingers entwined; her arm severed at the elbow, her disembowelled body lay a few yards away. A young boy of about eight scavenged her remains for any morsel of meat overlooked by those who'd torn the rich widow apart. With a tear in his eye, the impeccably dressed American took a few steps, taking care not to slip in Bernard's remains, and swung the chair leg like a major league hitter, dispatching the child to a more peaceful death than he had so far experienced.

As the terrified diners fought for their lives against increasingly overwhelming odds, three members of the string quartet continued to play a selection of hymns while the fourth, the cellist, slumped in his seat. A well-known American vaudeville singer, her long dress hiked up past her knees, sat astride his legs ripping the flesh from his face with her teeth. A plump, middle-aged woman screamed hysterically as she witnessed the once attractive soprano stuff one of the cellist's eyeballs into her mouth. Thick, clear fluid ran down her chin as the eyeball burst open with a popping crunch.

The plump woman stopped screaming and just stared at the ceiling vacantly as Esme, fresh from slaying Violet, broke her neck with one violent twist. She let the plump corpse fall to the floor among the abandoned handbags, gentlemen's scarves, and body parts now littering the expensive Axminster carpet, before she began to feed on the more choice cuts of meat. It took her a few moments to tear through the subcutaneous fat and locate the oversized liver, but the exquisite taste of the fatty organ made it all worthwhile.

The darkly lined and mottled corpse that, until a few hours ago, had been the bright and engaging maid, Esme Jackson, took her fill of the open platter of warm meat on offer. The vile, blood-soaked monster hunched over the dead woman's ample remains no longer bore any resemblance to the vivacious young woman who had turned many a young man's head as she pulled pints in the Belvedere Arms. All traces of her humanity were consumed by the plague that relentlessly ate away at her rotting flesh. When the food supply ran out, she would no longer be able to replenish what it consumed, and she too would die. Although for Esme, and those like her, death would come as a blessed relief.

But she had one more score to settle. A score felt so deep it left a mark on her soul, a mark that only Miss Wilson could expunge. Leaving the empty carcass for the scavengers, Esme staggered to her feet and headed purposefully towards Miss Wilson's office.

Pandora, her head tilted to one side, watched Esme weave her way through the pandemonium of the saloon from her vantage point on top of the grand piano. Having sniffed the air, searching for signs of danger, she joined the other scavengers stripping the rich, fatty meat from the bones of Esme's kill.

Fifty-four

A small group of passengers cowered in the lifeboat nearest to Moody. They were shouting at him and the few other crew members he had assembled on the boat deck, pleading with them to lower the boat into the still, dark water below. A few of the infected had already broken out onto the promenade, lured by the scent of fresh meat, and were steadily making their way towards his inadequate band of defenders gathered around the lifeboat's davit.

"There's only a few of them. Don't panic and make your shots count."

Moody was thankful for the revolvers issued, at the captain's orders, from the safe in the master-at-arms' office. Not that the order had come in time to save him or the rest of his search party, but it gave the surviving crewmen a fighting chance of defending the boat deck long enough for help to arrive.

A fresh-faced able seaman in front of him raised his weapon. With shaking hands, he pointed it in the general direction of the nearest plague-carrier, a tall, lanky woman with what looked like a bundle of rags clutched to her chest. He paused, staring at the advancing woman with pain and indecision in his eyes; he had not come to sea to shoot women, even if they were already dead.

"For God's sake, shoot her, boy!" The shout came from one of the passengers huddled behind the defensive semi-circle formed by the crew.

"I … I can't. It ain't right to go shooting people." The able seaman's voice was breaking under the strain as two large tears raced down his smooth cheeks. The woman with the bundle was only a few yards away, her eyes just dark, lifeless voids below her high forehead. The foul reek of death surrounded her like an invisible shroud.

"Move aside!" Callahan stepped up next to him, his arm extended towards the approaching corpse. A loud gunshot filled the air, and the creature toppled over backwards, a large hole in the back of its head. A cloud of white smoke hung in the air, and for a while, the distinct smell of cordite proved a pleasant alternative to the smell of rotting decay that had become so prevalent in such a short period of time.

The bundle the dead woman carried rolled free from her grasp as her body slumped to the deck, the rags unravelling enough to reveal the mangled remains of a baby. The woman, or someone else, had already taken several large bites out of the tiny body and ripped one arm out of the shoulder socket like they were pulling a succulent drumstick from the Sunday roast.

"Oh, sweet Jesus," muttered Callahan as he looked down at the child's remains. The young able seaman gagged violently and rushed to the ship's side, barely reaching it before his stomach turned inside out, hurling its contents into the sea

below. Several women in the lifeboat, able to see what had just occurred, started screaming, their delicate dispositions already frayed far beyond the norm.

"I say, this is most distressing." The well-spoken male voice came from the lifeboat. "I order you to lower this lifeboat this instant. I have some important friends at White Star, and I can assure you I'll see to it you never work for them again."

Moody looked at the man with contempt. "I do not expect to live beyond tonight. If the undead don't take me, the sea will. So, you see, I'm not worried by your pompous threats. He lifted his revolver, pointing it at the man huddled among the women in the lifeboat. "Now if you'd be so good to vacate your seat and make room for a lady, I would be most appreciative."

The man huddled lower in his seat, the bravado of a moment ago, gone. He stared back at the gun in Moody's hand, his eyes wide with fear. Moody didn't know if the man was more scared of the gun or the thought of staying on board the ship with the insane victims of a plague that rots the flesh from your bones as you walk. And, truth be told, he didn't much care. His instructions were to secure the lifeboats; women and children first.

Officer Moody pulled the hammer back with his thumb and hoped he looked like he knew what he was doing. He had never even fired a gun before and certainly never pointed one at someone in anger.

"Don't make me repeat my request, sir." The last word stuck painfully in his craw but his hand remained steady, the barrel pointing at the petrified man's exposed head.

"If I give up my seat in this boat then I'm agreeing to die, you pretty much said so yourself." The man's gaze flicked nervously between the revolver's cold steal and Moody's steely cold eyes.

"And if you don't, I'll shoot you." Moody's calm tone belied his anguish. Inside, the responsibility of his decision wracked him with guilt, but he stood resolutely behind it. "Not much of a choice I'm afraid, but that's where we are."

Another shot roared from Callahan's weapon, the sound reverberating in the cold night air, the smoke drifting down the promenade like a ghostly apparition. A few yards away another passenger, his darkly lined skin peeling away from his face exposing a subcutaneous maze of muscles and tendons, dropped to the floor; a clean circular hole in the centre of his wide forehead.

"Just shoot the motherfucker in his smug face and have done with it."

Callahan expertly flicked open the chamber of his revolver and inserted two bullets he fished from the pocket of his massive overcoat. Then, with a flick of his wrist, Callahan clicked the drum back into place, quickly scanning the promenade for nearby threats. He only lowered the gun when he was satisfied their position was, for the time being at least, secure.

"One last chance before I let my impatient friend here shoot you in the leg and leave you at the mercy of those creatures." Moody nodded towards a small group of the infected lurking around an open doorway close to their position. "I'm sure you would prefer to take your chances on your own terms?"

After a few moments of indecision, the man stood up and began to climb unsteadily from the lifeboat. A woman Moody assumed to be his wife began crying hysterically, her thin hands clutching at his leg, preventing him from leaving. He kissed her on the cheek then firmly pushed her away, deliberately not making eye contact as he swung his leg over the gunwale and jumped down onto the *Titanic*'s slippery deck.

"I'm entrusting my wife's safety to your hands. Please see that she gets off this cursed ship before anything evil can befall her." Without a second glance, he set off up the promenade in the opposite direction to the group of infected passengers. "I think," he shouted in a proud, strong voice, "I might like a drink and perhaps a fine cigar." With that, he disappeared into the gloom, leaving his wife crying uncontrollably on the shoulder of the stout mature woman squashed into the seat next to her who, in turn, valiantly tried to console her.

Moody turned to the ashen-faced able seaman who still clung to the railing, the front of his company issue overcoat splattered with his own vomit. "You are no bloody use to me here. Go to the bridge and inform the captain we have secured the lifeboats, but we won't be able to hold them for long. Take your revolver and bloody use it, on yourself, if you have to. Now hurry!" He watched as the frightened young man scampered away like an errand boy with a bright new penny.

"Good luck lad," he muttered under his breath before turning his attention to the white tunic emerging from the darkness. A steward jostled a small gaggle of women towards the protective cordon as Callahan watched them suspiciously, revolver at the ready.

"Good evening, sir," he said in a soft Scottish accent, addressing Moody. "Mr. Guggenheim directed me to escort these ladies to the lifeboats as the saloon, and indeed much of the ship, is no longer a safe refuge."

"Well done." Moody couldn't remember the steward's name so he quickly added, "Will there be more joining us?"

"Mr. Guggenheim and some of the men are holding those …" He paused, searching for the right word but evidently didn't find it, "things at bay; although, I doubt they will be able to hold out much longer, they have already suffered several losses." He delivered this news in the same measured tone he informed diners of the choice of soup of the day.

"They are protecting several ladies whom I shall return with shortly, God willing." Having safely delivered his charges into Moody's protection, he turned on his heel and walked briskly back in the direction from which he had come, leaving Moody and his men to help the new arrivals into the nearest lifeboat.

Fifty-five

Bridget felt numb. She cried when she first returned to the suite, but now there were no more tears to shed. Esme, or what remained of her, had undoubtedly saved her life earlier that evening, and not for the first time. Bridget couldn't help but wonder what would have become of her had not the beautiful young chambermaid, with a stubborn attitude and a dubious past, extended her the hand of friendship. What if she had not recognized a kindred spirit, separated only by their social position?

William's body still sprawled across the bed in the other room. It was the first thing she had done on her return, checked to make sure the bastard had stayed dead. She had prodded him several times, the last one in his left ear, with the pointed end of her parasol. She understood over the last few hours the dead had, quite literally, developed a habit of coming back to bite you. Dead or alive, or somewhere in between, she wasn't going to allow William to wreak his revenge on her, especially if it meant spending her final hours dining on human offal.

Then she had broken down and cried. She cried tears of fear for herself and her unborn child. She shed tears in grief for her dead friend Esme and finally, tears of relief when she comprehended that in all the slaughter and carnage on the ship, the unfortunate death of her husband would, like as not, go unpunished.

After her tears were spent, she went numb. She felt drained and emotionally exhausted.

Bridget sat staring at nothing, thinking of nothing. Lost in the frailty of her own existence, unaware of the dangers she still had to face if she were to escape with her life. The ship, fatally holed below the waterline, had begun sinking bows first into the freezing waters of the North Atlantic, the angle of the deck steadily increasing as more and more water flooded into the ship's forward compartments.

An intense banging on her cabin door roused her from her stupor. Fear gripped her heart, constricting her chest. She quickly searched for something to defend herself with but could only find her flimsy parasol. By then the banging had stopped. Bridget, parasol poised, approached the door. A sudden and loud knock forced her heart up into her mouth.

"Sir, madame. Please vacate your suite and make your way to the boat deck. Captain's orders." The voice was firm and friendly. Cautiously, Bridget opened the door, parasol pointing menacingly at the steward standing in the hallway outside. "I'm ordered to tell you that, for your own safety, you are to come with me to the boat deck."

"Are we sinking?" Bridget surprised even herself with her matter-of-fact tone.

"I'm not sure, madame. My orders are simply to escort passengers to the lifeboats where other crew members will be there to help you." He looked uneasy as he spoke, shifting his weight from foot to foot.

"I'll get my overcoat and be right out." Bridget closed the door as the steward moved down the corridor knocking on the other doors. When she returned, a small crowd had gathered a few doors away and were loudly discussing the evening's events. The ship listing to starboard and sat bow down in the water, the general consensus among the group was that the great unsinkable *Titanic* was, in fact, sinking. Many were also voicing their concerns about the hordes of flesh eating monsters roaming the ship in search of food. News of the hordes' arrival in the dining saloons and other parts of the ship had obviously spread rapidly, several reported hearing gunshots. With all this occurring at once people were understandably beginning to panic, and Bridget Grafton wasn't immune to the feeling of unease rippling through the small crowd.

The steward rushed towards them, a couple of elderly ladies, struggling to keep up with his pace, trailed in his wake. "Is that everyone from your cabin, Mrs. Grafton?"

"Yes, Captain Grafton joined Mr. Guggenheim for after dinner drinks and has not yet returned." The lie rolled comfortably off her tongue, a few of the other passengers looked at her awkwardly, wondering whether she was aware of the hordes rampaging through the saloon, killing everyone in their path. Bridget struggled to remain impassive as if unaware of the dangers facing her husband while her insides knotted up with guilt and fear.

The steward looked nervously at the other passengers for a few seconds, debating, no doubt, on whether to tell her of the evening's events. Then, obviously thinking better of it, began hurriedly directing the group towards the stairway taking them up and finally out onto the upper deck.

Bridget gave a soft, relieved sigh and smiled pleasantly at the two old ladies, offering the most infirm looking one her arm for support. Without looking back, she followed her companions towards what she hoped would be safety, leaving her dead husband's body to either be tragically lost in the ship's wreck or, less tragically, eaten by the rotting corpse of a working class immigrant. An ironically fitting end, she thought, for such an arrogant, bullying snob.

Fifty-six

Esme stared down at the torn and broken body of Miss Wilson with cold, lifeless eyes. The woman who had made the last few days of Esme's life a living hell had hidden in her office just off the main pantry. She had pleaded for her life, grovelling in much the same way she had made so many young women grovel for their jobs throughout her years as a head housekeeper for the White Star Line.

Her death had not been quick, Esme made sure of it. Miss Wilson died a slow and painful death as the chambermaid she had so despised in life broke bone after brittle bone in her aging body until she passed out from a combination of pain and blood loss. After that, Esme dragged the old woman's unconscious body from the safe confines of the office by her straggly, grey hair, before tossing her into a frenzied crowd of the hungry Hell hoard. She watched as they tore the thin, misshapen limbs from the Old Dragon's frail torso, finally sending her to the death she so richly deserved.

Then, driven by the instinct to feed, Esme followed the scent of warm blood, her senses picking up the rhythmic beat of life as she moved through the pantry and up the stairs towards the first class suites and the boat deck beyond.

Captain Smith stood on the near silent bridge looking out at the ocean that had been his life for so long. The dark expanse of water stretched to the horizon where it merged with the sky

that arched high above them. It was a cloudless night and the stars shone brightly, their light reflected in the water below.

The ship's bows were already submerged, the larger waves breaking against the superstructure which would ordinarily perch high above the waterline, but now threatened to topple forward with each wave. The ship would not be afloat much longer; Smith felt it in his old bones. He just prayed when the time came she would carry every last infected soul to the ocean floor.

"Sir?" He hadn't heard the fresh-faced sailor approach, but he took a moment to study his features. He appeared so young, a reminder of his responsibilities. A reminder of when he was a fresh-faced young able seaman, with his whole life ahead of him.

"Well? Do you have bad news for me?" He arched his eyebrow expectantly and tried to offer the youth an optimistic smile.

"I'm afraid I do, sir. Mr. Moody has secured the lifeboats but doesn't expect to hold them for long. The people, sir, they look dead, yet they still walk. They are getting closer to the lifeboats with every passing minute." As if to punctuate his point several distant gunshots disturbed the bridge's almost tranquil peace.

The captain's gaze returned to the darkness beyond the observation window, aware the eyes of every crewman on the bridge were on him.

"Gentlemen, Hell's demonic pirates may take this ship from us, but not as a luxurious flagship, but as their grave. I will, of course, remain on this bridge until the sea claims my soul. I thank you for your loyalty and service and discharge you from your duty." As he spoke, Smith looked into the face of each man in turn. Not one looked away. To the young seaman, he added, "I suggest you hasten to secure a berth on a lifeboat."

The able seaman replied with conviction, his voice strong. "I am neither a woman nor a child, sir, and therefore I do not have a berth on a lifeboat. However, I believe Mr. Moody could use an extra pair of hands to help launch those lifeboats."

Captain Smith nodded and with a feeling of immense pride, not just in that one able young man but his entire crew, saluted the young man so willing to accept his own death so others may live.

"Good luck, my boy." With the captain's best wishes ringing in his ears, the sailor hurried away to assist in the battle to launch the lifeboats.

Six decks below, Chief Engineer Bell and his men were fighting the same battle. Unaware of the extent of the chaos in the rest of the ship, they were fighting to keep her afloat long enough to allow rescue. Many stood waist deep in the freezing water still roaring through the gaping hole in the ship's hull. They crewed pumps and ran hoses trying to delay the inevitable while keeping the generators, providing vital electric light and power to the rest of the ship, running.

Steadily, the rapidly rising water pushed the survivors back, claiming compartment after compartment. With each lost compartment, with each door they closed, more men were trapped, subjected to the terrifying realization they were going to drown, leaving no corpse to be pulled from the savage sea, no body for their loved ones to bury.

Finally, aware their titanic struggle was in vain, Bell discharged his men from their duty. But by then, both he and his men knew any chance of salvation had passed, their escape routes already claimed by the rising water. Even if they could climb up through the dark decks without falling victim to the marauding bands of flesh-hungry killers, they would only find the lifeboats gone, filled with the women and children and, no doubt, the wealthy and titled. So they stayed at their post, aware it was for naught, but resolved to die a proud death with their shipmates at their side.

Fifty-seven

Bridget followed the small band of survivors down the dimly lit corridor. The lights were beginning to fail, some sections of the ship were already in darkness, and the temperature was dropping. The heating had failed, which Bridget surmised, meant the ship's boilers had failed, and if that was due to the collision allowing seawater to extinguish the furnace, then surely it was only a matter of time before the *Titanic* sank. She tried to cajole the old lady using her arm for support to move faster, urging her on with calm reassurance while her own fear danced a rousing polka in her chest. Having no idea how long it would take for a vessel this size to sink, she was in no mood to tarry.

The rest of the group were already some yards ahead, and Bridget worried they would become separated, losing their way in the dark. This would make them easy prey to the first slavering creature they encountered. She pulled on her charge's arm, urging her onwards with a reassuring smile, but in her anxiety to leave the shadowy corridor behind, she used too much force. The old woman stumbled and, for a precious moment, time stopped as she struggled to regain her footing, then she slumped forward as if propelled by some invisible force, dragging Bridget down with her.

The two of them crashed to the floor. Bridget, using her free arm to brace her fall, still felt the force of the impact. She heard a loud crack and in the brief moment of surreal silence that followed, she instinctively knew what had happened. Then, the old lady's anguished screams of pain broke the silence, confirming her fears.

Bridget pushed herself up onto her knees and looked down at the woman's horribly bent leg. Her long skirt covered the actual break but the right foot, protruding from under the hem, pointed out at a sickeningly unnatural angle, her toes pointing towards the ceiling while she still lay face down.

"Help me!" The woman pleaded between screams as Bridget carefully climbed to her feet, pushing the woman's desperate, imploring hands away. She knew the old lady's chance of escaping had been dealt a serious blow and to leave her meant condemning her to death, but she could not help her. She had to think of herself and her unborn child.

"I can't." Bridget turned away, unable to look her in the eye.

The woman's traveling companion bustled past Bridget, a Bible already open in her hand. "You go on, my child. Hurry! Or else they will leave without you. Time is of the essence."

Bridget set off down the corridor in pursuit of the steward and the line of survivors following him without a backward glance. From behind her, she heard the hysterical sobs of the injured woman, then they were drowned out by her companion's strong voice reading a passage from the Bible as she sat with her friend to await their fate.

Bridget hurried on, taking the stairs up to the boat deck two at a time, her breathing becoming deeper and more

laboured with each stride. Her back, thighs, and calves felt like someone had taken an iron bar to them. She offered up a silent 'Thank you' to William. He had inflicted more pain on her than this, more torture and mental suffering than any one person should ever experience and it had strengthened her body; strengthened her resolve. She kept moving, digging into that resolve, determined to reach the lifeboats. She had not come this far only to fail now. If Bridget Grafton was nothing else, she was a survivor.

Fifty-eight

Esme staggered out into the cold night air. Her breath would have made little wisps of condensation if her rotting lungs were still functioning. The last vestige of her humanity shrivelled with her internal organs as she finally succumbed to the virus putrefying her body tissue with increasing ferocity, leaving nothing but a decomposing shell dependent on fresh meat for its survival.

The remaining sources of fresh meat were gathering here, on the boat deck. She could sense its warmth; feel its pulse beating like a drum, calling to her. She started to move down the boat deck, drawn onwards by the lure of food, ignoring the half-eaten bodies and the cold, dead creatures feeding on them. Her desire was for a fresh kill; her only purpose was to feed.

A warm bodied figure stepped across her path in the darkness, its back towards her, unaware of her presence. The figure hurried to join a group moving towards the crowd at the far end of the deck. Esme smelt the emotions flowing from her new prey's skin like a rich, intoxicating perfume. Anxiety, apprehension, and fear blended with courage and determination to form a powerful musk.

She quickened her pace, closing the distance. There was something else, something different, something almost imperceptible: a second heartbeat. It was softer and quicker than the prey's own life-sustaining pulse, but she could almost feel its rhythm deep within her hunger.

Esme's fetid corpse had its prey in sight and wasn't about to be denied such a delicious prize.

Bridget stumbled on, the coldness of the breeze blowing across the deck catching her by surprise, drawing the air from her lungs. The ship's bow had sunk from sight, the aft slowly climbing into the night sky, setting the deck at an almost impossible angle. Large chunks of ice still slid wildly across the deck, threatening to upend anyone unlucky enough to be in their path, sweeping them to their death.

The lifeboats were close but to reach them she would have to run a gauntlet of the dead. They were closing in on the thin cordon of sailors protecting the davits and the small group of survivors crowded around the last few boats. The crewmen were using the lifeboats' long oars to ward off the horde, keeping them at a safe distance. Occasionally, more gunshots would rent the unnaturally quiet night as the diseased threatened to breach the cordon, forcing the crew to use the remains of their scarce ammunition to repel the assault.

As she got closer, the crewmen used the oars to lunge at the seething mass of decaying flesh, momentarily pushing it back to create a narrow gap. The steward frantically ushered the line of survivors through the gap, and Bridget, bringing up the rear, was just about to make a last desperate lunge through the gap before it closed when Officer Moody stepped towards her, revolver raised.

A bullet whistled past her ear, then the deafening roar of the gunshot rolled over her senses, disorientating her. She tried to focus on Moody, but her eyes stung from the blast of gunpowder blown across her face, her ears ringing with the shot's violent concussion.

"I've got you, Mrs. Grafton." Moody's voice was strong, comforting. His firm grip on her wrist, pulling her roughly into his strong chest felt more comforting still. She allowed herself to sink into his strong arms, overcome by the emotions of the last few hours, as he almost carried her through the gap to the waiting lifeboat.

Fifty-nine

Esme had closed to within a few tantalising yards of her helpless prey before she heard the soft metallic click. From over the shoulder of the strangely familiar figure staggering away from her—the scent triggered distant memories, memories of the emotions she no longer experienced—appeared the face of another warm bodied survivor. Driven on by the prospect of a kill and the desire to feed deeply on their soft flesh, she surged forward, her eyes fixed on the face of the man pointing at her.

Esme did not hear the revolver's second click or the sound of the explosion as the firearm erupted a few feet from her face.

For an instant, she saw the barrel flash. Then she plunged into oblivion. Blood, as thick and as black as the tar that liberally coated the ship's pulleys, rolled down her face from the perfectly round hole in her forehead. Then her body, finally at peace, slumped onto the icy deck.

Sixth Officer Moody pulled the confused looking Mrs. Grafton to his chest, not wanting her to see the young chambermaid's decomposing body leaking vile, putrid ichor across the deck. Time was short; he couldn't afford for her to panic or have a moment of sentimentality over the young servant who'd once, with a brighter soul than the creature she became, been her friend.

"I've got you, Mrs. Grafton," was all he could say as she negotiated the rapidly closing pathway between his men's oars. He wanted to say so much more. He wanted to tell her how his heart leapt whenever he saw her, how she had captured his heart that first night as they sat at the Captain's Table. But now was not the right time, and for him, time had run out.

More and more of the rotting dead were joining the throng around their precariously positioned perch high on the increasingly steeply sloped boat deck. They were literally caught between the Devil's cohorts and the cold, black sea. Behind him the sheer weight of the dead pressing forward in search of flesh caused the cordon to breach, allowing the creatures to drag his men down one by one.

Moody swept Bridget off her feet and swung her into the last lifeboat while shouting at the men manning the davits, "Lower away, while you still can!"

She clutched his coat as the lifeboat began to descend at an agonizingly slow pace. "Come with me?" She pleaded. Her face, beautifully luminescent in the moonlight, upturned to his, her bright eyes filled with fear. He leant in, kissing her for a brief moment that would last an eternity, then pushed her hands away as the lifeboat swung out over the icy waves far below.

Sixty

Bridget's outstretched arms still reached towards the gallant and dashing Officer Moody as the infected swarm overran his position. She watched, the salty tang of his kiss still on her lips, as the dead dragged him down. She couldn't turn away as they swarmed over his body ripping, biting, and tearing it apart so violently he did not have time to scream. Just as the boat dropped below deck level, and she would no longer be able to see their disgusting feast, another sailor, the dead clawing at his body, pointed his revolver at Moody and without hesitating, shot him in the head.

Bridget's thoughts returned to her dead husband, and she suppressed a smile. All-in-all, things had turned out very well. Her loathsome husband and his whore of a mistress were both dead, and any evidence implicating her in his death would soon sink to the bottom of the Atlantic. She stood to become a very rich woman, and as added insurance to her claim on the Grafton millions, she still carried a child. It did not matter it wasn't his; the rest of his family didn't know that.

The only fly in the ointment was Esme's death. She had been a resourceful and quick-witted ally, and Bridget owed her nothing short of her life. As the lifeboat finally splashed down into the churning sea surrounding the stricken vessel, she pledged to find Esme's sister, Charlotte—it was the least she could do to repay the debt she owed.

As the two crewmen assigned to the lifeboat began rowing steadily away from the sinking ship, its stern rising high into the night sky, Bridget Grafton greeted her fellow survivors with a polite nod. There was an elderly English lady wearing far too many diamonds sitting next to a younger woman who just stared out to sea with a faraway look in her eyes. A small group of middle-aged women, a few of whom Bridget recognized from the group rescued from near her cabin, filled the centre of the boat. A mother and her daughter huddled together in the stern.

Clutched in the little girl's arms, wrapped up tight in a woollen shawl, was a small, terrified monkey.

Author's Afterword.

Although I have played fast and loose with the tragic events of *RMS Titanic*'s only voyage, some people, places, and events are, for reasons of historical credibility, real. I have also, largely, remained within the voyage's timescale and events that occurred.

The words and actions of those characters whose identities I used are complete fiction. To this end, I have provided the following.

Captain Edward John Smith. It is believed he stayed on the bridge where, some claimed, he shot himself. However, to counter this, some report seeing him in the water where he swam to a lifeboat with a child then, ensuring the child was safe, swam away again. From what I have read about Captain Smith, I'm inclined to believe the second report.

His body was never recovered. He was 62.

Chief Engineer Joseph Bell. A Member of the Institute of Marine Engineers and the Royal Naval Reserve, Bell and his fellow engineers stayed at their posts. A memorial to their bravery still stands in Southampton.

His body was never recovered. He was 51.

First Officer, William McMaster Murdoch. He was on the bridge at the time of the collision and worked diligently to load the

lifeboats. One of the lookouts claimed he shot himself, taking responsibility for the collision, although this was the only evidence reported, it appears to have been hearsay.

His body was never recovered. He was 39.

Benjamin Guggenheim. He was indeed travelling with his mistress, Madame Aubart. Following the collision, his butler got him into a life jacket, and he escorted Madame Aubart to the lifeboats, but, accepting his fate, he returned to the cabin to dress for dinner and sat in the saloon drinking while the ship sank. Legend has it he said, "We've dressed up in our best and are prepared to go down like gentlemen."

His body was never recovered. He was 46.

Madame Aubart. A singer and only 24 years of age at the time, survived in Lifeboat 9. On 18th April, she sent a telegram to Paris which read, "I'm saved but Ben lost."

She died in 1964 at the age of 77.

Thomas Andrews. As the ship's designer and part of the Harland and Wolff's Titanic Guarantee Group, he had a complimentary ticket. Following the collision, he toured parts of the ship and advised the captain she would not stay afloat more than 2 hours. He spent that time encouraging people to wear life belts and make for the lifeboats. Last reports have him in the Smoking Room.

His body was never recovered. He was 39.

Bruce Ismay. The *Titanic* had been his brainchild from the start. He survived by securing a berth in Lifeboat C. The boat reportedly contained 11 men and only 2 women but had capacity for 32 people. The fact he survived didn't sit well with the public or the press, and he resigned from his position the following year.

He died in 1937 at the age of 74.

Sir and Lady Duff-Gordon. Allowed to take a seat in Lifeboat 1 by Officer Murdoch, they both survived. The lifeboat contained only 12 people, of which 7 were crew. Some wanted to return and collect more survivors, but Sir Duff-Gordon refused. The crewmen, on safely reaching the rescue ship *Carpathia,* each received £5 from Sir Duff-Gordon to compensate for their lost kit. I leave that for you to judge.

He died in 1931 at the age of 68, she in 1935 at the age of 71.

Countess of Rothes. Rescued in Lifeboat 8 in which she took a turn at the tiller.

She died in 1956 at the age of 77.

Master-at-Arms Thomas King. He helped passengers into the lifeboats.

His body was never recovered. He was 42.

The other characters mentioned are fictitious. Although there was an able seaman Davis on board, this was coincidental. His body was never recovered. He was 39. There was also a family with the name Astor (not Bernard), but again this was coincidental.

I did find reference to a Callahan being the only American on the *Titanic*'s crew but could find no mention of him in official records.

The Belvedere Arms was a real pub in Southampton from which people were recruited to work on board *RMS Titanic*.

1,513 people perished aboard the *Titanic*, but so many met their death with honour, their heads held high. Allen Gibson in his book *The Unsinkable Titanic: The Triumph Behind a Disaster* observed, "Her sinking was the last great act of chivalry, the curtain call to Old World pluck. She was never just another ship. In her one voyage she transgressed into culture through passengers rich and poor willing to forsake themselves for the survival of others, because doing so was simply the natural and correct thing to do."

Thank you.

Ash Hartwell.

2017

About the Author

Ash Hartwell was born in Maine but grew up in England where he still lives with his wife and four children. Having spent over a decade working in customer service he enrolled in University and trained as a nurse, spending a number of years working in an intensive care unit just outside London. He now breeds Cavalier King Charles spaniels with his wife, while writing his tales of horror. He is currently working on his own novel as well as writing short stories for a number of anthologies.

Ash Hartwell is a Fictioneer and member of a number of horror related Facebook groups. He is also a supporting member of the Horror Writers Association.

Other Works by Ash Hartwell

Printed in Great Britain
by Amazon